Your Truth or Mine?

Trisha Sakhlecha grew up in New Delhi and now lives in London. She works in fashion and is a graduate of the acclaimed Faber Academy writing course. In the past, Trisha has worked as a designer, trend forecaster and lecturer. *Your Truth or Mine?* is her first novel.

TRISHA SAKHLECHA

Your Truth or Mine?

PAN BOOKS

First published 2019 by Macmillan

First published in paperback 2019 by Macmillan

This paperback edition first published 2019 by Pan Books
an imprint of Pan Macmillan
The Smithson, 6 Briset Street, London EC1M 5NR
Associated companies throughout the world
www.panmacmillan.com

ISBN   978-1-5098-8626-5

1 3 5 7 9 8 6 4 2

A CIP catalogue record for this book is available from the British Library.

Typeset by Palimpsest Book Production Limited,
Falkirk, Stirlingshire
Printed and bound by CPI Group (UK) Ltd, Croydon, CR0 4YY

For Nana

When it all unravels, what will they believe?

ROY

London

Nothing has changed but everything is different.

I am standing here, in my beautiful kitchen, watching my beautiful wife cook what smells like an incredible breakfast, and I know nothing has changed. I watch her move, measuring, stirring, distractedly dipping her little finger in the batter to taste it, then wincing and snatching it back when she realizes she miscalculated the temperature. She's lost in her thoughts, earphones plugged in, moving to a soundless beat, pausing every couple of minutes to sip her coffee. I wonder what she's listening to. It must be something upbeat, peppy, I decide. I lean forward to try and decipher the hum that escapes her earphones and it surprises me how long I take to recognize the song. 'Way Back Into Love'. Our song. I remember listening to this years ago, both of us still innocent and desperately in love, cramped together on the narrow bed in her room, each with one earphone plugged in, the one on the right hearing the vocals and the one on the left hearing the beats,

singing along, trusting that love alone would be enough to
hold it all together. We were so naive, so stupid. Despite
the warmth of the kitchen, I shiver.

I force myself back to the present and gear myself up for
what is to follow. Mia looks happy. Relaxed. I walk up to
her and wrap my arms around her, burying my face in her
neck, smelling her hair, letting her blissful oblivion envelop
me, a momentary shield against the storm that is about to
rip through my life.

'Roy,' Mia calls out from the kitchen. 'Who is it? Roy?'

I hear the scramble of footsteps as Mia rushes into the
hallway to investigate. Her meddling buys me some time
to compose myself and, just this once, I'm truly grateful
for her interference in anything and everything that goes
on in my life. She cranes her neck to look past me into the
front porch and I realize I've only opened the door a fraction. I relax my grip on it, turning to look at Mia as I take
a small step back.

She looks terrified.

'What – what's happened? Is it Mummy? Addi? What's
wrong?'

She's panicking. Of course. She's done this before, I
think, and I am hit with a sudden urge to protect her.

The woman speaks first. She's small, slight, perhaps five
foot four, with tied-back brown hair, a round face and sympathetic, deep-set eyes. She looks out of place in her skirt
suit, standing next to the uniformed officer. She reminds
me of Mrs Sen, my primary school English teacher. Her

voice is hesitant as she addresses Mia. 'Mrs Kapoor?' Mia nods slightly, quickly, and she carries on, her voice more confident this time. 'Everything is all right, Mrs Kapoor. We're from the Metropolitan Police. We just have a few questions for your husband. May we come in?' she says, her gaze fixed on Mia. Another nod and I realize I can no longer refuse without looking like I have something to hide. I let go of the door and step back, giving them a proper glimpse of the hallway for the first time.

The woman introduces herself and the other policeman, but I don't register their names. We go straight into the dining room. They look around, taking in the high ceilings, the large windows, the newly installed open-plan kitchen. They glance at the array of pictures and knick-knacks on the mantelpiece, souvenirs from Mia's travels and mine over the years, shimmering under the unexpected winter sun. I can see the envy in their eyes. At thirty-one, I've already achieved more than they ever will. In other circumstances I might have let them look through the pictures, I might have even enjoyed showing off a little bit, but right now, right now I want them out.

'How can I help?' I ask, putting on my most convincing concerned-citizen smile and motioning for them to sit down as I pull out a chair for myself.

They sit down directly across from me, the dining table between us. I get a waft of something sweet and cinnamony from the kitchen and I realize I'm hungry.

I look around and see that Mia has occupied herself with the business of tea. She might like to think of herself as

Indian but she has all those telltale idiosyncrasies that come with being English, albeit half. Tea first. Always. Like *that* will solve anything.

It's the woman speaking again. I decide to call her Sen, the association with my harmless English teacher somewhat comforting. I presume her partner is a junior officer or constable. He isn't armed. His only job seems to be to make notes. He pulls out a biro and starts chewing on its end, his face contorting as he sinks his teeth into the unyielding plastic. He's tall but his shoulders are slightly hunched. He looks bored.

'Mr Kapoor, are you familiar with Emily Barnett?' she asks.

'Yes, we've worked together a few times.'

'Oh?' she says, waiting to see if I will elaborate. I don't.

'When was the last time you saw her?'

'A couple of days ago . . . Wednesday, I think.' I look at the calendar on my iPhone. 'Yes, Wednesday. I met her for a drink at the Swan near Archway station.'

'Ah, I see. Were you meeting for business purposes or socially?'

'Socially, I suppose,' I say, willing myself to stay calm. They don't know. They can't.

'Alone?'

'Yes.'

'And you haven't seen her since?'

Stay calm. They don't know. I repeat it to myself like a mantra but my heart is beating fast. I wonder if they can tell.

'No,' I say.

Mia's standing next to me now, the tea forgotten. I can see the cogs in her brain turning, working out that I lied to her about the press dinner at the Shard. I feel myself contract and shrink. That's the effect my wife has on me these days.

Sen leans forward, forearms resting on the table, hands clasped. 'When you met her, did Miss Barnett seem worried about anything? What did you talk about?'

There's a strange tightness in my chest. I can't focus. I can barely breathe. While I try to compose my answer, it hits me that I haven't yet asked why Sen's questioning me about all this and that in itself might be construed as suspicious.

'No, she was fine. Look, Ems – I mean Emily – is a journalism student. We've worked together on a couple of projects. We met because she wanted some tips on looking for paid freelance work. I haven't seen her or spoken to her since,' I blurt out. 'What's going on? Is she okay?'

Sen exchanges a quick glance with her partner and he jots something down.

'Miss Barnett was reported missing on Friday,' she says. Her voice is even, her face blank. 'We've been going door to door asking people if they remember anything that might help us and your name came up.'

I don't know what to say. I barely manage a squeak before Sen speaks again.

'What time did you leave the pub? Did Emily leave with you?'

'Yes . . . no . . . I mean, yes, we left at the same time, around nine p.m., but then we went our separate ways. I walked her to the end of the road. She lives nearby.'

'Did she mention any plans for the next few days?'

'No, no she didn't.'

'Right. And you said you've had no contact with her since then?'

I shake my head, not trusting myself to speak.

'Well, as you will understand, we are very concerned for her safety.' She glances up at Mia as she says this and places a flyer on the table. *MISSING*, it says in bold red letters.

'My details are on this. Please call me if you think of anything,' Sen says, circling a name and number on the flyer. Detective Inspector Brooke Robins. CID. Not Sen. Definitely not Sen.

'Of course,' I say, getting up to see them out. I bolt the door behind them.

Mia's sitting at the table when I return to the room. She looks up as I walk in. Her piercing green eyes are dark and muddled. The moment builds. I wait for her gaze to settle on me and when it does, I know that I'm done. I have to tell her.

It's starting to unravel, my love.

PART ONE

Three months ago

Jaisalmer/London

ROY

Jaisalmer

Just a hundred kilometres from the Indo–Pak border, there is a disarming sense of destiny in the thick air that permeates Jaisalmer. It's the city that should never have existed, the city built on shifting sand dunes, the city that rises, with its intricately carved sandcastles, from the depths of the Indian Thar Desert, only to disappear as quickly as it appeared. The end of the world, the locals call it.

I was picking Mia up at the train station and, as is the norm in India, the train was late. Punctuality – or, for that matter, organization – has never been a strong suit here. I tried to work my way towards the information desk, weaving through the hordes of people on the platform waiting to pick up relatives and friends, circling around chains of hand-holding children and the army of metal carts being wheeled by men with absolutely no sense of urgency, side-stepping the booksellers, *chai-wallahs*, and old men crouching around hessian sacks. I stopped when I saw the uniformed ticket collector.

'Is the Jaisalmer Express late?' I asked.

'No, no, it's on time.'

Yeah, right.

'When is it scheduled . . .'

My words faded into the cacophony of voices coming from everywhere. The ticket collector had already walked off with the brightly veiled woman on my right who had been begging for his attention. Perfect.

I plodded back to the *chai-wallah* and bought a cup of sweet milky tea and a packet of Parle-G biscuits. An empty train was pulling up on the other platform, the outsides of the coaches covered in graffiti and urgent, dark red paan stains. As the train came to a halt, I saw flashes of colour moving through the coaches, couples laying claim to the window seats, children clamouring onto the top berths, coolies with red, agitated faces demanding more money. Within moments, the empty coach in front of me was crammed with hundreds of people, all fighting for their six inches of space. A little girl stuck her head out from between the horizontal bars fencing the window and waved to someone. As the train jerked forward, she caught my eye and I realized she was waving at me, probably excited to see a man so clearly out of place amidst this chaos. I finished my tea and turned to look for a dustbin, the creepy face of the Parle-G girl staring up at me from the crumpled wrapper.

I hadn't been on an Indian train in years, preferring the ease of flights and road travel. But Mia, she loved it. She found air travel mechanical, grim. Trains, on the other hand, offered her a chance to curl up in a curtained cabin and watch the world thunder past. It reminded her of the old days, she said, when there were still four of them. Mia, Addi and their parents would fly to India every summer to see her mother's family and when they had had enough of the endless feasts with the nosy aunties and overbearing uncles, Mia's parents would wake up the girls in the middle of the night to catch the Himalayan Queen. They'd board the train half asleep and wake up to steaming mugs of tea and buttered buns just in time to see the hills rise through the dawn haze. It all sounded incredibly romantic, memories saturated with the simplicity of nostalgia.

A loud screeching noise cut through my thoughts. Indian Railways' chosen voice announced, in characteristic sing-song fashion, that Mia's train was going to arrive 'in approximately five minutes'. Finally! I hadn't seen Mia in weeks and it had been harder than I had imagined. Both of us travelled a lot so we were used to being apart but over the past few months it had felt like I had only seen Mia in passing. The last time I saw her was three weeks ago at Heathrow – she had just flown in after a week in Paris and I was due to fly out to Delhi that same afternoon. I smiled to myself as I thought of the few hours we'd spent huddled together in the Costa Coffee at Terminal 4, talking about everything and nothing, a married couple that would have looked like young lovers to a stranger.

The coolies had clustered together along the platform

preparing to get on the train as soon as it arrived and, sure enough, it pulled up in a matter of moments. There she was, my darling Mia. I was aching to touch her and smell her and drink her in but I stood back, knowing it was pointless to try and get close to the doors, and let Mia elbow her way to me instead.

'Sweetie,' she murmured as I caught her in a tight hug, 'this isn't Heathrow. Sweep me off my feet a little later?' She pulled away, a naughty smile playing on her lips.

'Come here,' I said, grabbing Mia as soon as we were alone in the room. 'I've missed you.'

'I've missed you too,' she said, trailing kisses along my jaw. 'Have we got some time or do you need to rush off to meet the crew?'

'I told them I'd meet them at half four,' I said with a groan. 'I'll need to leave in fifteen minutes.'

'Why don't I come with you? I need to see if my husband is as good in front of the camera as he says.' She pulled away slightly, dipping back and letting my arms support her entire weight.

'Your husband's better than he says, madam,' I countered, pulling her back in. 'But don't you want to rest? I don't mind if you don't come.'

'No, I'm fine. I'd rather be with you. Plus I have a litany of obscenities I've been ordered to reel off at George.'

I raised an eyebrow. 'Addi?'

'Who else?' Mia laughed, peeling my arms away from

her and quickly undressing to get into the shower. 'Find me an outfit that isn't creased, will you? Red case. I'll be quick, promise.'

'Mia! Roy!'

I looked up towards the sky, shielding my eyes with my hands, the sharp glare from the sun cutting through the dark lenses of my Ray-Bans. George stood on the terrace, waving like a lunatic. There was a shadow behind him as he leaned over through the crenellations. 'Mia! Roy! Over here!'

'Heard you, weirdo. Coming!' Mia yelled.

We climbed up the steep incline leading into the fort, pausing every few minutes to catch our breath and lean against the pillars of intricate carving depicting the many, many mythical tales that breathe life into this barren land.

When we got to the top, George was standing there with a goofy smile and his hands clasped behind his back. Ignoring me, he turned to Mia and bowed. 'My queen,' he said, presenting her with a small cactus.

'You may rise,' Mia said with mock seriousness before engulfing him in a hug.

'Georgie,' she exclaimed, when she finally tore herself away, her lips scrunched up into a pout. 'It's been too long.'

'It has, hasn't it? We've only got your bastard of a husband to blame for that, though,' George said as he landed a playful punch on my shoulder.

'Yeah, yeah, yeah.' I rolled my eyes. 'Mia,' I said as I turned, remembering George's shadow, 'meet Emily.'

'Emily's been helping us out on the shoot over the past

few weeks. She's my brilliant assistant cum location scout cum make-up artist all rolled into one,' George added, as the two women shook hands. 'Emily, why don't you fix Roy's face and I'll be with you guys in a sec? We'll start rolling in fifteen minutes. We have about an hour and a half before the light fades.'

'Okey-dokey, boss,' Emily said. 'Roy? Shall we?' Emily beckoned for me to follow her to the far corner, the only part of the terrace that the sun wasn't encroaching on.

'I didn't realize George knew your wife as well,' Emily commented as she rifled through her kit.

'Yeah, they've known each other since they were kids. Neighbours. Mia and I met through George.'

'Oh, I see,' Emily said as she pulled out a baby wipe. Her left hand rested lightly on the back of my neck while her right hand travelled across my face and neck in firm, confident motions. I could feel the heat of her fingers through the thin towelette.

She had been doing my make-up every day for the past two weeks but for the first time, this routine act felt strangely inappropriate. I looked around.

A few paces away, George had set up his camera. Mia stood with her back to him, looking out over the city.

'Have you got some water?' I asked, as Emily dabbed powder on my face.

An amber mist had enveloped the fort, refracting the sun's rays and casting a hazy, ethereal glow as if the entire city was aflame.

I took a slug from the bottle Emily handed me and

shook my head when she picked up the hairbrush. There was no need.

We were shooting the opening shot last. George liked to work the same way that I did with my essays – middle and end first and then the introduction. It's a subtle trick many new travel writers overlook.

Once we had wrapped up the shoot, we decided to walk back, zigzagging through the labyrinth of streets that connect the fort to the city centre, sampling some street food on our way. The pungent smell of *laal maas* and *mirchibadas* permeated the air thick with sweat and dust.

We stopped when we got to the crossroads.

'Emily, are you flying out tomorrow as well?' Mia asked, looping her arm through mine as George looked for taxis.

'No, there was a mix-up with our flights so I'm here for another two days,' Emily said, leaning over to add in a stage whisper, 'though I think George orchestrated it so he wouldn't have to fly economy with me.'

Mia laughed. 'No, come on, Georgie would never do that.'

'Taxi's here, Mia,' I interrupted.

'Okay, sweetie,' Mia replied. She turned to kiss Emily. 'Why don't you come along to the wedding? I bet you'd enjoy it.'

'I'd love to but I really wouldn't want to impose. The guest list must be drawn up already.'

'Don't be silly. It's an Indian wedding, everyone and their neighbour's invited. It's settled then, we'll see you and George tomorrow afternoon.'

ROY

Wednesday, 9th September

The morning went by in a blur. Mia woke me up at an insanely early hour, her slight frame pressing into me with uninhibited urgency.

'Roy,' she whispered, her voice hoarse.

More asleep than awake, I turned and kissed her. 'Mmm?'

'What's the time?' She quivered as my fingers found her under the duvet.

'Four – four fifteen? We have time,' I murmured, letting my words tickle her ear before they travelled further.

'Oh sweetie,' she said, her breath hot against my skin. I pulled her to me in one easy motion, the contours of her body fitting perfectly into mine, our hips rising and falling together in a familiar rhythm.

'We didn't have time,' Mia remarked with a laugh later as we rushed down, glowing and still a bit dazed. The first set of guests had arrived with the unseasonal rain at five a.m., straggling in with muddy shoes, shadows under their eyes, and a queer assortment of luggage that was ill at ease in the lavish hotel lobby. The lack of an airport in Jaisalmer meant most guests had had to travel on overnight trains from various parts of the country. As the hosts, Mia and I had the lovely task of welcoming them all with big hugs and even bigger smiles, looking past their dishevelled clothes and pretending their morning breath smelled of fresh lilies, all the while nodding sympathetically as they attempted to regale us with stories of survival amidst the wailing babies and snoring men they *all* invariably had in their carriages. Mia's mother and Addi had arrived late last night and while, as the bride, Addi got to sleep in, Mia's mother had come down before us, fresh faced and dressed characteristically in a silk *sari*, the *pallu* draped freely over her shoulder.

Before I had the chance to go over to greet her, I felt a sharp tug on my jeans. I looked down at a sleepy-faced toddler.

'Can't find Mummy,' he said.

Shit, what was I to do with him? 'What's your name?' I asked the boy.

'Can't find Mummy,' he wailed, more urgently this time.

I picked him up and looked around, trying to match his weepy face and distinctly wet bottom with the face of an adult who could be held responsible for him. I barely knew these people. I spotted Mia talking to a young, overeager couple and decided to turn him in to her.

'He's lost,' I said, interrupting Mia mid-sentence. 'And wet,' I added after I had safely passed the boy on.

'Thanks for the warning,' Mia said with a laugh. 'Roy, have you met Raj and Geeta? They're Aditi's friends from school. Geeta was just saying they're moving to London later this year – Anerley.'

'That's wonderful. Anerley's great, you'll love it,' I said as we shook hands. 'And it's just around the corner from us, so you'll have to let us show you around.'

'Oh, we'd love that. We should exchange numbers,' Raj began, nodding enthusiastically.

'Of course. I'll let you both get some rest just now, but let's catch up again later,' I said, before turning to Mia who was busy fussing with the toddler in her arms. 'I can see Sarita Aunty looking a bit lost there, darling. Do you want me to see if I can get her settled in?'

'Thank you,' Mia mouthed to me a couple of minutes later as I shuffled past, hand in hand with her great-aunt.

'Move over, lazybones. I need a nap before brunch,' Mia said as she climbed into bed later that morning.

'Hmmm,' I mumbled, still half asleep. 'How was it?'

'Tiring. Everyone was asking for you.'

'What did you tell them?'

'Just that you're a lazy old man,' she teased.

I tickled her lightly. 'Didn't hear you complaining this morning, Mrs Kapoor.'

'And . . .' She hesitated.

'Hmmm?'

'A few of my aunties were asking about our plans. You know how—'

'For?'

'A baby, Roy.'

There was exasperation in her voice. I didn't say anything.

'It wouldn't be such a bad idea, would it? We're settled now, we can aff—'

'Maybe. But first, sleep.'

The *mehendi* ceremony that afternoon was spectacular. In true Mia fashion, the affair was a riot of colours, scents, patterns and activity, every element coming together effortlessly in unlikely amalgamation. Every detail had been planned and executed to perfection. The arched pathway leading into the hotel courtyard was covered in crawling vines of yellow and orange marigolds and speckled with tiny glass lamps in a myriad of colours. *Dhol-wallahs* in identical hot-pink turbans and bright vests were lined up along both sides of the pathway, their faces animated, sticks perfectly in sync, drumming up an easy beat as people walked in. Brass bells were suspended from strings of flowers snaking through the trellises above them, offering glimpses of the clear autumn sky through the gaps between the blossoms. Guests clad in brightly coloured clothes and oversized sunglasses lounged on sofas scattered across the courtyard, moving to the enthusiastic beat of the *dhol* while sipping on Indian-themed cocktails. A small queue had formed along one side where the *mehendi* artists sat painting intricate scenes depicting all manner of exotic tales with henna. Though this was technically Addi's *mehendi* ceremony, Addi, Mia and my mother-in-law had all had their hands painted earlier that morning so they were free to dance and mingle with the guests.

The *dhol-wallahs'* excitement was contagious and even the most somber guests burst into a jig as they walked in. We spotted George, and Addi, James, Mia and I danced our way towards the entrance, our bodies mirroring the ever-increasing tempo of the drums, challenging them, and each other, to go wilder, faster. The closer we got, the more hypnotic the beats sounded, building us up into a frenzy, faster and faster, shoulders shimmying, heads thrown back, arms and shoulders moving in powerful jerks, faster, faster, faster, till all five of us collapsed into a hysterical heap of laughter.

'Oh my God. That. Was. Amazing,' Mia and Addi shrieked in unison, their arms held up, palms facing forward to protect the still damp henna.

'George, I never knew you could move like that, man,' James said, slapping George on the back.

'Don't forget I grew up with these two crazies, dude. Dancing was *not* optional,' George said, laughing.

James and I looked at each other in mock despair. 'We know,' we said, laughing as well.

'Oh, shut up, you two. I need water. Georgie, you've got some serious explaining to do. Why the hell aren't you staying for the wedding?' Addi reeled off, dragging George and James towards the bar.

Mia and I were alone at last. She had been so engrossed in her work and planning the wedding, it felt like I had barely seen her in months. Her hair had tumbled down to her shoulders. The delicate clips holding it back were clearly not strong enough to withstand such frantic dancing.

'You're gorgeous,' I said and tucked her soft brown hair behind her ears. There was a hint of sadness on her face.

'You okay?' I asked her. She nodded, her eyes focused on something behind me.

I glanced around, trying to look at everything through her eyes. The flurry of activity, the smattering of vibrantly dressed guests, the madcap decor – it was all one hundred per cent Mia. She had strived to create for her older sister the perfect wedding that she had herself been denied.

'I'm so sorry we couldn't have this, darling,' I said and, in that moment, I truly meant it.

'Oh Roy, no. I was just thinking about Daddy, that's all,' she said with a small smile, her sadness even more pronounced against the dizzying gaiety surrounding us. I reached over to squeeze her shoulder. It was incredibly frustrating that in India you were expected to hug virtual strangers but touching your wife outside the bedroom was still frowned upon. I settled for the next best alternative.

'Come on, let's get you a drink. I hear the margaritas are deadly,' I said and steered her towards the bar.

As dusk fell, hotel staff lit up little lanterns, bathing the vibrant colours from the afternoon in a soft yellow glow. Guests had started trickling back in, refreshed after a late afternoon siesta. The men hung back, dressed in smart suits and nursing drinks, whilst their wives flitted around air-kissing each other, heavy *lehengas* rustling and swishing around their ankles as they moved. Elaborately applied make-up and opulent jewellery had replaced the sunglasses from earlier. The excitement from the afternoon lingered and people congregated in little groups, waiting for Addi and James to arrive and the dancing to begin.

Something about a woman standing a few paces from me caught my eye. Perhaps it was the way her *sari* was pleated and pinned neatly. Or maybe the way she cocked her head to the left every time the man across from her spoke. I felt a flash of recognition and spun around, walking straight into my mother-in-law.

'Roy, *beta*, will you fetch Aditi and Mia? James is already here so we should start the *sangeet* soon.'

'Of course, Mummy. I'll go now,' I said. My mother-in-law had unwittingly provided me with the perfect excuse to walk away.

I hurried back to the main building, passing Emily on my way. Tall, blonde and dressed in a tight dress, she cut a striking figure amongst the conservatively dressed Indian women around her. George had left for Delhi earlier that evening and Emily was on her own tonight. I made a mental note to come back and find her later. Neither Mia nor I had spent much time with her at the *mehendi*. I didn't want her to feel left out.

I found Mia standing outside Addi's suite, checking her hair in the hallway mirror. She twirled when she saw me.

'Gorgeous,' I said automatically.

'You don't look too bad yourself,' Mia said, eying up my

reflection as I went to stand next to her. Even with heels on, Mia was a few inches shorter than me. I flicked off an imaginary speck from my collar. I was wearing a deep blue *kurta* with a black vest. The high collar of the vest highlighted my jaw, making it look sharper than it was. At nearly thirty-one, I could still pass for a twenty-five-year-old.

My blue-grey eyes caught Mia's in the mirror and I smiled. We looked perfect together. 'Your mum sent me to fetch you and Addi. Is she ready?'

'Should be. They were finishing her make-up when I last checked,' Mia said to me and then knocked on the door. 'Addi?'

'Coming,' Addi yelled back.

The rest of the evening was spent drinking and socializing. After the performances wound down, James began a drawn-out speech thanking the guests for coming and Mia and me for arranging it all. I caught Mia's eye and smiled. He had had too much to drink and went on for quite some time about finding love in a foreign land and striving for perfection in an imperfect world, some of it philosophical but most of it incoherent rambling. He began an analogy about snake charmers and lovers and I decided Mia and I needed another round if we were to get through this night.

When I got back with our drinks, James had moved on to dreams and ideals and Mia had disappeared. I scanned the crowd, trying to spot her bright orange outfit amidst the blur of colours. My eye finally rested on her petite frame but when I realized whom she was talking to, I decided to go a different way. Mia was meddling again and I wasn't in the mood for another argument.

I spotted Emily and walked over to her instead. The shifting light from the lanterns was bouncing off her silver dress, which made keeping my eyes on her face difficult. I wondered if she had been wearing this earlier.

'Is that for me?' Emily asked, nodding towards Mia's wine.

'Sure,' I smiled.

'Thanks. How are you holding up?' she asked, taking the glass. 'I've been watching Mia. She keeps getting pulled into conversations. I don't think I've seen her sit down for a minute. She must have a lot of patience.'

'She enjoys it,' I said.

'Really? I couldn't stand it. Too many people.' She paused and sipped on her wine. Mia's wine. 'Is your family here too?'

'Did you enjoy the performances?' I asked, the alcohol making me stumble over my words so they came out rushed, all tangled up in each other.

She regarded me for a minute before answering.

'Yes, yes, I did. I am shattered, though. I should head back,' she said. 'Do you need to stay till everyone leaves?'

I looked at Mia from the corner of my eye. She was still deep in conversation. 'No, I'll walk you to a taxi and then head up myself,' I said. I was done for the night.

There was a queue for taxis at the front porch so we decided to walk to the back of the hotel and poach a taxi before it entered the premises. It was a lot darker there than it was in the courtyard and my eyes took a few seconds to adjust.

Emily pulled out a cheap plastic lighter and a pack of Marlboro Lights from her bag and offered me one. I don't know what surprised me more: the fact that she smoked or that after almost ten years, I was aching for a fag. I had quit smoking when Mia and I got engaged, a step towards the changed man I had every intention of becoming. I lit up and held the flame for Emily. She shook her head and leaned in. It took me a minute to comprehend what she was doing. I lowered my head towards her and our cigarettes met, the spark from mine igniting hers.

Over the last two weeks, I had seen Emily as little more than a naive, vaguely interesting and somewhat pretty intern. In an instant, my perception transgressed into something more. I *saw* her now.

'We might have been better off joining the queue,' I said.

She shrugged, inhaling deeply.

'I've really enjoyed myself over the past few weeks. It's been nice working with you,' Emily said, looking straight at me.

The uneasiness I had felt at the shoot returned in an instant. I wondered how much longer we would have to wait for a taxi.

'Your work is amazing,' she said.

'I'm married,' I said, stupidly, even as my heart hammered on, the alcohol and the adrenaline melding together into one deadly combination.

She smiled.

'You're amazing,' she said.

She didn't look away. I held her gaze. It was all too tempting. Mia and I had settled into such a predictable, everyday love, this sudden wave of candid admiration felt liberating. Emily had the same devil-may-care spirit that I had cherished in myself years ago. I found myself wondering when I went from being fun and adventurous to sensible and boring. We stood there for what felt like hours, unmoving. The distance between us remained the same yet we were infinitely closer. Even the air between us felt electric. It was as though a barrier had been removed. I wanted to reach out and see if the girl standing in front of me was real. I knew I needed to leave but I couldn't. I was frozen to that spot, braver, bolder under her gaze. Where earlier I had struggled to keep my attention focused on her, I was now struggling to take my eyes off her.

A stray curl had escaped her pinned-back hair. I lifted my hand and brushed it away from her face, letting my fingertips graze her cheek as I tucked it behind her ear. That simple act turned into something else and, before I knew it, my lips were over hers in reckless abandon.

MIA

Drunk James is hilarious. You're REALLY missing something.

'. . . and, you know, love can be strange. It's like, one day you're fine and the next day . . . it's like . . . the next day . . . you're . . . you're . . . beyond fine. You're awesome . . . you're . . . like a ninja . . . and you're getting married in this magical land . . . and it's exotic, like *Arabian Nights* . . . and then . . .'

Wish I could've stayed!! Must get together when everyone's in Londres. Boarding now. Look after E for me, will you?

I stared at George's text, certain that Emily was the latest in his string of naive girlfriends. I thought back to the *mehendi* lunch, and how Emily had been looking on as George and Roy discussed camera angles and narrative structures, her eyes wide with awe and wonder, and just a sliver of rebellion; how George had alternated between ignoring her and pulling her into the conversation. I groaned inwardly. Why couldn't he find someone his own age for once? I sent George a quick reply and walked over to Addi. She covered her face in mock shame when she saw me.

'Come on! You do realize you have blackmail material for the next decade, don't you?' I said, linking my arm with hers.

Addi rolled her eyes, feigning annoyance. 'Now you know why he's always on driving duty.'

'. . . there's camels and genies and ninjas . . . and snake charmers . . . I mean . . . you could find a genie . . . or a ninja . . . on a camel . . . It's all written, guys . . . You know what I mean? It's all written . . . fate . . . even snake charmers . . . you see . . .'

James was on a roll.

'Umm . . . I think I might have the next two decades covered,' she said before both of us burst into laughter.

'Have you seen Mummy?' I asked when we had recovered. 'I ran into Uncle Bill earlier. He was looking for her.'

'Uncle Bill?' she asked, looking at me. 'I didn't think he would actually come. Aunty Jane too?'

'Yep,' I said.

Addi looked as perplexed as I felt. As a child, I had adored Uncle Bill. With his broad build and spectacled grey eyes he reminded me of Daddy, but things had been tense with him over the past few years. Mum and Addi had never really got along with him, and Aunty Jane was a bit – how should I put it? – eccentric.

Addi shrugged, her attentions already back on James. 'Well, I need to see Mum anyway. I'll tell her. Where's Roy?' she asked.

'Gone for refills,' I said, pointing to my almost empty glass. My eyes sought him out amongst the people gathered around the makeshift bar. 'Looks like he might be a while.' Geeta had intercepted Roy. She was gesturing wildly, clearly trying to make a point. Roy was nodding along, hands in his pockets. He looked towards the bar briefly before turning his attention back to Geeta. I almost laughed out loud. To anyone else, it would look like Roy was listening intently but after nearly ten years together, I knew he was blanking her out, itching to get away. Everything I loved about India – the chaos, the sense of community, the traditions – Roy hated. He had surprised me with his limited knowledge of rituals and conventions when we started planning Addi's wedding. You wouldn't think he had grown up here. James was probably more at home in India than Roy was.

I spotted Emily standing alone in the corner and I made my way over to her, stopping en route to exchange jibes with groups of friends and relatives. Despite the cool desert breeze, Emily had taken off her shawl and draped it over one arm, showing off a rose-gold mini-dress with a plunging V-neck – the kind of style I'd sell to an Essex boutique.

'That's a nice dress,' I said, reaching over to feel the fabric. Polyester; about £6.50 FOB; probably made in Vietnam or Cambodia to benefit from the GSP, though once we had the Euro hub up and running, I could get the same price from Romania *and* bring in the shipment quicker. I caught myself slipping into work mode and changed the subject in my head.

'I'm so sorry we haven't spent much time with you. It's been so manic.'

'Please don't worry about it. I'm just happy to be here. It's such a different—'

'Mia, someone said Roy's mother is looking for you,' my cousin Mansi interrupted. 'Somewhere there.' She waved towards the main hotel block before wandering off.

'Sorry,' I said to Emily with an apologetic smile and hurried away from one forced conversation to the next.

'Ma, how are you?' I asked, bending over to touch my mother-in-law's feet.

'I'm okay, Mia. It's certainly a lively party, isn't it? So . . . free.' She shuddered. 'Not like how our family does things. But of course your family is *different*.'

'How was your trip?' I asked, trying to keep it light.

'Tiring. I was expecting Siddhant at the station.'

It took me a second to clock on that she meant Roy. No one called him Siddhant except his parents. He had switched to his middle name when he moved out of his parents' house years ago. I had only ever known him as Roy.

'It's heartbreaking when your only son cuts you out of his life. His father can't even talk about it. Did you speak to him?'

I did speak to Roy. Several times, in fact. His response was always the same.

'Give him some time, Ma. I'm sure he'll come and visit you as soon as he can. He's just so busy right now,' I said.

'Too busy to come and see his parents?' Her voice went up an octave. 'I've been so unwell. My blood pressure . . .'

I tuned her out.

Roy had vanished as soon as he saw me talking to his mother so I didn't even have a drink to soften the edges. I had always loved how stubborn and idealistic Roy could be. But God, did I hate it when he left me to deal with his mother. It was like being in a hostage video. Smiling outside, dying inside. In the first few years, I had really tried. Roy's relationship with his parents, or rather the lack thereof, bothered me to no end and I had made it something of a mission to try and fix it. I was so excited about the idea of having an additional family; I had thought they'd be thrilled to have me too. Needless to say, they weren't. Roy stood his ground and they stood theirs. Roy's parents' refusal to accept a 'half-breed' cemented his aversion to them. The fact that I was the only reason Roy was still connected to India was an irony lost on his parents.

Roy and I had had a big argument when I was finalizing the guest list for Addi's wedding. He didn't want to invite them at all and, I have to admit, I considered it. His mother made everything so complicated. But in the end convention won over convenience. It was bad enough that his father hadn't come; if his mother had also been missing, there would have been way too many questions. Everything had been perfect so far. There had been no major disasters, everyone was having a good time, I was amidst all my favourite people and I wasn't going to let my mother-in-law's melodrama ruin any of that. So I did the only sensible thing you can do when you're being held hostage – I switched her to mute, put on a sympathetic smile and nodded along.

I woke up with a groan the next morning. My head was throbbing. It was early. Roy was already awake. He was sitting up in bed, frowning at his phone.

I snuggled up to him. 'You disappeared last night.'

'I know, I'm sorry. I was so wasted, I just came up and slept. You were out for ages.'

I must have muttered something incoherent then dozed off because when I came to again, Roy was sitting next to me, freshly showered, holding a Nurofen and a steaming cup of coffee.

He planted a kiss on my forehead. 'Here, take this.'

I checked my phone. It was quarter past ten. We had organized a city tour and traditional Rajasthani lunch for the guests. Everyone was supposed to meet in the lobby at half ten.

'Don't even think about it,' he said, reading my mind. 'I'll manage the guests. You just relax and spend some time with your mum and sister. I've ordered pancakes for you.'

Just like that, the flash of irritation from last night disappeared and I resolved to deal with my in-laws better. Roy may be temperamental but this was the man I loved. He was flawed, yes, but then so was I. This was my Roy. The man I had so easily fallen in love with and quickly married. Moody? Yes. Restless? Extremely. Short-tempered? Sometimes. But always kind, always gallant and I loved him despite my many, many insecurities, his hang-ups and all the little complexities that made up our marriage.

'You're too good to me.' I gulped down the Nurofen and dragged myself out of bed. I felt like shit. Every muscle in my body was aching. I'd had seven – no, wait, eight – drinks last night. And then there were the shots. Even my eye-lashes felt heavy, glued together. I must have left my make-up on. Oh well.

Roy was getting ready to leave when I emerged from the bathroom.

I kissed him before climbing back into bed. 'Thank you.'

'Hey,' he said, his voice cracking with tenderness, 'I love you.'

ROY

Thursday, 10th September

I love you. *I love you?*

I closed the door softly behind me.

Guilt wracked through me. I couldn't believe that I had betrayed Mia and then acted as if nothing had happened; that I had kissed Mia and told her I loved her, as if I hadn't kissed another woman just last night.

You're amazing, Emily had said.

Just thinking about it . . . it hit me again. The regret. The nausea. The utter, complete shame of it all. Unfamiliar tears pricked my eyes. A reminder of how different this was to my little indiscretions with past girlfriends. This was Mia. My wife. My beautiful, fragile, would-do-anything-for-me wife. Fuck.

Fuck.

I wanted to go back in time and shake some sense into myself. I couldn't believe I had been stupid enough to walk off with Emily like that, drunk as I was. I knew that girl was trouble.

You're amazing.

This would kill Mia.

Sure, things had been tricky recently. Mia was always anxious, we had both spent too much time focusing on our careers and not enough on each other, and then there was the never-ending situation with my parents. But despite all the usual disappointments that came with marriage, Mia and I . . . we loved each other. We were happy.

We were *successful*.

I had gone and ruined all of that.

MIA

Thursday, 10th September

A stack of pancakes and two cups of coffee later, the bassline of my hangover dropped to a gentler, more manageable hum. It was almost soothing, this quiet buzz in my ear, a reminder of the madness that had ensued last night. I smiled to myself. It was real. I hadn't imagined it. It had been a great night. I hummed as I showered and dressed. I had arranged to meet Addi downstairs at midday – I was a bit late but Addi wouldn't mind. Most of the guests were away so I could dress casually. I threw on my favourite Alexander Wang jeans and a linen T-shirt and stepped into my plimsolls. No heels, thank you very much. My feet were still sore from all the dancing last night. A quick slick of lip balm and I was ready to go, armed with my iPad, some Post-its and a pen.

I checked the time again as I waited for the lift, squinting at the scratched dial, the watch on my wrist much older than me. It used to be Dad's when he was a student and I'd inherited it from him. The mahogany leather was curling up and peeling off in ripples after years of constant use. I frowned at the deep horizontal ridges branching out from the hole I'd had added in. They were threatening to split the strap in two. I had been refusing to get the strap changed for years but I'd probably have to concede soon.

Dad had been austere in his possessions and, aside from his books, most of which had gone to Addi, there wasn't much in terms of personal effects for either of us to hold on to. Mum had had a big clear-out the day after the funeral. Uncle Bill and Aunty Jane were always around in those days, and I remember overhearing Aunty Jane telling Mum to leave it for another day. It was too soon, she had said. But Mum had been stoic, adamant. She found it painful coming across all of Dad's things, she said. She kept forgetting he wasn't coming back and she couldn't have a breakdown every few hours, not with two little girls to look after. In just one afternoon, Mum and Aunty Jane had folded up all of Dad's clothes and stacked them up in boxes, ready to be sent to Iraq or Burma or one of the many refugee camps Mum sent things to every year. I had presumed the watch went in one of those boxes to some far-off camp so when Mum gave it to me, six years later, on my thirteenth birthday, wrapped up in pale blue tissue, it had been a welcome, if tearful, surprise. I had raced up the stairs to show Addi, laughing and crying at the same time. Daddy's watch had been a constant companion ever since, staying firmly clasped around my left wrist for most of the last sixteen years. I intended to wear it to my thirtieth next year.

As if on cue, the lift doors opened and I all but walked into Uncle Bill.

'Didn't you go for the city tour?' I asked, giving him an awkward half-hug as we traded places.

'Did you tell your mother I was looking for her last night?'

'No, sorry, I—'

'Tell her to come and find me,' he said. The lift doors closed and his looming figure disappeared down the corridor.

The decorators had started by the time Addi and I reached the ballroom. We had agreed on a clean blue and cream colour scheme for the wedding – a stark contrast to the kitsch theme of the *sangeet* and *mehendi*. Though we had hired a specialist decorator for this evening, I was nervous about whether the crew would be able to deliver everything I had asked of them. It hadn't been possible for me to fly down before the wedding and I'd had to brief them via Skype. The flurry of activity in the ballroom was a good sign and I let out a breath I hadn't realized I was holding. When I had requested hydrangeas, delphinium, anemones and roses, the florist had politely reminded me that they were in the middle of a desert and then swiftly sent me an invoice reflecting the air freight and 'convenience' charges. Nothing was impossible in India as long as your pockets were deep.

The flowers had arrived in insulated boxes that morning and the florist was busy arranging them into bouquets.

Addi and I walked to the centre of the room, where someone had laid out printed copies of all the pictures from my Pinterest board next to large-scale printouts of the ballroom's floorplan. It had been a nightmare procuring these – hotels were nervous about these things after the Mumbai shootings.

'Wow! This looks great,' Addi said, crouching down to leaf through the pictures.

'You're welcome, sis,' I said, walking around to look at the centrepieces. I had requested that each table have a slightly different bouquet of flowers in the vintage crystal vases. Same but different.

Addi trailed behind me as I scribbled notes and stuck them to the vases where the arrangement wasn't up to scratch, the neon orange of the Post-its jarring against the pastel flowers. 'Are you still seeing the same therapist?' she asked when I put my pen away.

I nodded. Huge brass urns had been lined up against the backdrop of the sandstone pillars, overflowing with bundles of cream- and honey-coloured roses.

'Is it helping? Any more episodes?'

The French doors leading onto the terrace had been flung open and the terrace itself was lined with hurricane lamps and tea lights. We stepped outside. Two men on stepladders were setting up the *mandap*, where Addi and James would make their vows to each other. They were draping swathes of cream silk around the wooden frame, stretching, tossing the fabric, and then pulling it taut. Stretch, toss, pull. Stretch, toss, pull.

'Not since last year . . . April. James was right about her being a good fit. She does . . . she just gets it, you know? More than any of the others . . . and I feel better, more in control,' I said. I turned to look at her. 'She's a good therapist, Addi.'

The man on our right teetered on his ladder and I took a step towards him. He pulled, shifting his entire body weight onto the fabric and using his feet to stabilize the stepladder before resting on it again and resuming his three-step routine. Stretch, toss, pull.

'Hey, this is not about getting a review for James's colleague! You're my baby sister and I *am* allowed to worry about you. Especially if you still haven't told Roy?' Addi persisted.

'I can't. You know what he can be like.'

We made our way back inside, the mid-afternoon sun still too harsh on the terrace. A young girl sat cross-legged on the floor, carefully unwrapping clear-glass orbs and placing a tea light in each, ready to hang them around the *mandap* once the drapes were done.

'I know, darling, and I understand keeping it from everyone else. But you can't keep lying to your husband. Roy practically worships you, and everything that happened . . . it's so far back in the past, he's not going to care about anything except being there for you.'

'Yes, but he can be so narrow-minded sometimes. Roy is very . . .' I sighed. 'He just thinks therapy is for crazy people, you know? He'd look at me differently. I don't know if I can take that.'

Addi put her arms around me and gave me a squeeze. 'Oh Mia. I could ask James to talk to him? Maybe if he heard it from a doctor . . .'

I looked around the room. Everything was as it should be and the decorators seemed to be running on time. The room would be ready by five p.m., they said, an hour before the first guests were set to arrive.

'No. I'll tell him myself, Addi. I just need some time,' I said, standing back to examine everything one last time before we left.

It looked perfect but I could sense the familiar anxiety sneaking up.

Something wasn't right but I couldn't quite put my finger on it.

ROY

For once, the absurdities of social life in India entertained me immensely. I posed for countless family photos with near strangers, all of us hugging each other and grinning like long-lost friends when we had met barely twenty-four hours ago, our one hundred per cent natural fake smiles immortalized against the backdrop of the tourist high-lights: the centuries-old fort cannon, the gilded window in the *haveli*, the arch of the Jain temple. The excessively friendly chatter that was usually a source of irritation distracted me and made me feel normal again.

Sightseeing accomplished, I bundled the guests into SUVs to go to Kuldhara, a ghost town thirty minutes away from the city, where Mia had arranged a sit-down lunch. I'd come across Kuldhara when I was researching locations for my Condé Nast series and had mentioned it to Mia one day over dinner. The next thing I knew, she had arranged a traditional Rajasthani meal for the guests amidst the myth-ical ruins.

I climbed into the last car in the convoy. The driver was wearing a bright green shirt and mirrored sunglasses – Ray-Mans, as per the logo on the top right corner.

'Kuldhara, please. Can you overtake the other cars?' I had to get there first to ensure everyone knew where to go.

'Yes, yes, worry not.'

He zigzagged his way forward on the narrow road, dodging cars coming from the opposite direction with a slap on the steering wheel and some mild abuse. In a matter of minutes, we were leading the convoy.

'Very hot in desert,' he said.

'Hmm.' No matter where you go, people seem to love talking about the weather.

'You Delhi? Mumbai?' he probed when I didn't reply.

'London,' I said, looking out of the window. Why are Indians so nosy?

'Look Indian,' he said.

A pause. He swerved to avoid a herd of camels. Small dunes had cropped up on either side of the road. We were heading deeper into the desert.

'Know story Kuldhara? Strange place.'

'Uh-huh.'

'Ruler of Jaisalmer wanted to . . .' he traipsed on.

I closed my eyes and leaned back in my seat, pushing it back till it was almost horizontal. Not only had I heard the story countless times by now, I had researched it and shot a segment on it. I didn't need to hear it from him.

I checked my phone. I had sent Emily a text earlier that morning telling her I was sorry. The kiss was no more than a drunken mistake. I loved my wife. I valued my marriage. I had asked Emily not to come tonight. This was more than three hours ago and she still hadn't replied. I wondered if she'd stay away.

She was a sweet girl, Emily. Perhaps in another world we could have been together but here, now, I was with Mia and I had to focus on that. There was too much at stake. I wasn't about to mess up my marriage like I had all my other relationships.

I was considering texting her again when the car jerked forward. We had arrived at the transfer point. We had to walk the rest of the way. I got out of the car and motioned for everyone else to follow. I felt like a measly tour guide.

'About two hundred years ago, the residents of Kuldhara abandoned the village. No one knows where they went or why. There are a couple of theories, but the most popular seems to be that the governor of Jaisalmer, a man called Salim Singh, fancied the village chief's daughter and ordered the chief to send her over to his house in the city,' I started, my words rehearsed from the filming a few days ago.

'So what? That was pretty common back then, right?' one of Mia's cousins interrupted.

The angry glare from the sun pierced into my neck as I led the group through the crumbling walls of the once thriving community. I paused to take a sip from my water bottle. The queasiness I was feeling had nothing to do with the heat.

'It was, but this man was known to be malicious and the

young woman was something of a rebel. They say she vanished overnight, taking the entire population of Kuldhara, fifteen hundred people, with her.'

A few people were taking selfies with the sandstone staircase that stood in the middle of what must have been a house. No roof, no walls remained. The staircase was leading nowhere. I waited for them to finish before moving on.

'No one's lived here since?'

'No. Allegedly, the residents buried some treasure within the village before they left and cast a curse condemning anyone who attempted to dig for it or inhabit the land.'

'That's so creepy, man. What's the other story?'

'That Salim Singh picked up the girl and had the village evacuated.'

In both stories, Salim Singh was the villain and the girl the victim. In both stories, the girl disappeared without a trace. I wondered if anyone had ever asked him for his version of events.

I could feel the hot sand burning my feet through the thick soles of my trainers and I quickly led the group towards the dilapidated ruins of the community centre where lunch had been laid out. After elaborate Rajasthani thalis and sandy tea, we set off towards the cars, anxious to get back to the known comfort of the hotel.

I adjusted the direction of the air-con vents and checked my phone as soon as we were on our way. Still silence. I waited. I typed another text, then deleted it, then typed it again before deciding to put my phone away. We were halfway to the hotel when my phone beeped.

i understand roy. i'm sorry too. i let my feelings for you get the better of me. didn't mean for it to happen. enjoy the rest of the wedding and thank you for being so sweet. i'll see you in london xxx

Emily dealt with, I tried to devise a way to tell Mia about the kiss, break it to her gently, but every script I ran through in my mind sounded more contrived than the last. I thought back to my conversation with her mother last night. Mia already had so much to deal with right now; I didn't want to add to her worries. If I told her about last night . . . Mia saw the world in black and white; her inflexible morals would turn a kiss into something far more licentious. She would be devastated. She would be furious.

She wouldn't let it go.

Telling Mia would only complicate things. It was just a kiss, after all. Emily's lips had been on mine for a mere second. It wasn't even a kiss really. It was a glitch – an insignificant, minor glitch – and it shouldn't matter in the course of a marriage, I reasoned. A non-kiss didn't matter. No one had seen me. I loved Mia. I wasn't lying. That's what mattered. I'd got drunk and made a mistake. Granted, it was a huge and incredibly stupid mistake, but I had fixed it. Emily had agreed to stay away tonight and I didn't have to see her again. George could always find another assistant. It was really not a big deal and there was no point bringing up something that would only cause Mia more pain, I decided.

My decision made, a deep sense of relief followed in its wake, the significance of that one moment with Emily fading easily into swirls of rosy desert sand.

By the time I returned to the hotel, my hair was stuck to the back of my neck, my skin was clammy with grime and my head was throbbing from the sharp desert sun. I swiped my key card and flung the door to Mia's and my suite open, wanting nothing more than a long shower and a few uninterrupted hours in bed. What I got instead was this.

Mia was leaning against the edge of the sliding doors that separated the bedroom from the sitting room. She had her back to me. My mother-in-law was sitting on the sofa, clutching one of Mia's lists and a pen. The glass coffee table in front of her was littered with papers. It looked like yet another wedding crisis and it wouldn't have fazed me had it not been for my mother. She was sitting on the sofa next to my mother-in-law, wearing a concerned smile.

'*Namaste*, Mummy,' I said, addressing my mother-in-law first before walking over to my mother for the more formal greeting that Ma preferred. 'You look well,' I said as I bowed down to touch my mother's feet, dainty under her stiff silk *sari*.

Mia turned around when she heard me and gave me an apologetic shrug. She was on the phone.

'Roy, good you're here, *beta*. We were just running through the check-out schedule and travel arrangements for the guests leaving tonight. Your mother kindly offered to help.' My mother-in-law smiled at Ma. 'She's so good with organization.'

My mother is terrible with organization. She just wanted a way in.

I forced a smile. 'Sounds like a task. I'll leave you to it.' I walked quickly towards the bedroom, ready to slide the door shut.

'*Beta*, we could use your help.' Ma. She was wearing her characteristic my-son-disappointed-me expression.

My eyes darted to my mother-in-law. She set her spectacles down and gave me a watery smile.

She had been nothing but kind to me all these years.

I settled down on the armchair across from the mums and smiled one of my perfect son-in-law smiles.

'Of course,' I said, picking up a handful of tissues from the side table and wiping the sweat off of my face and neck. 'How can I help?'

'There's been an accident just outside Jodhpur. Train got derailed.' She paused before going on to explain. 'It was a goods train so no casualties. But all trains going through Jodhpur tonight have been cancelled. We're going to have to arrange road transport for everyone flying out from Delhi tomorrow. Mia's speaking to the hotel manager about rooms and extending check-out times.'

She passed the guest list to me.

About forty guests were scheduled to fly on the nine p.m. Delhi to London flight tomorrow. Emily was on the same flight. I wondered if she knew about the cancellations. I'd have to call her and make sure she was okay.

'Have we looked into hiring a bus?' I asked.

'The concierge says we can't find an air-conditioned bus at such short notice,' Mia said, hanging up the phone and disappearing into the bedroom. She reappeared a moment later, handed me an Evian and perched on the arm of my chair, peering at the list in my hand while I drained the bottle.

I had driven down from Delhi with Emily and George. Twelve hours in a 4x4 going at eighty-five miles per hour. That had been some ride.

'SUVs?' I suggested. 'If we get ones with luggage carriers, we should be able to fit seven people in each car. It shouldn't be much more expensive.'

'That would work,' my mother-in-law said. 'What did the manager say about the rooms, Mia?'

'As long as they check out before eight a.m. tomorrow, they won't charge us anything extra for up to fifteen rooms. For the rest, it'll be half the day's tariff and we can keep the rooms till midday.' Mia beamed. She was a great negotiator. She insisted the entire concept of fixed prices was a hoax built up to fleece gullible civilians. 'But we've got to run through the list of rooms with him right now.'

'That's great. Why don't you guys go down and sort out the rooms? I can speak to the car service in the meanwhile,' I said. For all our failed attempts at telepathy, I was hoping Mia would get my drift this time.

It was thanks to her that my mother was even there to begin with, so I felt no guilt at all in letting Mia deal with whatever drama was coming next.

'Sounds like a plan.' Mia got up and straightened her T-shirt. 'Shall we go down, Mummy?' she asked her mother and then turned to mine. 'Ma, why don't you come too? I wanted to show you the spa. They've got these amazing ayurvedic treat—'

My mother held up a hand, silencing Mia mid-sentence. 'I feel a bit ill. I'll rest here.'

I took a deep breath. Why did my mother have to be so difficult? All through my childhood, that hand had kept me at bay, disciplining me, silencing me, distancing me. Now she wanted a relationship? Tough chance.

Mia and her mother left and I busied myself with phone calls. I rang Mia a few minutes later to let her know eight cars were booked for six thirty a.m. tomorrow.

'You've lost weight,' my mother said when I hung up.

'Hmm . . .'

I sent off a quick text to Emily.

'I saw your article in the *National Geographic*. It was . . . interesting. It's good to see you pursuing real writing. Are you doing anything else for them?'

'No. That was a one-off. I'm working predominantly with *Vogue* and *Harper's Bazaar* right now.'

I could see the contempt creep up my mother's face – the son of the country's top neurosurgeon and an award-winning economist writing fluff for womens' magazines. I had been raised to excel and excel I did: at disappointing my parents. It was their own fault.

'And the documentary?'

'A web series for Condé Nast.'

'Oh.'

'Mia mentioned you've had another book published?'

'Yes, have you seen it? Dr Manmohan Singh came for the launch.'

Of course he did. Manmohan Singh – ex-prime minister, economist and her dear friend.

'Great, I'll pick up a copy.'

The pause seemed to stretch for ages. So much had happened, neither of us knew what to say to one another anymore.

'How's Papa?' I asked finally.

'Why don't you ask him yourself? You haven't been home in a long time.'

'I've been busy,' I said.

For fifteen years? Her unspoken accusation hung in the air.

A sigh.

'He's better. He misses you.'

'Never heard him say that.'

'He's your father, Siddhant. Everything he did was for you. Can't you at least try to forgive him?'

MIA

'Hey, we're ready,' I said into the phone, looking at the rows of wedding favours Mummy and I had lined up in her room. By the window on the left were three rows of neatly wrapped boxes. The smallest boxes contained miniature horse-drawn carriages in pure silver, to be given to a handful of people – Addi's and my in-laws, Mum and Dad's siblings, aunts and uncles; the slightly bigger boxes contained silver-coated metal trays filled with dried fruits, intended for first cousins and close friends; the third row was split between envelopes of cash for nieces and nephews, tiered based on their position in the family tree, and traditional *bandhani saris* and silk ties for distant cousins and friends. Across from these, on the right-hand side, were the beige and gold paper bags that Roy and I had spent the previous evening filling up with boxes of Haldiram's sweets, *makhanas* in sheer gold pouches, and hand-written thank-you cards.

I started putting the boxes into gift bags and labelling

them as I waited, wondering how much damage control I'd need to do tonight. Roy's mum had insisted on spending the entire afternoon with him, holed up in our suite.

'Are you okay?' I asked Roy as he pushed a luggage trolley in five minutes later, parking it in the centre of the room.

'Mummy?' he asked, looking at the organized chaos around me. He waited for me to shake my head, then added, 'It was just the usual drama. Let's not talk about her.'

Silently, we started arranging the bags on the trolley.

'I'm sorry, sweetie. I tried to—' I began but he cut me off.

'I know,' he sighed, leaning over the army of glittering bags to reach for my hand. 'I'm sorry too,' he whispered.

'Finally,' Addi greeted us from her spot on the sofa. She was wearing a fluffy white dressing gown over her *lehenga* blouse and skinny jeans. One woman was painting her toenails, while another was fussing with her hair. The table in front of her was covered in make-up, hair products, tools and accessories. Her *lehenga* and *dupatta* had been laid out on the armchair next to her. 'Did you bring the jewellery?'

'Right here,' Roy said, pulling out two velvet boxes from an H&M bag. He held them out towards Addi, but the hairstylist pulled her back.

'Don't move,' the hairstylist commanded and Addi rolled her eyes.

'Bet James isn't being held captive,' she muttered.

'Bet James isn't looking half as stunning,' Roy said, handing one box to me and opening the other one himself.

I set them both down on the floor and crouched down next to Addi, taking her hand and slipping on the bangles and the rings one by one.

'Can I get you something, Addi?' Roy asked, hovering beside me. 'A glass of water, tea?'

'Wine, please, white,' Addi said instantly. 'I'm parched.'

Roy laughed and walked over to the fully stocked sideboard – bride's privileges – and poured her a small glass, then started fiddling around in the drawers.

'What are you looking for?' I asked, getting up to help Addi with her necklace, just as the hairstylist announced she was heading out for a cigarette, dragging the make-up artist with her.

'She'll need a straw, won't she?'

I smiled. No other man would have thought of that. 'Oh, they haven't got any in here,' I said. 'I'll go and get one from the coffee shop; housekeeping is too slow.'

I could hear Addi and Roy talking about me when I got back a few minutes later. I couldn't help but pause outside the door.

'I can't thank you enough, Roy. I know all this can't have been easy.'

'Don't be silly. It was nothing, and you know Mia, she did most of the work anyway.'

'Maybe, but there's no way she could get through this week without you. It's always been hard for her, admitting she needs help . . . and with everything—'

I pushed the door open, uneasy at the slant this conversation was taking, and both Roy and Addi jumped as I marched in, armed with a couple of straws and a plate of cheese.

'So,' I said cheerily. 'Wine?'

ROY

I watched Mia as she stood in front of the mirror, her shoulders rising and falling rapidly, as if her lungs were trying to get in sync with her brain. She lowered her head and squeezed her eyes shut, fingers digging into the upholstered chair in front of her. She had changed into an ivory *lehenga*, embroidered all over with small white flowers. Her dull gold blouse was modest, but clung to her in all the right places, and was fastened simply with a sleek bow in the middle of her back. Her bright red *dupatta* lay crumpled on the floor. She had been trying, for some time, to drape it.

She looked so beautiful, and so, so broken.

She obviously had no idea I was in the room or her perfectly-happy-perfectly-fine mask would have stayed firmly in place. I wondered, not for the first time, just how much Mia hid from me about her problems with anxiety.

I stood there for a few more seconds, and then, when I could stand it no longer, I went up to her and held her, burying my head in the back of her neck, my arms crushing her chest. I breathed her in. Flowers and rain. That Mia smell. The guilt hit me out of nowhere and I tightened my grip around her. I felt her tense up, then relax in my arms, and only when her breathing matched my own did I let her go.

We looked at each other in the mirror and Mia gave me a small smile.

Wordlessly, I picked up her *dupatta* and handed it to her. She tucked one end into her waistband, and then together we twisted the deep red fabric around her torso, draping it over her shoulder. She handed me a pin and I secured it to the back of her blouse, my fingers grazing her back as they fumbled with the tiny gold clasp.

'There,' I said, stepping back, 'you're perfect.'

MIA

Addi's wedding party was a flamboyant four-day affair. Mine was non-existent. When Roy told his parents we were engaged, they forbade him from marrying me. They said it would bring shame to the family, me being half English and all. Eager and obstinate, I decided, the way only a love-smitten twenty-year-old can, that our love was stronger than their hatred. We would wait. They would come around. It was all very *Romeo and Juliet*. But when, after eighteen months of tense Skype conversations, Roy told me his mother had announced they'd found the perfect girl for him, I conceded defeat. Their already fractured relationship crumbled. We agreed that a large wedding would lead to more friction and embarrassment for everyone involved – his parents wouldn't attend nor would they let any of their family attend. Moreover, we were both at the beginning of our careers and entirely broke. So two years after Roy proposed, we married in an anonymous civil court in Udaipur on a bleak Friday morning. I wore a simple red *sari* and Roy wore a grey suit – his only suit. We danced and drank champagne with a handful of people at my mother's house afterwards and flew back to London the next day. Whenever anyone asked why I had opted for such a small affair, I said both Roy and I had wanted an intimate wedding.

'You look amazing!'

The compliment turned me around. I air-kissed James's mother and got caught up in superficial banter. The evening was a mosaic of fragmented memories. People I had known all my life waltzed in and out of focus: the aunty who used to send sweets every *Baisakhi*, the uncle who loved taking Addi and me boating, the cousins we'd tie *rakhis* to every year. Snatches of conversations, high-pitched laughter and convivial jokes wafted about the ballroom. Everyone was busy putting on a show. The doting mother-in-law here, the perfect husband there. Where did it all end?

At dusk, we all moved to the terrace, wrapped up in silk scarves and pashminas. Once Addi and James were seated in the *mandap*, the fire was ceremoniously lit. Mum, Roy, the priest and I poured spoonful after spoonful of ghee into the cauldron, the dancing yellow sparks licking its curling edges, until the flames swelled, soaked in incandescent orange. Mum and I stepped back.

Roy placed Gangajal and flowers in Addi's palm and put her hand in James's before the priest tied them together with a bright red silk *dupatta*. No one saw what happened to me in that moment. Roy had just given Addi away.

Daddy should have done this.

Addi and James stood up for the *phere* and Addi began translating the verses for James.

'With this first circle, we vow to look after each other materially for as long as we shall live . . .'

Addi looked breathtaking in her deep red *lehenga*. Her eyes were glistening with unshed tears but her voice never wavered. My heart drummed. Deep breaths, Mia.

'. . . with the second circle, we vow to cherish and honour each other's physical, medical and emotional needs . . .'

Friends and relatives gathered around the *mandap* and showered rose petals on Addi and James as they walked around the fire. Everything stopped.

'. . . the third circle binds us together spiritually until all eternity . . .'

All eternity. It wasn't as simple as 'till death do us part' in Hindu marriages. Years ago, young widows would jump into their husbands' funeral pyres, so that even death couldn't separate them. *Sati.* The devoted wife, whose life belonged to her husband, even in death. Despite all our efforts, Mum had remained single for the past two decades. Was it undying love or simply cultural conditioning? Was this what marriage meant?

Something was digging into my palms. I looked down. My fingernails. No. *No.* Not now. Not again. Please.

'. . . we vow to live in happiness and harmony, share both joy and sorrow, and be content in a life of mutual love, trust and understanding . . .'

His part done, Roy came and stood next to me, his hand resting lightly on the back of my neck. I tried to slow my breathing down. I closed my eyes. Settled. I leaned into Roy.

'. . . with the fifth circle we seek the blessing of the gods for healthy children and vow to raise them to the best of our abilities . . .'

Did it matter that Roy and I never read our vows out loud? We never even had vows. Just many, many I love yous, the promise to always be faithful and a laminated piece of paper.

'. . . we promise each other unwavering support and a lifetime of togetherness . . .'

The priest's chanting rose to a crescendo, his mantras drowning out everything else. Roy slipped away to answer his phone. I focused on the flames. Indigo. Orange. Indigo. Orange.

'. . . with this final seventh circle, we vow eternal love, loyalty and fidelity to each other . . .'

ROY

Thursday, 10th September

I had never seen Mia as heartbroken as she looked that evening.

After the ceremony, all of Addi and James's closest friends and family assembled in the foyer to see them off. I stood between Mia and her mother as Addi threw fistful after fistful of rice over her shoulders, the white grains fluttering over her red *dupatta* to rest on the ground. Addi stopped walking when she got to us, pulling her mother and then me into a quick hug, before coming to stand in front of Mia.

'It's just—'

'I know,' Mia said, cutting Addi off and pulling her into a tight hug.

They stood like that for a long time, both sisters clutching on to each other, the significance of the moment so large that they could neither ignore nor acknowledge it.

After a few minutes, James stepped forward and wrapped his arm around Addi, murmuring something to her and Mia as he gently pried them apart.

As Addi climbed into the car, I turned to look at the trail of white she had left behind her, marking out a clear path: away from her old family and towards her new one.

MIA

Thursday, 10th September

'Hey,' Roy said, steering me towards the lift. The guests had all gone up to their rooms and hotel staff were clearing the lobby, ready to wind down for the night. 'You know Bristol's only a few hours away, right? She's moving closer to us, sweetie, not farther.'

Addi had been in America for the past two years. After the honeymoon, she and James were heading to Chicago to pack up. They were planning to move into their flat in Bristol before the new year. But my sense of loss had little to do with physical proximity. This was Addi moving on; it would be the start of her own family, one that would come before anything or anyone else, even me.

'I know,' I sighed.

'I need to nip around to Emily's hotel,' Roy said. 'She needs money for a taxi to Delhi.'

'Do you have to?' I said, trying to keep the neediness out of my voice. 'We could get the hotel's car service to send another car.'

'That would be complicat—'

A man yelling interrupted us.

' . . . No, NO. It's *my* brother's house. If you think I'll let you get away with it . . .'

Roy and I hurried towards the voices. Uncle Bill had found my mother.

I intervened, looking from my mother to Uncle Bill. I had never seen him this angry, nor her this anxious.

'What's going on? Is everything okay?'

'I'll tell you what's going on, Mia. I've already lost—'

'William, please.'

'Oh. Oh, I see,' he said, looking from me to Mummy. 'Must protect poor little Mia. She's not a baby anymore, Rekha,' he sneered. 'How are you going to hide this from her when the solicitors come knocking? You have no right to do this. I will not let you,' he spat and stormed off.

A handful of people had gathered in the corridor. There were no guests there, only hotel staff and decorators.

I moved closer to her, filling the empty space that Uncle Bill had left. Mummy looked frail, defeated. Roy put an arm around her to steady her.

'Mummy, what's the matter?' I asked, keeping my voice low.

'Mia, *beta*, it's nothing. You should go to your room. Roy must be tired.'

'No, we're fine. What solicitors?'

'We'll discuss this later.' She started to walk off. 'I think I'll go to bed too.'

'No, Mummy. What's going on?' I pulled her into one of the supply closets, closing the door behind the three of us.

That's when she told me, in between sobs, that she was planning to sell the house in Bristol. Dad's house. The only thing we had left of him.

'Were you even going to tell me?'

'Sweetheart, of course I was going to tell you. We thought it would be best—'

'We?' I looked at Roy. He squirmed. So he was in on this.

'You've both been keeping this from me?'

'Mia, *beta*, calm down. I was going to tell you. I just thought it would be best to wait till the wedding was over.'

'Well, it's over now.'

'Mia, just listen to her. Mummy's obviously very upset—' Roy started. I held up a hand and turned back to my mother. This was between us.

'I don't get it. It's our home!'

'Mia, things have been a lot harder than—'

'I don't care,' I shouted. 'I don't care. Uncle Bill is right. You can't sell it. Is it the money? We can help, you know. Roy and I. And Addi and James too.'

I waited for Roy to jump in and say something – of course we would help – but he didn't.

'Mia, please, listen to me. We can't hold on to the house anymore. I'm doing this for you, *beta*.' She tried to hold me like she used to but I wasn't little anymore. I wasn't weak.

'No.' I shook her off. 'NO. Don't try to pin this on me. It took you five minutes to get rid of all of Daddy's things and now you're doing it again. But this time, I'm old enough to know better and I won't let you.'

ROY

Thursday, 10th September

I seemed to have escaped my family's dramas and entered another's.

'Don't do that, don't walk away from me,' Mia said, following me into the bedroom.

'Will you just calm down, please,' I said, slipping off my tie and unbuttoning my shirt.

'No, I will not. You lied to me!'

'I did no such thing. Your mother came to me with a problem, and I gave her some advice.'

'A *problem*? So that's what I am?'

'You're twisting my words.' I tossed my shirt on the floor and turned around to face her.

'And you're ignoring mine,' she shot back, rooted to her spot by the luggage rack.

'Mia—'

'This is what you do, you just decide what you think is best for me and expect me to fall in line.'

'Mia!'

'Why are you yelling at me?'

'Move.' She stepped aside and I rummaged through my suitcase for a T-shirt. 'I'm just trying to make you listen,' I said through gritted teeth. Things had been so smooth for so long, I'd almost forgotten what Mia could be like when she didn't get her way. 'I think you're blowing this out of proportion.'

'I really don't care what you think right now,' she said. 'We're supposed to be a team.'

'There is no team, there's only me trying to make allowances for your—' I stopped myself. I took a breath. I'd been trying my best to be supportive all week, but sometimes Mia made it so hard. 'I don't think we should say any more, Mia.'

'No, I don't think we should.'

We stayed like that for a few minutes, me leaning on the dressing table, and Mia slumped on the bed, her *lehenga* and the *dupatta* I had helped drape crumpled beneath her, the silence and the weight of her expectations stifling us both till I could stand it no more. I pulled out some cash from the safe and stuffed in into an envelope.

Mia was intent on blaming me for her mother's secrets and it was clear that as much as I wanted to help her, I couldn't. Not right now, anyway.

I decided to go and sort out Emily's taxi. I told Mia where I was going and why, that simple fact lending credibility to my honest intentions. I would give Emily the cash, make sure the car was booked, the driver reliable and then come back to the hotel.

It was all perfectly innocuous.

Emily had called me during the ceremony, her voice full of apologies.

'Roy, I'm so sorry to bother you. I tried to book a car for tomorrow but they've refused to accept my card and I haven't got enough cash left to cover the fare. I hate to ask . . .'

She had gone on for some time until I'd interrupted her and told her that of course I'd help.

Emily was waiting in the lobby when I got there.

'I tried to call you. The concierge has left for the night,' she said, pointing to the clock on his desk. It was just after one a.m.

'Yeah, I forgot my phone at the hotel. Is the car booked?'

'The receptionist is checking with their car service. He shouldn't be too long. Should we get some coffee? You look knackered.'

She was wearing a pair of shorts and a vest. My gaze wandered. I looked away. 'It has been a long day. Which way is the cafe again?'

'It's closed. Let's go to my room?' she said and started walking towards the stairs. She turned when I didn't follow.

'Why don't I give you the money and you can just email me the receipt or hand it over to George when you see him.'

'You sure you don't want some coffee? I feel bad dragging you—'

'No, it's late and Mia's waiting,' I said, suddenly anxious to get back to my wife. I pulled out the envelope from my pocket and handed it to her. 'This should cover it. Be safe and text me when you reach Delhi.'

I turned to leave. Things were complicated enough. I didn't want to say or do anything I couldn't take back.

'Thanks, Roy! Don't be a stranger,' she called after me.

MIA

Friday, 25th September

London

The day's events replayed in my head while I drove. Chris, my annoyingly efficient sourcing assistant, had deemed the weekly sales meeting a fit platform to announce that he wanted to move to the new Eastern European hub. The 'change in scenery' would allow him to move on, heal, start afresh, and help set up the new arm of the business, he had hastened to add, looking at the perplexed faces of all the heads of departments.

I overheard the interns from Merchandizing talking in the toilet less than an hour later.

'There must have been signs. People in happy marriages don't cheat.'

'I know, right. But his wife's hot. I heard the other guy is an underwear model. Chris, on the other hand . . .'

Signs. If he had seen signs, wouldn't he have done something, you fools?

They shushed when I came out of the booth.

'We don't like gossip in this office.' I smiled at them in

the mirror while I washed my hands. They were infants, barely out of high school. What did they know of marriage? 'Now, didn't you girls have a report to hand in to me this afternoon?'

I had taken Chris out to lunch afterwards and the whole story had come pouring out over a bottle of overpriced Bordeaux – he refused to touch our usual Chianti. He had found his wife in bed with the Italian waiter from their local cafe. They were in love, she had exclaimed, while Al Pacino had pulled his trousers on at record speed. Just seven months ago she had professed to love and honour Chris in front of the whole world. Were people really this fickle?

You could work on it, see someone, I had suggested quietly. You took vows. People do come back from these things. But Chris was adamant. Inconsolable but adamant. I had given him a *friend's* therapist's number just in case and told him to take a few days to think about it. If after that he still wanted to move to Istanbul, I'd make it happen.

My phone vibrated on the passenger seat and I stole a glimpse as I swerved into the familiar driveway in a nondescript part of Bromley. It was Mum again. I hadn't been taking her calls so she had resorted to lengthy messages. It was always the same thing: I miss you; I'm doing this for you, etc., etc. A conspiracy of lies.

I felt a flicker of guilt as I deleted her lie and built my own.

Just going into a meeting with the team. Home by 9. Chinese tonight?

Three dots appeared instantly after I pressed send. Then disappeared. Then again. And once more before Roy settled on a response.

Okay. I'm seeing the editor tonight 😟 Promise you'll pick up the crispy duck?

Roy could be so grumpy sometimes it made me smile. It's one of the things I've always loved about him.

You got sick the last time! Such a baby ♥ I'll get it, but no more than 2 pieces for you!

My therapist, Natalie, had refused to see me when I rang her for an appointment yesterday. I'd already been to see her four times since we got back from India. She was worried about dependence. I would have thought my request for another session this week would please her – wasn't their clients' grief arguably what made therapists rich? – but it seemed Natalie wasn't seeing pound signs. It took a fair bit of persuasion, but eventually she agreed to see me. I had known all along she would; sales is my forte after all. But usually I'm the one making money not the one shelling it out.

I walked up to her front porch at two minutes to seven. Natalie always left the porch door open for clients to come in. She would open the door to her office and wave me in at precisely seven o'clock – not one minute before – after her previous client left through the back door.

I settled in on the armchair, eyeing the pale green box sitting on the mantelpiece to my right, directly below the large photograph of an anonymous beach. A clock ticked on behind me. Her office was so sparse – there was little else in the room except two matching leather armchairs, each with its own side table, a floor lamp, that picture and a few plants – I wouldn't have thought Natalie was the kind to indulge in Ladurée macarons. A gift from her husband, I presumed, as Natalie sat down in the chair across from me and crossed her legs.

'So, Mia, how are you today?' she asked, flicking open her notebook.

And so it began.

I walked out through that back door fifty minutes later, feeling drained. What had started out as a conversation about my marriage had somehow, inexplicably, settled on my parents'. Voices from the past invaded my head, tugging at memories that were best left alone. I got into my car and sat there for a few minutes, letting it all run through me.

Natalie had left me with a question: what are you afraid of?

I reversed out of the driveway and swerved onto the street, turning right at the junction. Scenes from the last few days played out in my head throughout the twenty-minute drive home.

Roy and I were in that pseudo sweet spot that you settle into after a really big fight. He hadn't apologized and I hadn't forgiven him. We had just sort of decided to ignore it had ever happened. Move on. We were having hot make-up sex – the best kind – without having really made up. We laughed at silly jokes only we could understand. We watched bad TV and ate too many takeaways. We were each in our own bubble. It was just like when we had first met except back then we had circled each other, full of longing, hoping we would collide. Now our conversations circled each other, full of longing, and we were terrified they would collide. He mentioned his dream of hiking glaciers for a year and I pretended not to hear him. I mentioned my dream of starting a family and he pretended not to hear me.

What was that, Natalie? What was I afraid of?

On Saturday, 26 September at 01.30 a.m.,
Emily Barnett <emilybarnett1994@apple.com> wrote:

R,

receipt for the car attached. i've got some dosh left over as well, how will i return it? tried getting in touch with G, but think he's in LA atm.

i'm sorry to bring this up again but i can't get that night out of my head. can we meet? i know you don't want to and i said i understood but i'm going crazy here. i need to talk to you.

also i've been thinking about going it on my own, i've attached a short film which i just couldn't resist showing you. kinda experimental but it resonates with my life right now. do you have any advice about going freelance or know anyone who can commission some shorts? can't wait to hear your thoughts.

thank you thank you thank you.

Em xxx

On Sunday, 27 September at 09.11 a.m.,
Roy Kapoor <roy_kapoor@me.com> wrote:

Emily,

It's good to hear from you.

I do see something of you in that film.

I suppose the best advice I can offer is this – be true to yourself and pursue your passion, wherever that may lead you. Rules can and must be broken. That is what creates authenticity and provokes emotion. I can't imagine you would have any trouble with that 😀

Of course we can meet. Perhaps we both need some closure . . .

And I'm sorry I was so blunt that night. I didn't know what to do. However complicated, my marriage does mean a lot to me.

En route to Paris for the day as we speak. It's wonderfully moody. Reminds me of you.

Roy

ROY

London/Paris

A meeting left wanting is the promise for another.

For a while now, I had been working on a proposal for a year-long travel project. I loved working as a freelance writer but with grudging passion. Yes, I got to travel the world but it was rarely on my own terms and never quite artistic enough. In striving to be completely different from my parents, I had somehow ended up exactly like them: settling for a career that was lucrative financially but not creatively. The freedom I had craved as a teenager toyed with me, seemingly within my grasp but eluding me all the same.

This project would change all that. I would be able to explore the abstract side of travel, blurring lines between genres, disciplines and mediums, culminating in a multidisciplinary exploration of some of the world's most extreme landscapes. Part memoir, part fiction, this was an ambitious project and I was nervous and excited in equal measure to see it through. I had sent off the proposal to a handful of editors earlier this year. Sara Morgenstern, a hotshot New York editor, had got back to me, suggesting we meet up during her upcoming Europe trip. She was spending a week in an apartment in Le Marais and had invited me over for weekend brunch. Very chic and *very* American. Mia and I had resolutely avoided speaking about both the meeting and my project. We had spent the forty-five minutes it took us from our house in Crystal Palace to the station discussing the last episode of *Grey's Anatomy*. Meredith Grey and Derek Shepherd's problems were code for our own. After we had pulled into the drop-off bay, Mia had leaned over and kissed me passionately. Over the past few weeks, sex had been good. Really good.

I re-read the email from Emily while I waited to go through security at St Pancras. I considered my reply. Even though nothing could happen between us, I still owed it to her to meet her one more time and talk about what had happened in a mature manner. There was no point in leaving things unresolved. The clarity would only help us both put it behind us.

I checked the departures board. I wanted to pick up a proper coffee for the train. Even in first class, Eurostar's coffee was terrible.

The woman in front of me seemed to be struggling with her suitcase. She was holding up the queue.

I tapped her on her shoulder. 'Do you need a hand?'

'I . . . umm . . . no . . . yes, actually,' she mumbled. 'Yes. Thank you,' she said, finally letting go of her case and turning to look at me. She was plain, her face void of any make-up, long black hair pulled up in a humble ponytail. The faint bruises along her right cheekbone were the only hint of colour on skin so pale I could see the ghosts of veins criss-crossing her forehead.

'No problem,' I said, lifting up the case with one hand. It didn't budge. I laughed. Both hands. 'What have you got in here?'

She looked at her feet. A hint of sadness hung about her.

'Good intentions,' she turned to say softly before walking through the metal detector.

Sara was everything you would expect a New York editor to be. What she wasn't, however, was interested in my project. Not as it stood in any case.

After brunch, we walked over to a cafe just off Rue Payenne. We sat at one of the tiny wrought-iron tables that had been lined up along the achingly cool cobbled courtyard.

'The thing is, Roy, as much as I enjoyed reading your proposal, I don't know what to do with it,' she said, pausing to order our coffees. '*Deux noisettes, s'il vous plaît.*'

She waved off the *garçon* with a practised flick of her hand and then went on to list everything that was wrong with my proposal.

'Your itinerary leaves little room for delays or detours, which, being as experienced as you are, you will know are unavoidable. Realistically, your one-year project could take anything between fifteen and eighteen months, plus post-production, which shoots up the budget by at least forty per cent. Just the logistics, the team, the budget, the sponsors – it's too complicated to pull off, especially for someone who is still relatively unknown.'

She paused to light a cigarette.

'You're a talented man; your piece on Reykjavik in the July *Vogue* was fabulous. Why not stick to what you do best? A more accessible version of the same idea – go to a couple of these places, but stay in hotels. Go to the extreme landscapes you've researched, but with a guide. Interact with people there. Go to the local hotspots. Tell your readers how they can have these experiences too. That's what great travel journalism is about.'

A drag.

This was a Yale philosophy alumna talking.

'Send me a revised proposal. It can still be a travel memoir, just lose the fable-istic soul-searching aspect. Do a few top ten lists. That I can work with. That I can sell, and for good money.'

MIA

Bristol/London

I was getting coffee from a vending machine when my phone rang.

'Addi! This has to be the longest honeymoon ever. Are you in Bali now?'

'I know. I'm sorry I haven't called. We're in Hanoi right now. Flying to Bali tomorrow. It's so beautiful here, Mia. You would love it. And the food . . .'

'Can't be better than the gourmet doughnut I just picked up at the service station,' I said, looking at the disgusting mess I had bought. I took a bite. Ugh. No.

Addi laughed. 'Service station? Where are you going?'

'Bristol,' I said, before I could stop myself. Shit.

'Oh. How come?'

'I'm meeting a friend for lunch,' I lied. 'And, um, I thought I'd go check out the house while I'm there.'

'Mia . . .' She paused. I could hear the worry in her voice. 'Don't. Is Roy with you?'

'No, he's away.' I took a sip from the Styrofoam cup. It

tasted burnt. I dumped my unfinished coffee and doughnut in the bin and walked back to my car. I'd stop at a proper cafe in Bristol. 'Relax, Addi. Natalie suggested I go there. She thinks it'll be good for me.'

'Really? Well, all right, but leave if it gets too much, okay? We should have done this together,' she said. There was a loud crackling sound. 'I think I'm losing signal, Mia. Listen, have you spoken to Mummy? I called her yesterday and she sounded upset. Is everything okay?'

'Yeah, everything's fine. She was probably just tired,' I said.

I could hear James in the background. He sounded far away.

'Okay, darling. You're right, I'm just worrying about nothing. I must run now, but call me later, okay?'

'Sure,' I said and hung up.

Everything was not okay. But even though we hadn't spoken, Mum and I had a silent pact. No one says anything to Addi till she's back. She deserved a break.

I locked the front door behind me and went straight into the kitchen. Over the years, tenants had refurbished more or less the entire house, but this room was exactly as I remembered it. I set my keys down on the breakfast bar in the middle of the room. I blew on the scratched marble surface and swirls of dust rose up and danced under the sharp beam of light coming in from the window, glimmering like specs of gold and silver glitter. Here one moment, gone the next.

Memories swam in the air, filling the empty room with glimpses of my childhood. Addi and me sitting there, legs swinging, as we ate our cereal before school. Dad picking me up and twirling me round and round, till I shrieked with laughter. Mummy plaiting my hair with pink and green ribbons for Holly's party. Mum and Dad whispering to each other, while Addi and I pretended to do our homework.

I walked around, letting the musty smell settle into my skin. The last tenants hadn't looked after the house; there were cracks in the walls, mildew, and the fittings in the bathroom had layers of rust on them. I went from room to room, voices from my childhood filling my head, memories from a different life seeping into me, crawling under my skin. I stopped when I got to Daddy's study at the back of the house. Mummy had closed up this room before we went to India, using it as a storage space for anything that couldn't be packed into our suitcases. She had said we'd come back for everything in a few months but we never did. The room stayed locked. The estate agent said he opened it every time there was a changeover of tenants to make sure there was no damage. Was there anything left to damage?

Natalie asked me last week if I idolized my parents' relationship, if I was trying to model my marriage on theirs. I had never looked at it like that but yes, I said, I suppose so. They had been a unit. They had been happy. *We* had been happy. Until the day before my seventh birthday, that is, when my father's car somersaulted across an empty motorway, destroying itself and our family. He had died instantly. Cardiac arrest. He didn't suffer, they'd said. She asked me if I was carrying guilt. If, perhaps, I was punishing myself. No, I lied, vehemently, angrily. Why would I punish myself? I wasn't carrying any guilt. I just missed him, that's all. And why did we have to keep circling back to my father anyway? I demanded. My problems had nothing to do with him.

The door rattled when I pushed it open.

The room was packed. I walked around the polythene-clad furniture to the far corner where Addi's and my matching pink bikes stood next to an island of neatly stacked and labelled boxes – *Kitchen, Crockery, Books, Cassettes, Linen, Rekha, Mia, Addi, David.*

David! I moved the boxes that were on top of it and pulled out Daddy's box. Did we still have some of his things left? It was taped up. I ran back to the kitchen with the box and yanked the tape open with my keys. Files, paperwork for his car, insurance, old notebooks, calendars. Nothing personal but this was his stuff! I decided to take it back with me, along with my own box, so I could take my time looking through it all. I carried the boxes to the car and placed them carefully on the back seat.

As I drove back towards London, my thoughts returned to the large pink box sitting in the corner of the room, still undamaged, the printed text on it just a little faded after twenty-two years. I hadn't told Natalie that the police had found a gift-wrapped package on the back seat – the doll's house Dad had promised to get me for my seventh birthday. Wasn't it strange that my miniature house had stayed intact through it all, ignorant in its bubble-wrapped cocoon of the damage it had caused while my real house crumbled from the inside out?

Roy was already waiting at the pick-up point when I pulled up.

'Hey,' he said, climbing in and flinging his bag in the back.

'Hey, sorry, the M4 was blocked. Overturned lorry,' I said.

He grimaced. Roy hated driving even more than I did.

'I didn't get time to pick up food. Do you want to order in?' I asked, trying to steer us out of the bay and onto the main road.

He hadn't noticed the boxes on the back seat. Or he had and he'd chosen to ignore them.

'It's fine, I ate on the train.'

'How was Paris?'

'Disappointing. She isn't interested.'

An SUV was holding up the lane in front of us. Roy drummed the dashboard impatiently. I played with the radio till I found a song I liked.

'I'm sorry, sweetie. Did she say why?'

'It'll take too long, it's not commercial enough. She suggested I turn it into a top ten list.'

'Hmm, maybe she's right? You're too busy for this right now anyway.'

The SUV jerked forward and we moved out of the bay and into the steady flow of black cabs.

'What's that supposed to mean?'

'Just that you have enough going on without having to worry about this too. With all the commissions, your new video segments and all the travelling I have to do, we hardly see each other anyway. I miss you. You can go back to this project in a couple of years, can't you?'

'No, I can't. I need to do this now while these regions are still unexplored,' he said.

A grey mist had started pressing down, blurring the view. I flicked on the wipers. *Don't make assumptions, Mia; be more forgiving*, Natalie had said. I tried.

'Okay, sweetie, I'm sure someone else will be interested. Have you spok—'

'We could fund it ourselves,' he said. He turned the music down and carried on, mistaking my stunned silence for encouragement. 'Think about it. We could dip into our savings, remortgage the house, I go away for a year. You can visit me once every couple of weeks, whenever I'm at a hotel. We'll get to see some of the best landscapes in the world.' He paused and smiled. 'And once it's done, no more long projects. We'll settle down and start planning a family.'

I couldn't believe it. Had he just tried to trade his year off for a baby? I tightened my grip on the steering wheel.

'No.'

'Sorry?'

'No,' I repeated, a little louder this time. 'We said we would help pay for Dad's house with the money. This project can wait till you find funding.'

'You can't impose things on me, Mia. And *we* didn't say we would pay for the house. You did.'

There was resentment in his voice. I didn't get it. Couldn't he see how important this was? I couldn't let my family be blown apart again. We had to get through this together.

'Don't you want me to protect my family?'

'It's a house, Mia.'

'It's my *home*. It's all I have left of—'

'And a dead investment. Listen to your mother, there's a reason she wants to sell it. We can't help, even if we wanted to. She's made up her mind.'

'She'll change it.'

'It's amazing how selfish you can be.'

Let it go, Mia. Don't push him. Don't risk your marriage over this.

But that one word, spoken so carelessly, undid me. I couldn't stop.

'Seriously? You knew I went to Bristol today and you haven't even bothered to ask me if I'm okay. Now you're telling me that my childhood, my family, isn't important enough and that all our money should go into a project that basically no one wants and that will keep you away for God knows how long, and you're calling *me* selfish?'

The silence that followed seemed to buzz. We drove quietly for the rest of the trip home. Neither of us knew how to back down from an argument. I was worried that this time I had gone too far.

Roy unbuckled his seat belt as soon as I pulled up outside the house.

'Roy, please,' I pleaded. 'I'm just trying to hold everything together here.' I looked at him, searching his face for the man I loved, the man who used to love me. 'I'm trying to hold *us* together.'

'By forcing me to stay?'

On Sunday, 27 September at 11.15 a.m.,
Emily Barnett <emilybarnett1994@apple.com> wrote:

thank you for taking the time to give me proper advice. everyone else just tries to convince me one way or another. i know where my passion may lead me and that scares me.

i'm sorry for contacting you again. i really am. i'm not as strong as i thought i was but i promise i'm trying.

when can we meet?

xxx

On Sunday, 27 September at 10.55 p.m.,
Roy Kapoor <roy_kapoor@me.com> wrote:

Being strong doesn't mean not talking about what you're feeling. Being strong means facing reality and embracing it, getting to know yourself, your dreams and desires and being at peace with them. Fear is good; it means your passion, whatever it may be, matters. Don't stop chasing it.

Crystal Palace Park, 3 p.m. day after tomorrow?

ROY

London

Emily was waiting for me at the entrance when I got there.

We walked around aimlessly for a while, following the looping gravel path. The park was busy for a weekday afternoon, full of people trying to catch the last of the summer sun. Toddlers rolled around in the grass, small creatures lost in their own world, while their mothers lounged on benches, keeping half an eye on them. Dog-walkers strolled clutching Styrofoam cups of coffee, Labradors in tow. An old man walked in slow motion, holding on to a walking stick with one hand and a young girl with the other. The girl, probably his granddaughter, kept leaning over and speaking into his ear. Every time she did that, he nodded and smiled.

The activity around us, the *normalcy*, masked that bizarre uneasiness that seemed to appear whenever I saw Emily.

I stole a sidelong glance at her – she was wearing a pretty summer dress and strappy sandals. A small leather bag hung from her shoulder with a denim jacket thrown over it. I wasn't sure how to bring up the kiss. We had been speaking to each other in fonts and pixels for so long I was finding it difficult to vocalize my thoughts. She spoke first.

'So, that night, I'm sorry. I am. But—'

'Look, don't worry about it,' I interrupted. 'We were both drunk and we got a bit carried away. That's all. It doesn't have to mean anything.'

My words sounded rehearsed and utterly insincere.

'I know it doesn't,' she said. 'It can't.'

She stopped and turned to face me.

'But the thing is, Roy, I don't regret it,' she said. 'That night, that kiss, everything, it was exhilarating. I haven't felt this way in a long time. And I – I can't stop thinking about you.'

I didn't know what to say. I had deluded myself into believing meeting with Emily would kill things when in reality it was doing the opposite. It *had* been exhilarating. Of course it had.

A bunch of kids were playing Frisbee a few feet from us. Behind them, a young couple was kissing, oblivious to everything around them. Teenagers. They didn't care who saw them. They could do anything they wanted, anytime they wanted, no consequences. They were free. They had a few more years of optimism ahead of them. Crushed dreams and cynicism would come later.

'Did you know there's a maze here?' I asked Emily.

I didn't know what I was doing. I wanted to stop, to turn around and walk back to my home, my wife and all our familiar problems. I also wanted to taste that freedom again. I wanted to pull Emily to me, right there, amidst the Frisbee kids and lazy dog-walkers, and kiss her. I ran my hand through my hair. I had no idea what I wanted.

'Really?'

'Yeah.' I pointed towards the far end of the park. 'It's beautiful but hardly anyone ever goes there. One of London's rare secret spaces.'

'Show me.'

We walked silently for a while, along the vaulted terraces and past the famous dinosaur sculptures. We circled the lake, heading deeper and deeper into the park, until we reached the fields. The grass was taller than I remembered it, sun-drenched after the long summer and interspersed with weeds and wild flowers.

I looked at Emily, eyebrows raised. She nodded and I led her through the field, trampling the knee-deep grass as I went. It fought back, prickling me through my jeans. I turned to look at Emily behind me. She was walking with both her arms stretched out, trying and failing to keep the blades away from her legs.

A large metal arch announced that we had reached the maze. We walked through it towards the dense labyrinth of hedges.

There were two identical paths on our right and left. I instinctively took the one on the left. There was an overwhelming scent of something, pine perhaps, emanating from the hedges. We pushed our way forward through the winding trail, searching for the next connecting path. The back of Emily's hand grazed mine as we went further into the maze. The trail got narrower, forcing us closer together; the path became lost in shadows and overgrown branches. I could no longer hear the noises from the park filtering through and other than the slight rustle of the leaves, mine and Emily's breathing was the only sound I was aware of. We stopped when we reached a dead end.

I knew where this was going.

I let my fingers brush Emily's as I turned to face her. I took her hand.

'Shall we turn around?' I asked, running my thumb along the inside of her wrist.

'We could,' she said. She moved closer, our bodies still not touching. I placed my hand on her waist, lightly. I could just about feel the suggestive curve of her back.

I spun her around. My hand was still on her waist. Our bodies were still apart.

I leaned in and whispered into her hair, 'This is even more intoxicating than I imagined.' I paused, breathing her in. I stepped away. 'But I cannot do this, Em.'

She turned around, confused.

'My marriage . . . it's complicated,' I said. 'It's not always easy but . . .' I trailed off. I was rambling.

'I don't expect you to leave her, you know.'

I looked at her, taken aback.

'I would never mess with your marriage. That is not what this is.'

This girl constantly surprised me.

She took a step towards me.

'She can never know,' I said.

We were inches apart now. I was breathing differently. We both were.

'I know,' she whispered.

For the first time since I had met Emily, I allowed my eyes to wander, taking their time. Her bright blue dress had little flowers printed on it. It was short, just skimming her thighs, held up only by two tantalizing straps. I couldn't tell if there was a bra underneath. It staggered me how badly I wanted to find out.

A slight smile was tugging at her lips.

One tiny step. That was all I had to take to feel her skin on mine. To lift her dress. Push her thighs apart. My crotch tightened. I realized then that my mind had been made up long before we entered this maze. I had just been biding time, working up to it. The walk, this maze, it had all been foreplay. It was as simple as that.

I took the step, pulling her to me, kissing her, touching her with unbridled urgency. Her back. Her shoulders. Her breasts. Her hands were in my hair, on my neck, darting down my chest, pushing me away, unzipping me, pulling me back in, closer. Closer. So much closer. She moaned when I lifted her leg and pushed her thong to one side. My fingers dug into the back of her thigh as I entered her. She told me to go harder, deeper. She begged me not to stop.

And so I didn't.

MIA

London

'I can't take your price to the sign-off, Mia. Design House is giving us a maxi-dress for a similar price. We need your dress to sit around the eleven-pound mark,' Jo's voice echoed, bouncing off the bare walls of the meeting room.

Mike was sitting opposite me, scribbling furiously. He slid his notepad across the glass table. He had circled the magic number three times. I nodded and spoke into the speakerphone.

'I understand, Jo, but the style you've picked is a complicated one and you *know* it doesn't always come down to consumption. The CMT on the panels alone is nine pounds! I've already brought our margins down to nothing for you.'

Mike was nodding eagerly. I got up and walked to the window. The street below was already filling up with shoppers. Oxford Street had proclaimed that Christmas was here. In October. People needed little more than a nudge to throw money away.

'I'm looking at the dress right now, Jo. I don't know how my design team managed this, but it looks exactly like the panelled skater dress that everyone's been talking about. You know the one from the Paris shows? Was it Moschino? Wait, no, that's Milan. Umm . . . Balenciaga?' I paused, pretending to think.

Jo's been in trade meetings all week, there's no way she would have looked at the shows. Neither had I.

'Hmm . . . are you thinking of the McQueen number?' she asked.

'Yes! That's the one. You're *so* good with these things,' I gushed.

'I see the similarity now that you mention it,' she added. I could almost see the smug look on her face. Buyers are so vain.

'Look, you've got a potential bestseller on your hands. If you can sign off the orders today, we'll get the shipment to you for mid-December. You'll have it on the floor before McQueen's factories even start cutting.' I paused. 'You could easily get away with a fifty-quid retail on the dress if you promote it right.'

'That's all very well, but I still need a better price. It is a mini-dress after all.'

Mike had got up too. He was pacing the floor. We really, really needed this order to go through.

I took a deep breath and looked at Mike, willing him to calm down. I punched some numbers into my calculator.

'I know, I know,' I said, keeping my eyes on him. I sighed. 'Okay, how about this – I can bring it down to fifteen twenty-five *if* you think you can up the quantity to eighty thousand pieces? Now, I know that sounds like a lot,' I added, before she could object, 'but we can stagger the deliveries for you – December and the end of January perhaps? Launch it post-Christmas and run a back-in-stock promo in Feb? That's the only way I can get this price past management.'

'Are you sure that's the best you can offer?'

'Afraid so.' I perched on the arm of the sofa, swinging my legs.

'I'll get back to you after the sign-off,' Jo said.

'Of course. Let's talk more this evening.'

'What the fuck was that?' Mike demanded as soon as I hung up. He was clutching on to the chair, leaning on it with all his weight. 'I told you to agree twelve fifty. We need this order.'

Mike and I were a 'team'. Technically, he was my manager but we'd been on the same pay grade for a while now. We were also gunning for the same promotion. *Awkward*.

I picked up my notebook and checked my watch. I was running late. 'Fifteen twenty-five gets us over forty per cent,' I said, as I slipped out of the room.

'Oh, just tell him to sod off. What would his price have made?' Roy asked. We were at our usual table in the Waterstone's fifth-floor cafe.

I looked up, surprised at this sudden show of support. Perhaps Natalie had been right after all. Things had been tense since that night in the car and in my session yesterday she had suggested – insisted really – that I arrange a casual lunch with Roy in a 'safe' environment. Take some of the pressure off. Show him we were still a unit.

'Twenty-eight per cent. Company minimum is twenty-three so twenty-eight's not bad.'

'But it's not forty per cent.'

'It's not forty per cent,' I agreed, smiling. 'And if Jo bites, the increased quantity will mean we make nearly five hundred thousand pounds. As opposed to Mike's a hundred and eighty.'

'What if she doesn't go for it?'

'I'll have to go back to her with some story and agree to a lower price. But if she's already placed it with another supplier . . .' I paused. Shit. What if she placed it with another supplier?

You'll be fired, the voices in my head murmured. *You'll lose everything.* I silenced them and focused on Roy.

'Mike will run to the board, get the sales director post, get rid of me,' I reeled off. It sounded a lot worse out loud than it had in my head. My confidence from this morning evaporated. Jo could easily move the style to Design House or Cubus or any of the vultures that had set up shop in east London in the last year. They would jump at it. Mike would get directorship. I'd get fired. Shit. Shit. Shit. What had I done?

Natalie's voice popped up in my head. *Come on, Mia, what's the worst that can happen?* I pushed her away. Even Natalie couldn't be right all the time. *The worst that can happen is a fucking catastrophe.*

I took a deep breath and tried to slow my brain down. There was a strange poster with illustrations of windows on the far wall of the cafe. It was new. I started counting the windows. I was up to twenty-two when Roy spoke.

'Hey, you.' Roy put his hand on mine and squeezed. 'Don't overthink it. You're far better at this than Mike and everyone knows that. Remember the Christmas party?'

I nodded. Roy was right. At the Christmas do last year, Elizabeth Pritchard, one of the founding board members, had waved me over to the top table and insisted I sit next to her. I had spent the evening chatting with everyone on the board while Mike glared at me from his usual table. After his fourth glass of Prosecco, Harvey Shaw, another board member, had leaned over and whispered, 'We're looking forward to having you on this table permanently, Mia. Just keep doing what you're doing.' I had gone home on a high and fallen asleep repeating everything to Roy on loop. I woke up the next day to snow in the garden and an unprecedented annual bonus in my bank account. We paid off the bulk of Roy's student loan and booked a chalet in Zermatt that week.

I shook the thoughts away and squeezed back.

Roy's tenderness touched me. He always knew what to say to make me feel better. He had seen how upset I was and decided to put our argument behind us, no questions asked. Couldn't I do the same?

If everything went to plan, I could finance his project next year *and* help with Dad's house. That would solve everything. I was going to tell Roy this when I noticed the waitress, Anna. I smiled at her as she placed a large slice of cake and two forks between us. We dug in.

Another thought occurred to me: a year apart might make us stronger but it could just as well be the last straw. It could be the final blow that would break us irreparably.

ROY

'Thanks, Anna. Give our love to Janey,' I said as Mia and I walked towards the lift.

We'd been coming here for years. Mia had made me work hard to score that first date and I had known instantly that the usual dinner and drinks was not an option and a stroll along the river or a trip on the London Eye was a cliché. Plus there was the issue of money – I had none. So I had picked her up from her student halls one afternoon and we'd wandered through Soho chatting easily about her course, my last submission, and the challenge of finding a good cup of *masala chai* in London. She'd been surprised when I'd steered her into Waterstone's, my hand resting automatically on the small of her back. I thought we were drifting aimlessly, she had said with a smile. We'd spent the rest of the afternoon flirting over Fitzgerald and Hemingway and then climbed up the five flights to the cafe for coffee. The layout and scale of the place had changed dramatically over the past few years but we'd continued coming here. It had become an easy tradition, one of so many that made up the DNA of our relationship, though these days Mia usually had to rush back to work. Browsing through the bookstore had become something of a solo foray and Rumi and Rilke had replaced Fitzgerald and Hemingway.

The Poetry section was tucked away in an alcove on the first floor. I was leafing through the new Rumi edition when I heard a phone ringing behind me. I turned to see a woman bent over the table showcasing modern poetry. Long black hair veiled her face. She had deposited her bag on top of the books and was rifling through it, emptying it out, presumably to find the offending phone. She looked vaguely familiar. She must have found the phone and turned it off then because it stopped ringing. Just before I went back to my book, she looked up and our eyes met. In an instant we agreed we didn't recognize each other. I heard her walk off a few minutes later.

Emily had emailed me yesterday, asking if I wanted to meet up. The guilt I'd been tiptoeing around all week had finally kicked in last night and I'd been fighting it all day. I knew why I was drawn to her – the admiration, the excitement, the respect . . . it was all so electrifying. She had made her position clear, but before I agreed to see her again, I needed to figure out if it was worth risking my marriage over a short fling. Whatever Mia's faults, we had been together for nearly a decade and I needed her in my life.

I picked out another book and decided to make my way

over to the till. I paused briefly to look at the display table. A small leather-bound book wedged between the stack of Kate Tempest and Michel Faber caught my eye. I remembered seeing the woman pull this out of her bag earlier. I picked it up. Tiny gold letters announced the title: *LIKE THE SEA*. It looked worn, the navy leather slightly discoloured. I hesitated and then opened it. Perfectly looped letters covered entire pages in black ink. Words and phrases leapt out at me, a few that I recognized – snippets from poems I could recite verbatim – but most of these permutations were new, words arranged in a manner that felt both unknown and familiar at once.

> *they sit watching the clouds gather*
> *quietly over the valley*
> *puckering the sky, guarding*
> *the peaks, hiding*
> *joys and catastrophes within*
> *the earth craves the sun*
> *and the moon the earth*
> *strangers yesterday, lovers today*
> *known phrases float from unknown lips*
> *not even the clouds know*
> *if they harbour rain*

I went over to an armchair in the corner and sat down, leafing through the notebook with an urgency that mystified me. Every page held poems that stirred me in ways I hadn't known were possible. There was the sensation of something clicking into place, as though somehow these words alone were reigniting a longing that I had long forgotten existed.

I was immersed in a poem about crossroads when a shadow darkened the page.

'I believe that's mine.'

I looked up. The woman from earlier, the poet, was standing in front of me. I stood up, hastily snapping the notebook shut.

'Yes . . . I . . . Your writing . . . it's—'

'Personal.'

'Oh. Of course. I – I didn't . . . I found it on the display table and I—'

She snatched the notebook out of my hands and turned to the first page. She held it up for me to see.

PRIVATE. PLEASE CALL 07598 636544 IF FOUND.

'I'm so sorry. I didn't see that,' I said.

She regarded me for a minute, then turned around and walked off towards the staircase, stuffing her notebook in her bag as she went.

I found myself rushing after her.

'Are – are you following me?' she demanded, spinning around to face me before I could say anything.

It took me a second to grasp what she was insinuating.

'What? No,' I said. 'Of course not. Look, I'm really sorry I read your work without your permission, but your writing . . . it's sublime. I – I couldn't stop myself.'

'Well, you should have,' she snapped back.

'Have you published anything?' I persisted.

'Just – please just back off.'

'Hey, I'm sorry if I upset you. I'm a writer too, and I was just curious,' I said, taking a step back, hoping that would put her at ease. Something passed over her face and I added, a bit more softly, 'Have you showed these to anyone? An agent or publisher?'

'No,' she sighed. 'I only started writing last year.'

I nodded, fixing my gaze on her pale face. I was amazed at how deeply this woman's writing had touched me, at how much I *cared*. She started walking down the stairs and I followed. 'It's hard. I was the same when I first started writing. But you're a natural. And these poems . . . you really should get them out there.'

I walked with her all the way to the ground floor, talking at her, telling her about my own experiences from when I was starting out, and with every step, I could sense her softening towards me.

'Do you really think people would like these? My poems?' she asked, incredulous, as we stepped out of the bookshop.

'Yes! Anyway, it can't hurt to try, can it?' I smiled, strangely satisfied.

Outside, a light rain had begun to fall, no more than a slight spray, but enough to turn the quickly dampening pavement dark. I pulled up the collar of my jacket as we lingered under the awning, talking about poetry competitions and readings. It was still bright but lamps had started flickering on up and down the street. My gaze settled on a young couple seated at the window seat of the cafe across the road. They were sitting quite close together, each lost in their own world, the woman staring out of the window and the man looking at his phone. There was a detached intimacy between them that can only come from years together. I caught broken glimpses of them through the steady stream of traffic in front of me until the stark red of a bus obscured them from my view. I sought them out again a few seconds later when the bus moved. They were sitting in the exact same position, doing the exact same things, not touching but still connected, stuck in a single moment of their lives that would stretch on forever. I turned my attention back to the woman standing beside me. Despite the chill in the air, I unwrapped my scarf and stuffed it into my pocket, finding the soft wool oddly suffocating.

'Well, it was nice to meet you,' she said, hesitating.

'Which way are you headed?' I said. I couldn't shake the feeling that I knew her from somewhere.

'Waterloo.'

'Ditto. Shall we walk?'

She nodded and we fell into step together.

'Why did you start writing poetry?'

'I'm not sure, really,' she said. 'It happened quite organically, I think. I sat down with my notebook one day and the poems just started writing themselves.' She smiled, looking straight at me. The stark contrast between her pale skin and black hair rendered her otherwise ordinary face striking. 'Is that strange?'

I smiled. 'That's how the best poems are written. It's a dying art.'

She nodded. 'Sad, isn't it? The most evocative form of writing yet the most often overlooked.'

'Most people skim through one poem in thirty seconds and dismiss the entire genre.'

'People dismiss what they don't understand,' she said. 'I have a friend that I sometimes exchange books with. I loaned her a copy of this new anthology a couple of weeks ago and the next time we met, she was frantic. What does it mean? she kept asking me. The words are beautiful, but what do they mean?' She paused as we crossed the road, and then carried on. 'You see, for me the beauty of a poem is that it's unfinished. I love that its meaning lives in the space between words. But for her, and she's an accountant, it was incomplete. It asked a question but didn't provide the answer. Do you know what I mean?'

I regarded her for a minute. I had never before had such a conversation with a stranger. I decided to go with it.

'Absolutely,' I said, 'that's what I'm always telling my wife. You can't fit poetry in a neat little box, you don't read it the way you would a novel. You hear a poem; you feel it, smell it. And then you find your own truth in it.'

'What does your wife say?'

'Usually, it's something like, all right, sweetie, let me just finish my Stephen King and I'll give Dickinson a shot.'

'And does she?'

'Never.'

She laughed.

We walked along the Strand and turned right towards Waterloo Bridge, passing the dimly lit Somerset House on our left, quietly reclaiming its stature after the madness of fashion week.

'So what about you? Have you always wanted to be a travel writer?'

'More or less,' I shrugged.

'Aha, and do you love every minute of it?'

'I suppose I do.'

'You sound convincing,' she smiled.

'It's just hard,' I found myself saying, after a few moments. 'For me, travel has always been about freedom, and curiosity, and even when I'm on assignment, I like taking my time, and slowing down to experience things. But we live in an age of endless choices. And even before I've achieved one thing, I'm hankering after the next. It can be disorientating.'

'I know what you mean. Wanting something, whether it's a new book or a career or intimacy, is terrifying, but it's also beautiful. I want to be content, but also, I would worry if I didn't crave new experiences from time to time. It would make me feel, I don't know, numb in a way.'

I nodded. We were walking side by side, the conversation flowing so naturally it felt like we had known each other for years. I found myself compelled to speak to this woman with an honesty that astonished me. And yet we hadn't even introduced ourselves. Or perhaps it was because we hadn't introduced ourselves.

It was strange.

It felt like I was talking after an eternity of silence.

The night had started to settle in. Across the river, the

London Eye buzzed with activity, its lit-up pods turning slowly in an incomplete circle, disappearing into the black clouds that floated above us. I glanced at the woman walking alongside me as we crossed the bridge and the sensation returned that I knew her from somewhere.

'I'm sorry, this is going to sound strange, but have we met before?' I ventured.

'No, I don't believe we have.'

'Oh.'

'Well, anyway, this is me,' she said, pointing to the bus stop across the street. 'It was nice to meet you.'

'Likewise,' I said with a small wave.

I watched her walk to the bus stop, looking twice at everyone around her as she queued up for the bus, clutching her wallet in one hand, and holding on to her handbag with the other. It was just as she was disappearing into the bus, her movements peppered with a strange mix of grace and fear, that I remembered where I knew her from.

On the way home, I found my thoughts returning to Emily. I knew what I had done was wrong. Everywhere I looked there was evidence to that effect. But I found it hard to associate the image of a cheating husband or a sordid affair with what had happened in the park that day. And wasn't it like the woman said, I reasoned, craving new experiences was what made us human, alive? I had spent so long trying to fit myself into the mould of the perfect husband, I had forgotten why I'd moved to London in the first place. I had given up on my dreams and convinced myself that the stability that marriage brought was more important. But weren't the ability and the means to savour every moment a necessary condition for happiness? It seemed naive to expect any long-term relationship to remain perfect throughout when the people in it were constantly evolving. Shouldn't we expect instead that, like in life, there would be mistakes made, times when one or the other partner would go off course? Why should it even matter as long as no one got hurt? The more I thought about it, the more obvious it seemed that not only was it unfair to expect Mia to be everything, it was impossible. There was nothing wrong with seeing Emily as long as it didn't hurt my marriage.

As long as Mia never found out.

MIA

Mike was waiting for me in my office clutching a pint-sized Starbucks cup when I walked in.

'You're late.'

I checked my watch. 'It's six minutes past nine, Mike,' I sighed. 'What's up?'

'Jo didn't call back, did she?'

'Not yet.'

I must have checked my phone a thousand times since yesterday. Nothing. I had all but convinced myself it was because her meeting had run late until I saw her tweet at half six last night.

Isn't it great when everything just falls into place? Best sign-off ever. Can't wait for our X-mas range to hit the stores!

Did that mean she had dropped our style? Or worse, placed it with someone else?

I reached around Mike to put my bag and my own regular-sized coffee on my desk. I shrugged off my leather jacket, waiting for him to move so I could sit down.

'You need to stop being so goddamn arrogant and just call her. Give her what she wants. Harvey will not be happy if we lose this order.' Mike stormed out of my office and into his own across the floor, cutting through the maze of open-plan desks that stood between us. Every trained Sourcing and Merchandizing eye darted from him to me. I closed the heavy glass door, which provided little more than a false sense of privacy, and reached for my phone. It was time to eat humble pie.

Voicemail.

By lunchtime, I had reviewed my spring-summer sales projections, emailed three potential new buyers and pulled up two factories on inflated prices. I still hadn't heard back from Jo. I didn't think my stress levels could shoot up any further until I saw Roy's mother's name flashing on my phone. Just what I needed.

'Mia, I've tried calling Siddhant but his phone goes straight to voicemail. Do you know where he is?' her voice crackled in my ear.

'He's on a press trip in the Atlas Mountains, Ma. He probably doesn't have mobile signal. How are you?'

Somehow, over the years, lying to Roy's mother had become so natural I didn't even pause to think of excuses anymore. Roy had travelled far more in these phone calls than he had in real life.

'I need to speak to my son.'

'He'll be away all week. Can I help?'

There was a long pause.

'Hello? Ma, can you hear me?'

'Yes. Well, I've been invited to chair a seminar at Oxford University next month.'

'That's great. Congratulations.'

'Yes, yes, thank you. Papa and I will be in Oxford for three days. We'll visit Siddhant and you for a few days afterwards.'

Shit. This was not something I was prepared for. Roy and I were finally in a good place again and his parents visiting . . . that would screw everything up. But Ma wasn't asking. I saw Chris hovering outside my office and waved him in.

'Of course, that'll be lovely. Do you know your dates yet?'

'The fifth to the eighth of November.'

'Let me just put that in my diary.' I paused and audibly flicked through some papers. 'Oh no, Ma. We're away at a wedding that week. It's such a shame, we would've loved to—'

'We'll be in England for a few days. We can plan around your dates. Get Siddhant to call me as soon as he's back.'

'Kill me now,' I said to Chris when I hung up.

'Roy's mum?' he asked, leaning on the door frame.

'Uh-huh.'

'I don't know why you put up with her. She sounds like a right bitch.'

'I wish I had an option.'

He opened his mouth to say something but I beat him

to it. I knew what was coming. Chris thought Roy used me as a buffer with his mother, which Roy totally did, I just didn't want to hear about it right now.

'What's up?' I asked.

'I'm going to go pick up lunch. Want anything?'

'Ooh, yes please,' I said, digging around in my bag for my purse. My hand brushed up against something hard and I pulled it out. It had been sitting in there for days. 'Actually, I'll come with you . . . Do you mind if we take a slight detour?' I asked, waving Roy's iPad at Chris.

We stepped out of the office and into the steady stream of shoppers on Oxford Street.

'Madness, isn't it? Who even knew there were so many people in London?' Chris said whilst we waited at the four-way crossing at Oxford Circus.

I laughed and nodded. Kylie Minogue had switched on the Christmas lights last week and people kept stopping to look at them. They weren't even on yet. Wait a few hours, will you, I felt like saying to the woman who was struggling to hold on to a baby buggy full of shopping bags with one hand while taking a picture with the other. The crowd thinned as we crossed over onto Regent Street.

'How are things with Alanna?'

'Fucked. She's at her sister's. Or so she says. I can't be bothered anymore, to be honest.'

'Oh Chris.' I reached out and squeezed his arm.

'I'm leaving her, Mia. Can't be with a woman I don't

trust. I was going to wait until next week, but I might as well tell you now. I've made up my mind about Istanbul.'

'Are you sure about this? I—'

'What?'

'Never mind. I'll speak to Harvey once we know what's happening with the Eastside order.'

'Thanks,' Chris said, pulling out a cigarette. 'What were you going to say earlier?'

'Oh, nothing.'

'What? Go on.'

I let out a small sigh. 'I don't want to overstep, Chris, and what Alanna did . . . I can imagine how devastating that must be . . . but people make mistakes. And they can come back from those mistakes if they're given the chance. You both took vows. In good times and bad, remember? If you leave now, you may not have a wife to come back to.' We stopped outside the Apple Store and I turned to look at Chris. 'She might move on.'

'We also vowed to be faithful. Those are just words, Mia. Not everyone looks at marriage the way you do. And as far as having a wife waiting for me, I don't care. I'm done.'

Chris waited outside whilst I went into the Apple Store to drop off the iPad. Roy had been working in the kitchen last week when I'd walked in with the groceries. I'd placed the bags on the table and, in doing so, knocked over a glass of water that had proceeded to seep into the iPad. It had died quietly while we unpacked the Sainsbury's bags.

'It can take between eight and ten weeks and even then, I don't know if we'll be able to fix it. The damage is pretty extensive,' the Apple guy said, handing me a sheet of paper. 'Fill that in clearly, please. How did you get water on the device again?' He looked at me like I was an imbecile. I checked his name tag. Rick.

I smiled at him.

Working at the genius bar doesn't make you a genius, Rick. Accidents happen.

'That's okay, just do your best,' I said, scribbling down my name and address on the form.

We were in the queue at Pret when my phone rang. Finally.

'Hey,' I said, popping my head into Mike's office. He was chin-deep in a burrito. 'Jo called. We've got the order. Fifteen pounds.'

'That's – that's great. Well done.' Even the salsa smeared on his face couldn't mask his sour expression.

'Thanks,' I smiled, turning to leave.

'Have you told Harvey?'

'I'm going to see him now.'

'Wait, I'll come with you,' he said, reaching for a napkin and wiping his mouth. In my five years here, I had never seen him abandon his lunch.

We took the short flight of stairs up to the management floor. The muffled sound of our footsteps as we walked to Harvey's office filled the silence that had fallen between us. I had only been up here twice since the refurbishment earlier this year; they had really gone for it – floor-to-ceiling glass windows, plush carpets, leather upholstery, the lot.

Harvey waved us in as soon as he saw us. I smiled at his secretary, Yvonne, on my way in. She must have told him why we were coming up.

'Mia, Mike, I hear you have some good news?' Harvey beamed.

Mike rushed in before I could say anything, speaking through the perma-smile he reserved for board members. 'We've sealed the Eastside deal, Harvey. Half a million. Forty per cent.'

'Excellent, that's a good few quid!'

'Thanks, Harvey,' I stepped in. 'It was touch and go for a moment there but I spoke to the buyer this morning and, thankfully, we've clinched it. The official orders should be with us in a few hours.'

'Just what I like to hear, well done.'

Harvey gestured towards the leather swivel chairs across from him.

'And we've got plenty of time for the shipment so it should be all smooth sailing from here on,' Mike said once we had both sat down.

'Well, not quite. They were keen on a pre-Christmas launch so I've had to agree a quicker lead time. End November ex-factory for hit one and mid-Jan for hit two,' I said.

Mike's eyes focused on me. 'I didn't realize you had amended the terms,' he said, his smile still in place. 'That's cutting it quite close.'

Harvey leaned back in his chair. A slight frown was beginning to punctuate his face.

'It's only a couple of weeks less than our usual leads. Nothing our factories can't handle,' I said.

'Where are you placing this?'

'Isla Apparels. Turkey.'

'Bit risky, considering the Euro hub is so new. We may need a trip,' Mike chipped in. 'Make sure everything's in order, talk the factory through compliance, etc.' He paused. 'Why don't you go over there for few weeks, Mia?'

'That's a great idea, Mike. We need to look at training the new staff there anyway. But I was thinking we could send Chris instead. I spoke to him this morning and he's willing to relocate there for a while. He can train the new staff and monitor the order there and I can oversee things at this end. What do you think, Harvey?'

'Are you sure he can handle it? We've heard murmurs about a breakdown . . .'

'That's just office gossip. You know how vile it can get. Chris has been on enough trips with me to know the drill and I can always fly over if he needs me.'

ROY

Tuesday, 6th October

I could hear Mia in the kitchen when I stepped out of the shower. I pulled on a T-shirt and joggers and went downstairs. She was busy assembling a salad. A bottle of red wine stood open on the counter.

'Someone's in a good mood,' I said, walking over to pour a glass for myself. I took a sip. Mia's taste in wine was impeccable. A far cry from the vodka-guzzling girl I'd first met.

She turned and gave me a peck.

'We got the order!' she grinned. 'Harvey was pleased to say the least.'

'Brilliant. Mike?'

'Mike *said* he was pleased and then he suggested I go to Turkey for a few weeks.'

'Bastard. What did you say?'

'I managed to dodge him,' she said, setting the salad bowl on the table and checking the oven. 'We're sending Chris instead. How was your day?'

'Good. I spoke to George. Looks like they loved the video segments. They want us to draw up a plan for a twelve-part series.'

'That's great, sweetie. Well done.'

'Hmm,' I mumbled, taking another sip.

'So . . .' she began. She turned towards me. Her face had taken on a pained look. I looked away, flicking through the stack of takeaway leaflets on the table that seemed to grow higher every week.

'We need to talk,' she said. She was leaning against the counter, almost-empty wine glass in hand. My heart raced. I found myself wondering if she had somehow found out about Emily.

'Roy,' Mia said.

I looked up. I forced myself to calm down. I reminded myself that she had looked perfectly happy just moments ago.

'Ma called this morning,' she continued, twirling her glass.

I allowed myself a small sigh. I summoned my voice. 'Yeah, I had about ten missed calls from her. Where did you say I was?'

'Atlas Mountains.'

'Good. What did she want?'

'She and Papa are coming to the UK next month. They want to come and visit us.'

'What?'

'I told her that would be lovely but—'

'You told her what?'

'Roy, please, just hear me out. I tried to get out of it – said we were away that week – but she just said they'd move their dates to suit us,' she rushed. 'I didn't know what else to say.'

'So you invited them to come and stay with us instead? Have you lost your mind?'

'She invited herself!'

'Yeah, I'm sure she did.'

'You *know* your mother. She doesn't ask.'

'And I know you! Always fucking meddling.'

'I wasn't meddling! She called me because you didn't answer your phone. I was trying to—'

'Spare me the bullshit. This is what you've wanted for years.'

'You think I like playing referee between you and your mother? I wish you'd man up and speak to her yourself. Why can't you just put the past behind you so we can all move on?'

'I'll speak to her when I want to speak to her.' I closed the distance between Mia and me and slammed my still-full glass on the counter. The wine swirled and sloshed, threatening to spill out. In the background, the oven beeped.

'Stop trying to fix my family.'

MIA

I can't breathe. I CAN'T breathe. I look around for something, someone to hold on to. I close my eyes and try to focus on staying afloat. I can feel the water rising. The pool is shrinking, closing in on me. I snap my eyes open. I look at my hand, now barely over the surface of the water. It tires, wanting to drop down. I channel all my energy into keeping it there; just a minute ago I was waving frantically. I scream out for help but all that comes out is a strangled gasp. There's water in my mouth, in my ears, swirling through me, filling up my lungs, hammering against my chest. I'm trying to think, come up with a strategy, but all I can think about is Roy. Where is he? He never leaves me alone in the water. I look around again. He was here just a minute ago. Where did he go? I can't breathe. I need to breathe.

I woke up with a gasp. My eyes flicked open and I kicked off the covers, suddenly hot. Next to me, Roy was snoring softly. I touched his shoulder, letting my hand linger for a few seconds, but he didn't stir. I checked my phone: four forty-five a.m. I slipped out of bed and went downstairs to the kitchen. The wooden floor felt cool under my bare feet. I clutched the counter in front of me as I gulped down a glass of water.

The vividness of the dream had left me shaken. My heart was in my ears. I gripped the worktop harder, my muscles tightening with the effort. I shook my head. Finally, as the remnants of the dream started to slip away, I managed to breathe again.

Natalie was going to have a field day with this one.

'Hi,' I spoke into the phone quietly, a few hours later, 'it's Mia. Could we pencil something in for this morning?'

She must have registered the quiet terror in my voice because for once, without any of her usual talk of dependence or overwrought schedules, she agreed immediately.

'Okay, so, Chris, if you could look at flights and a hotel for the first week, I'll get that signed off tomorrow. Susie, could you please liaise with Design and QC for artworks and specs. I'd like to get the tech packs over to the factory ASAP. Helen, let's run through your notes on the compliance manual tomorrow afternoon.' I snapped my notebook shut. 'Any questions, give me a shout,' I said. I allowed myself a quick look around the table before getting up, trying to decipher if anyone had smelled my panic or noticed my dwindling attention. The emergency session with Natalie had calmed me down but even so, I had caught myself slipping a few times during the meeting. So I had sped through it all, delegated more than I usually would and brought in distractions in the form of pastries. Everyone was busy taking notes, half-eaten croissants and muffins in front of them. The cliché about people in fashion starving themselves was just that – a cliché and utter bullshit. No one says no to a free treat. I picked up an almond croissant and walked out. I still had the rest of the day to get through.

ROY

'You go first. I'll see you soon,' I said, zipping up my jeans. I smoothed back my hair in the mirror. Emily nodded and slipped out quietly.

It turns out a handicapped toilet is as good a place as any for sex – lots of space and plenty of handles and railings for leverage. The discreet basement location was a bonus. I walked out of the toilet, up the stairs and out of the cafe, after a mere two minutes, undetected. I nodded to Emily on my way out. She was sitting at the table by the window with a menu open in front of her.

I had barely reached the end of the street when my phone beeped.

same time, tuesday? xxx

I smiled to myself. I must be really good.

'I'll get that,' I said, reaching for the bill. I caught the waitress's eye and held up my gold Amex. I turned back to George. 'Do you have any thoughts on the team yet?'

George leaned back in his chair, hands behind his head, legs stretched out on one side of our window seat. At six foot four, George struggled to fit into any regular-sized space. 'I still need to work through the budget with the producers, but I was thinking of bringing Adrian on as first AD and Gill for art and creative. Emily can still assist with locations, but we'll need to get a local scout on board too,' he said.

'Ah,' I nodded, pretending to consider it.

'There you go.' The waitress handed over the card machine to me with a wide smile. Add gratuity? I pressed 'No' and punched in my code. She was doing her job – one she was paid to do – no need for tips. I handed the machine back to her and the smile disappeared.

'What were you going to say?' George asked when she'd left.

'It's nothing,' I said, pushing my chair back. 'I'm just a little surprised you want to bring Emily on. It's your call of course,' I added.

George's face was intent as he nodded. 'No, I know what you mean.' He paused, getting up to slip on his jacket. 'She can be a bit OTT and we need someone with a bit more tact for Africa.'

I felt my phone vibrating in my jacket pocket and pulled it out. My mother's face flashed on the screen, interrupting my line of thought.

'Just something to consider,' I said, frowning. I debated letting it go to voicemail but she would just ring Mia and I didn't want to risk *that* again. For all I knew, Mia would invite them to move in with us.

'I'm sorry, I have to get this,' I said to George, before speaking into my phone. '*Namaste*, Ma.'

'Siddhant? I've been trying to reach you all week. Did Mia tell you?'

I sat back down and mouthed an apology to George as he walked off with a wave. The waitress scowled at me from across the room. I motioned to her to bring me another coffee.

'Yes, Ma. I've been travelling.'

'How was your trip?'

'It was fine.'

'Will you be coming to India soon?'

'No.'

'Did Mia tell you I've been invited to chair a seminar in Oxford?'

'Yes. Congratulations.'

'Maybe you could come to Oxford for the talk? It's on . . .' I heard the rustle of papers as she paused and a mental image of her bent over her desk flashed before me. 'Tuesday the third of November, ten a.m.,' she continued.

I pushed the image aside as the waitress plonked a flat white and another bill in front of me. I wasn't the teenager waiting for his mother to look up anymore. 'I don't think so. It's a working day.'

'Oh. Well, anyway, we'll come and visit you. We can spend some time together then. All of us. As a family.'

There was a hint of desperation in her voice and I couldn't help but wonder if her distress was more than just a ploy. 'I'll probably be travelling.'

'Yes, Mia told me you are going for a wedding. I will ask my secretary to coordinate dates with her. We will see you in a few weeks, *beta*.'

I hung up and sipped my coffee slowly, trying to hold my space on the table for long enough to clear my head. Ma sounded determined and short of refusing to see them outright, there was nothing I could do to avoid seeing my parents. Perhaps that is what I should do, I thought. They – *he* – certainly deserved it.

An image of my father flashed across my thoughts. It was always the same: him standing in the living room, telling me to clean myself up and stay in my room. I slumped back in my chair and gazed out of the window. The street outside was starting to fill up with bankers and estate agents, all anonymous in their identical black suits and matching Bluetooth headsets, rushing to get back to their suburban existences. A cushy job, a large house in zone forty, a trophy wife and two perfectly well-behaved children. They were clearly living the dream I had passed up on.

A woman in a red jumper and leggings caught my eye, standing out in the army of suits. My eyes followed her as she walked past the window and entered the cafe, oblivious to my scrutiny. She looked familiar. I caught a proper glimpse of her face as the waitress led her to a table along the wall, directly across from me.

It was the woman from the bookshop.

I paid for my coffee and walked over. She had a notebook open in front of her. I tried to resist taking a peek.

'Hi.'

She continued writing. I hesitated.

'Hi,' I said again, bending down to touch her arm lightly.

She looked up with a start, panic clouding her face until recognition wiped it away a second later. She snapped her notebook shut. 'Oh, hello. Strange running into you here.'

'Certainly a coincidence – unless you're following *me* of course?' I teased.

She gave me a bemused look. 'Indeed,' she answered.

'Do you work nearby?' I asked her.

'Sometimes. I'm a freelancer.'

I waited for her to elaborate and then, giving up, 'What do you do?'

'I dance. Contemporary ballet.'

I looked at her lithe frame, long hair, and the air of fragility that surrounded her. It made sense. Everything about this woman whispered poise.

'I remembered,' I muttered.

'Excuse me?'

'I remembered . . . where we first met – before Waterstone's, I mean.'

'I don't think—'

'Eurostar. I helped you with your bag?'

'Oh.' She frowned. 'Oh yes, of course. I'm sorry, I was in a state that day. I don't remember much about that journey, to be honest.'

She looked troubled. I found myself wondering what had made her so. 'I've had days like that. Were you travelling for work?'

'No.' She hesitated. 'I had to go and see an ex. It ended . . . badly.'

'I'm sorry to hear that.' I stepped to one side to let a waiter pass.

'Thank you,' she said, then after a moment of thought, 'I guess I wasn't who he wanted me to be.'

'Are we ever?'

The woman shrugged.

'Anyway,' I said, 'I'd better be off. It was nice seeing you again.'

She nodded but said nothing.

As I turned to leave, her last comment still stuck in my head, I realized I still didn't know her name. It was absurd. I went back to her table. This time she saw me coming and looked up, her colourless grey eyes regarding mine directly.

'I'm Roy, by the way,' I said, holding out my hand.

She smiled and took my hand.

'Celia.'

MIA

Friday, 16th October

I gave an involuntary sigh as I stepped out of my heels and snuck in, closing the door softly behind me. Even though the lights were off, the milky glow from the window illuminated the room enough for me to find my way around. Chris's leaving drinks had stretched on longer than expected and I had texted Roy halfway through the evening to tell him not to wait up. Still, I had fooled myself into believing he would.

Roy stirred when I opened a drawer.

'Hey,' Roy murmured, 'come to bed.'

'In a minute, sweetie.' I was still wobbly from the cocktails. I pulled out a clean T-shirt and walked over to the bed.

'What's the time?'

'Half two. Go back to sleep.' I knelt down to kiss him lightly before tiptoeing into the en-suite. By the time I came out, he had rolled over onto his stomach, fast asleep. Next to him, on the nightstand, his phone lit up to announce a new message and then went black again.

Roy had come to bed full of apologies a couple of days ago. He had spoken to his mother and knew it wasn't my fault. He had overreacted; would I forgive him, please? Of course I would. I always did.

Natalie had been pleased when I told her. She said it was a sign we were both invested in the relationship. She had compared it to one of Mum and Dad's arguments I had told her about, using it as an example. Every marriage has its ups and downs, she had said, but what mattered was that we were using honesty and trust to get through it. I had felt the same kind of pride that I did when my year four teacher gave me a gold star in the spelling test.

Yet I could feel the familiar wash of panic swirling up my chest and all I wanted to do was pick up Roy's phone, sitting naively on the nightstand, and check what he had been up to. It took herculean effort to make myself turn away.

Don't be that woman. Go to bed.

I reached for my bag and pulled out my own phone. No new messages.

I emptied my handbag on the dresser, found a half-eaten Kit Kat and finished it off, all the while thinking about Roy's phone.

Pathetic.

I went over and knelt by my wardrobe, feeling around in the back until I found an empty box. I pulled it out, folded my handbag in it, and manoeuvred it behind all the other neatly stacked and labelled boxes. I left the package I had picked up earlier that night tucked away in the inner pocket and went to bed. I thought of the nondescript alleyway I had walked to, heart pounding, to pick it up, the almost wordless exchange that had followed and the relief I had felt walking back to the station uninterrupted. I was hoping I wouldn't need to use it, but I felt calmer knowing it was there, nestled in the folds of last season's Chloe, just in case things got out of control.

ROY

Tuesday, 20th October

'I hope you had a pleasant stay with us, sir. Hope to see you
again.'

'It was perfect, thanks,' I said, pulling out my car keys
and heading to the car park. It had been yet another great,
if exhausting evening. I hadn't been able to sleep after
Emily had left and ended up watching *Eternal Sunshine of
the Spotless Mind* into the early hours. All I needed now was
some coffee, I thought, climbing into the car.

Emily and I had been meeting frequently over the past
few weeks, the rules of our non-relationship clearly estab-
lished. We met only on weekdays. We never ate anything.
We hardly spoke, and emailed each other only to arrange
these meetings. We quickly tired of empty car parks and
anonymous back alleys. I started booking cheap hotel
rooms more and more frequently – sometimes two or
three times a week. It didn't matter how drab the pictures
looked or how far I had to drive. The more remote, the
better. Glynview, the Imperial Inn, the Duke's Arms. All

tacky business hotels with tired staff, a supermarket break-fast spread and patterned curtains. I never wrote about them, of course. Emily joined me everywhere, sexy lingerie in tow. With her, nothing was off limits. By now we had an easy routine set up: I would arrive first, mid-afternoon usually, check in, order room service. Emily would breeze in a few hours later, past the reception, with the air of someone who knew exactly where she was going. Her confidence was astounding, the sex exquisite. She never stayed over. It was perfect.

I put on the radio and checked the sat nav: ETA 15.35.

I glanced in the rear-view mirror and reached for my phone.

On my way back. Missed you. Movie and takeaway tonight?
Mia's reply was instant.

Missed you too ♥ ♥ Sounds fab, see you later.

I smiled. Perhaps I had stumbled upon the key to a happy marriage.

'I can't believe you enjoyed that,' Mia said between mouth-fuls. It still surprised me how much she could pack away in her tiny body. 'Nothing happened in the entire film.'

'What do you mean nothing happened? There was all this stuff going on under the surface.' I leaned over and grabbed the last slice of pizza from the box that was sitting on her stomach.

'Mmmm,' she said, 'yeah, but I just kept waiting for all that under-the-surface stuff to explode, you know? I mean Sofia Coppola's great but in this movie, basically, they both went to Tokyo, ran into each other, had a few drinks, a few laughs and then flew back home. I mean, come on, give me something! Real life is not like that.'

I laughed.

'Seriously? Real life is *exactly* like that. And you're one to talk, you keep everything hidden away. Now,' I said, lifting Mia's legs off my lap and getting up, 'I think we need some ice cream.'

I checked my phone on the way to the kitchen. I always kept it on silent these days.

'Chocolate chip or coffee?' I called out.

There was one missed call. I dialled back.

'Chocolate,' Mia yelled back.

'Hi,' I whispered into the phone.

'Hey.'

'I'm at home. Is it important?'

'Well, depends how you look at it.'

'Ems, what is it?' I tried again. 'You know I can't talk at home.'

I pulled out two bowls and spoons.

'I was just thinking about you,' she whined.

'Oh. Yes, me too. Look, I've got to go. I'll text you tomorrow, okay?' I shot back, hanging up before she had a chance to say anything. Perhaps it was time to get a second phone.

I pulled out the ice cream tubs and scooped some chocolate ice cream into two bowls, adding a scoop of coffee as well to mine. I could never pick.

MIA

Thursday, 22nd October

'So I really think once Addi chips in, we'll be able to buy my mum out. I mean, I need to speak to her obviously, but Addi's going to be as upset about this as I am. She'll want to save the house.'

'You sound very confident,' Natalie said.

'I've spent all morning at the bank, it's looking good.'

'Right. And that's great. I just want to make sure you aren't relying too heavily on anyone, even your sister.'

'I'm not. And anyway, this is a non-issue,' I said, eager to change the subject. Natalie could be quite a buzzkill sometimes. 'You said there was something you wanted to discuss?'

'Yes, I had a call from James the other day,' Natalie said. 'I understand that he and your sister are moving back?'

'Yeah, they arrived last week.'

'Ah.'

'What?'

'I'm just curious as to how involved you see them being

in your life going forward?' She paused. 'Specifically in relation to our work here?'

'Why?'

Natalie flinched, but then continued after a minute. 'James raised a few concerns about my approach, which are all valid from his point of view, of course. But this is the kind of thing I was concerned about when you first came to see me. As your therapist, it would be unethical if I let anyone influence your treatment plan without checking with you first.'

'It was about Bristol, wasn't it? This isn't James. It's my sister getting protective about me. I'll speak to her.'

'Mia, that's not what I'm saying. Of course your sister will worry about you. And considering how long James and I have known each other, it's perfectly natural for him to reach out. My primary concern here is you. How do you feel about your sessions with me?'

'We've been over this, I've never felt this comfortable with a therapist before.'

'And your trip to Bristol?'

'It was fine! I mean, I was upset, and sad, but then I was going to be. We've been working towards this for years now, and we both agreed that I was as ready as I was ever going to be, right?' I looked towards Natalie and she nodded. 'Addi's just . . .' I sighed. 'You have to understand, before I came to you . . . Addi's seen me at my lowest, and she's seen me struggle, for years, so she worries about anything that might tip me over the edge.'

'Of course.'

'She thought my going to Bristol by myself was a bad idea, she must have told James, and so James called you. It's my fault. I should never have told her.'

'No one's blaming you, Mia.'

'No, I know.'

'I only wanted to discuss this so that you and I could come to an agreement about how to proceed. You know it's typical practice to review treatment plans from time to time. Would you feel more comfortable with another therapist? Someone who isn't connected to your family at all, perhaps?'

'No,' I said. 'With all due respect, Natalie, I think you're overreacting here. I'm fine, I'm happy with my progress, I don't think going to Bristol was a mistake, and I'd like you to carry on being my therapist. Now, can we just move on, please?'

ROY

Friday, 23rd October

'What are you doing?' I woke up wincing. Mia was right next to me, her face inches from mine. I flipped onto my side and pulled the duvet up to my chin. 'Did you just bite – Ow! Mia!'

'Happy Birthday,' she whispered, before bursting into giggles and slipping out of bed.

Mia was in the kitchen making coffee when I went downstairs. She handed me a cup, leaned back against the counter and then looked me up and down. Very dramatic.

'Thirty-one. That's it, you're officially old now.'

I rolled my eyes. 'Whatever,' I said, unconvincingly.

We were both playing familiar roles, but something was amiss. I could see that Mia sensed it too. She turned around and started moving things – all my favourite dishes – from the hob to the table and I sat down. I didn't know when it had started, or how, but Mia had been taking the day off for my birthday for years. It seemed we were sticking with tradition this year as well.

'So tonight, do you want to go to that place in Forest Hill?'

'Could do,' I said, scrolling through my phone to look at the couple of texts and Facebook messages that had come in since earlier that morning. I'd spent the bulk of the last hour on the phone – my parents, James, Addi and Mia's mum – and Mia had inserted herself in all the conversations save for the last, when she suddenly remembered she had to send some urgent emails for work, and I ended up making excuses for her. Mia loved to analyze my relationship with my parents, but she refused to see what she was doing to her own. Ironic, considering her mother was actually nice.

'Roy,' Mia said, when I looked up. 'Living room.'

MIA

Friday, 23rd October

I stood in the doorway and let Roy pass, barely able to contain my excitement.

I watched as he scanned the room, his eyes finally resting on the gift-wrapped box on the coffee table. He turned to smile at me, then knelt down on the floor and ripped it open.

Roy went through each item with the requisite exclamations – the binoculars, the sun visor, the rolls of film – until he got to the bottom of the box and found the plain white envelope with his name on it.

'What's this then?'

I shrugged. 'Open it.'

He gave me a strange look, and then opened the envelope slowly, almost as if he was scared to see what was inside.

I watched his face run through an entire symphony of emotions as he flicked through the papers, reading everything twice.

'Mia, is this for real?'

'Of course it is. Do you like it?'

I had printed off an itinerary for a trip across Namibia. I'd been working on it for months now, researching, costing, organizing. Starting at Windhoek, we'd travel through the Namib Desert and the Etosha salt pan, spend a night at the Mowani Mountain Camp in Twyfelfontein, fly over the Skeleton Coast, visit the Cheetah Conservation Camp and then drive through the Sossusvlei dunes. Everything was booked and paid for, so Roy could just enjoy himself. He had been obsessing over Namibia for years.

He walked over and grabbed me for a kiss. 'I love it. When am I going?'

I tried not to flinch. He didn't mean it like that. I know he didn't.

'June, next year. It's the only time I can take three weeks off,' I said cautiously.

His smile wavered for a fraction of a second as he took this in.

'Amazing,' he said, giving me a peck before letting go. 'Thank you.'

ROY

Tuesday, 27ᵗʰ October

'So where are we going?' Emily asked, wriggling into her jeans.

'I can drop you off at the tube station,' I said, twisting to put on my seat belt just as her hand found its way back on my knee.

'Or we could get some dinner? I'm starving after all *that*, and maybe if I had some more energy . . .'

I turned to face her. The top three buttons of her shirt were still undone, her bright pink lace bra peeking out. Irresistible. I forced my eyes up to her face. Young and earnest. The stab of guilt took me by surprise.

'I can't, sorry.' I lifted her hand and placed it on her leg. 'Edgware or Mill Hill?'

It was just gone five when I got back to the house, but I found myself looking up as I parked to see if Mia was back. The darkened kitchen window told me she wasn't. Mia and I had disagreed on this since the day we moved in together:

she would go into the kitchen as soon as she got home, turn on all the lights and put the kettle on – even though most of the time she'd go straight up to the bedroom, leaving the lights on and the kettle boiling. She found it comforting. I found it wasteful. For some strange reason, thinking about it brought a smile to my face. I let myself in, switched on the lights, and then put the kettle on.

I had barely taken off my coat when my phone beeped. It was Emily. Already. She wanted to know if we could meet again the next day. Even though I had nothing else on, I said no.

I put my phone away and started clearing a week's worth of clutter from the coffee table – crumpled-up tissues, a half-eaten chocolate bar, bad magazines, an old newspaper. I'd spent the afternoon at the National Gallery and couldn't resist picking up the new *National Geographic Journeys of a Lifetime* book. I pulled it out of the carrier bag and set it down on the newly tidy coffee table. I went back into the kitchen with the rubbish, and instead of sticking everything in the same bin – another thing Mia and I disagreed about – I surprised myself by splitting it into what was recyclable and what wasn't.

I decided to take it one step further and took the bins out, then went for a run. I was on a roll.

On Monday, 02 November at 06.23 p.m.,
Emily Barnett <emilybarnett1994@apple.com> wrote:

here's a link to the song I was telling you about the other day. listen to it, think of me, show me how it made you feel the next time we meet.

show me.

E xxx

On Wednesday, 04 November at 02.07 a.m.,
Emily Barnett <emilybarnett1994@apple.com> wrote:

haven't heard from you and wondering if everything is ok? my friend Ali is doing the pr for a new club in soho. it's opening on friday and she's put a bunch of us on the guest list. i know you said no weekends, but can you sneak away? for me?

i miss you. can't wait to see you xxx

On Thursday, 05 November at 11.32 p.m.,
Emily Barnett <emilybarnett1994@apple.com> wrote:

hellooo???

On Friday, 06 November at 10.32 a.m.,
Roy Kapoor <roy_kapoor@me.com> wrote:

Emily, sorry I haven't been in touch, there's quite a lot going on right now and I've been busy. Enjoy the gig tonight. I'll call you when I can.

Roy

MIA

The temperature turned on us overnight, the long summer drowned out by a bitter chill as November rolled in. I felt a shiver run through me as I waited for Natalie to return to the room.

'There you go,' she said a few minutes later, handing me a mug of peppermint tea.

'Thanks.'

'Where were we?' she asked, reclaiming her spot opposite me.

I held the mug with both hands, letting the steam cloud my face as I sipped. I put the tea on the table next to me and looked at Natalie.

'I had that dream again, the one about drowning.'

'Okay.'

'I feel like I want to ask him. Just put it out there, you know. And every day I decide I will. But . . .' I trailed off.

'But you don't?'

'No.'

'Why is that?'

'I don't know. I guess I'm scared of what he might say.'

'Hmm.'

'It just doesn't make sense,' I burst out.

'What doesn't make sense?'

'Why I'm so anxious now . . . Everything's better. Roy and I are in a good place again. Addi's back. Work's great. I've got a plan for the house. Everything is fine. But I'm – I'm not.' I sighed. 'Do you remember when I called you from India, a few months ago? Everything was falling apart but I managed to hold it all together. So why can't I do that now?'

'Well, maybe you're just tired,' Natalie theorized. 'Like you said, you have been holding everything together. That can be exhausting.'

'Yeah, maybe.'

I picked up my tea and took a small sip. Better.

'Can we go back to your sister's wedding for a minute?'

'Why?'

'Well, for one, you've been avoiding speaking about that night.'

'No, I haven't. I told you everything.'

'You told me what you found out, not how you found out or how you felt about it.'

'I don't see how that's relevant.'

'Trust me, it helps. Just talk me through it, when you're ready,' Natalie encouraged.

I nodded, allowing the memory of that night to resurface, clawing its way into my brain.

'After Addi's *vidaai*, and the argument with Mum, we went back to our suite. Roy kept trying to talk to me, explain, but I didn't want to hear it. The fact that Mum was selling the house was bad enough, but for Roy to have kept it from me. It was all too much. I just needed some time to, I don't know, process?'

Natalie nodded and I carried on.

'We were arguing, and I think I . . . maybe I pushed him too far. Roy said he had to go and give Emily some money. For a cab. I wanted him to stay with me. I just wanted to . . . um . . . just get in bed, sleep it off, you know?' I paused, steadied myself. A familiar ache filled my chest. 'But I was so angry, I didn't say anything. He left and I went to bed alone. He was gone maybe ten or fifteen minutes when his phone started ringing. He'd put it on charge in the living room when we got in and he must've forgotten to take it with him. It was past one a.m.; I thought if someone's ringing this late, it must be urgent. So I got out of bed and went into the living room but by the time I got there, it had stopped ringing.'

Natalie leaned forward, frowning. She sometimes behaved like a talk show host, leaning forward now, reaching out to pat my arm then. I wished she wouldn't. This wasn't some primetime drama. This was my life.

'I punched in Roy's code to see who it was. Em –' I stuttered. 'It was Emily. She'd also sent him a message and I – I opened it. It was sickening. I felt like this – this desperate, prying wife. She'd texted to tell him the concierge had left for the night and signed it "Em, xxx". Just reading that, I knew something had happened between them.'

I paused to steady my voice, carrying on after a minute. 'I scrolled up and there it was: Roy's text to her, from that morning. He'd kissed her. While I was fending off his mother, my husband had been kissing an overconfident, entitled, stupid little sl –' I cut myself off, telling myself that the insult was too shameful to utter aloud, that it was beneath me to judge her even if she deserved it.

I tried to focus on Natalie instead; she was leaning forward waiting for me to continue. I looked away, her scrutiny making me uncomfortable.

I couldn't find the words to describe the quality of the pain I had felt when I had read those messages, but as I recounted the events of that night, it reappeared in a flash, choking me, the tears stinging my eyes. The dull ache from a few moments ago sharpened its focus, twisting itself into my chest, deeper and deeper, into something else entirely, something darker that seemed to paralyze me and bring me alive all at once.

I let out a small sob.

It was time for me to stop pretending.

MIA

Natalie held out a box of tissues, the diamond on her finger glinting in the afternoon light. I shook my head and fixed my gaze on the picture behind her, trying to compose myself.

'Roy and I, we never had secrets, you know? We used to tell each other everything, but all of a sudden, there were all these things he was – he was hiding. All these lies. I remember staring at that message for what felt like hours. I just sat there, reading it again and again. It felt like my whole life was falling apart. I was so angry. I'd invited her to be a part of my sister's wedding. I was *nice* to her. And she – she . . . the ungrateful bitch.'

I closed my eyes. I pictured Emily in that slutty gold dress, shawl tossed aside, cleavage on display. I realized that even though I had been acting like it was all in the past, that I was fine, I wasn't. I was furious at her, and at Roy. The only difference was that I loved Roy, and I hated her. Everything had been perfect until she came along. She had caused so much damage, and worst of all, she had got away with it.

I found myself picturing her getting run over by a car, or getting shot, or even quite simply being publicly shamed, humiliated, called out for the monster that she was.

Never before had I wished someone serious harm, but as my brain came up with more and more heinous scenarios to place Emily in, I realized I was enjoying it. It didn't matter how, I just wanted her to pay, to realize that her actions had real consequences. The strength of my resentment terrified me and I snapped my eyes open.

'. . . but you decided not to confront Roy,' Natalie was saying.

'No. I heard Roy's key in the door and I had a moment, a fraction of a second, to decide what the rest of my marriage would be like, and I realized I had to trust him. He had told Emily it was a mistake and I had to believe that. I had to believe my husband.'

'That's an interesting choice of words.'

'Sorry?'

'You said you *had* to believe your husband.'

'Well . . . yes. Isn't that the point of a relationship? Trust?'

'Trust, yes, but not fear.'

'It wasn't fear.'

'I see. And you still feel that way?'

'Yes.'

'Then why bring it up?'

'So I don't have to keep carrying a secret around?'

'What do you –' Natalie began.

'I keep –'

'Sorry, carry on, please.'

'I keep thinking back to an argument Mum and Dad had when I was little. Dad was angry because Mum had been keeping something from him. I remember thinking, even as a little girl, that if Mum had been honest they wouldn't have fought.'

'What were they fighting about?'

'I don't . . . I can't remember exactly,' I said, even as snatches of the memory lingered before my eyes. I pushed it away. 'Does it matter?'

'No, no, of course not. This recurring dream, what do you think it means?'

I sighed. 'I don't know, Natalie. That's why I'm here. What do *you* think it means?'

'Well, it seems to me like you have a subconscious fear of loss and abandonment.'

'I'm sorry?' I said. Roy hadn't abandoned me. He was here. We were fine. Didn't she get it? The problem wasn't Roy; it was Emily.

'Sometimes when we refuse to acknowledge our emotions or our anxieties, they can find other ways to manifest – recurring dreams, panic attacks, et cetera. Considering everything you've been through recently, and your history with dependency issues, I think subconsciously you're viewing a confrontation with your husband as a means of reassuring yourself that he won't leave, which in itself is a risky move. But Mia, feeling rejected or abandoned in a situation like this is perfectly normal and that is something we can work on here, together, okay?'

I nodded. Yes. Okay. Together.

On Tuesday, 10 November at 08.10 a.m.,
Emily Barnett <emilybarnett1994@apple.com> wrote:

why haven't you returned my calls? are we still on for tomorrow? call me back please.

ROY

'*There* you are,' Mia gushed when I walked in. 'We were worried you'd been held up.'

'Sorry, the meeting ran late,' I lied.

I noticed my parents standing by the hostess station, looking on as though they were waiting to be introduced. Mia turned towards them and I followed. I had considered inventing an urgent press trip when my mother's secretary emailed over their itinerary but something told me they would just extend their trip to suit my travel plans so I settled for a day-long meeting instead.

'*Namaste*, Ma,' I said, leaning in to give her a quick hug. She had a grey overcoat on over her trademark silk *sari*.

I gave my father a brusque nod. That was the best I could manage.

'If you'll follow me,' the hostess said and we trailed her into the restaurant, weaving through a large table of girls in high spirits and higher hemlines, a couple on what looked like an awkward blind date and the usual happy-hour release of pesky estate agents in suits. 'Here we are,' the hostess announced with a flourish when we got to our table. 'Would you like to give me your coats?' she asked us as we stood around trying to decide who would sit where.

'Yes, thank you,' my mother said, unbuttoning her coat and handing it over to her. Mia followed suit and I spied the telltale black beads of a *mangalsutra* peeking out from under her top as she unwrapped her scarf and sat down. It wasn't even real; she had ordered it online two years after we got married, in preparation for a day like today so she could play the perfect *bahu*.

The waitress placed menus in front of us as soon as we sat down. I ended up across from my father and Mia across from Ma.

Time stretched as Mia fussed over my parents, using small talk and bad jokes to mask the tension that shrouded the table. I let her carry the conversation.

At some point, the focus shifted to me. Mia was telling my parents about the video segments with George, how it was 'really quite a big deal' and that webcasts were bigger than TV nowadays.

I was unravelling my dinner napkin when my father spoke.

'Mia, did you know Siddhant was enrolled in medical college before he decided to become a writer?'

Mia looked at me, unsure of how to handle this unexpected turn in the conversation. This was clearly not the happy reunion she had ordered. 'Yes, he mentioned it,' she said finally.

'He wanted to be a cardio surgeon. He got into the best medical programme in the country,' he went on, his voice cool, measured. 'Siddhant was always very bright, right from when he was a little boy. He wanted to be just like—'

Oh, come on.

'You wanted,' I muttered, going back to my napkin.

'What was that? Speak up, son,' my father reprimanded and I automatically sat up straighter. Years of conditioning did that to you. I placed the napkin on my lap, running my hands over it to smooth it out.

'*You* wanted me to be a surgeon. I didn't. I never wanted that life for myself.'

'Yes, you've made that very clear. I suppose you've got everything you wanted now?' My father's eyes locked on mine, challenging me.

Seconds passed. I glanced around the table. Mia was fidgeting with her watch, Ma was scrutinizing the drinks list and my father was glaring at me. What did he want from me?

The waitress appeared by my side and introduced herself, oblivious to the relief she offered. Were we ready to order the drinks yet? Some wine, perhaps? I placed our order: a diet Coke for Mia, wine for my father and me, and lemonade for Ma.

'So what's good here?' Ma asked when the waitress had left.

'The grilled chicken's great,' Mia chimed, the two women manoeuvring us back to polite conversation.

I turned on the shower and stepped in, letting the hot water run over my back.

I had everything I wanted, he'd said. Everything I wanted. How dare he? He had made sure I didn't, *couldn't* have anything when he kicked me out.

My father had been furious when I came home after my first term at med school and announced that I wasn't going back. It was dull, restrictive and regimental; I wanted to be a writer, I had insisted. I've been accepted on the creative writing programme at Columbia University, I told him. He threatened to kick me out of the house and cut me off if I went through with it. Later that night, my mother had stood in my room, watching me fit whatever little I could in my holdall. I had stormed off to a friend's house on a high fuelled by testosterone and teenage angst, promising never to return.

I had gone back a few weeks later when the letter from Columbia arrived. The director of the writing programme had written back to me. Though they couldn't give me a scholarship, he wrote, he was very excited to offer me a place on the course with the promise of an unpaid internship at the *New Yorker*. He had called me a gifted new writer with a compelling voice that defied my age and upbringing. My father had laughed and told me he would ring the dean at med school and get them to take me back. If I did well in the finals, he would let me go on a writing workshop in the summer. It could only help with the medical papers I would have to publish over the length of my career, he reasoned. I went straight back to my friend's that night and left for good a week later. I had seen my parents a couple of times since then but any chance of a real relationship had been wiped out that day. I had spent the last fifteen years running – from them, from India, from my culture, from myself. An announcement to no one listening that I was free.

I turned off the shower and reached for the towel.

This wasn't everything I wanted. It didn't even come close.

The fifty grand that my parents had refused to shell out had cost me my career and them their only son.

Mia was sitting on the bed, smoothing lotion over her legs, when I stepped out of the bathroom, a blast of hot air following me into the bedroom. I towelled off and pinched some lotion off her.

'You okay?'

'Uh-huh,' I replied, putting on a T-shirt and boxers.

'Roy, sweetie, you can't let him get to you like this.'

'I know but he just makes it so . . . hard,' I sighed.

Mia got up and wrapped her arms around me. 'Hey, it's only two more days,' she said.

I nodded. She was right. Two more days and then I didn't have to see them again.

'Come to bed, it's cold,' Mia said, before climbing into bed herself.

'In a minute. I'll get us some water,' I said and went downstairs to the kitchen, closing the door behind me. I filled two glasses with water and set them on the counter. I pulled out my new, disposable phone from behind the cabinet and punched in my code. Seven missed calls and three texts in one hour. Emily was getting out of hand. I shot her a quick reply, turned off the phone and went back upstairs to my wife.

MIA

Wednesday, 11ᵗʰ November

'*Namaste*, Aunty, *Namaste*, Uncle.' Addi bowed down to touch my in-laws' feet before grabbing me in a hug. 'Mia. Happy Diwali!'

James traipsed in a few minutes later.

'Parking in London is a nightmare,' he said, leaning over to kiss me on both cheeks. He looked around. 'Where's Roy?'

'At a meeting, he should be back soon,' I said. 'Have you met my in-laws, James?'

James shook both their hands and sat down on the armchair across from them, sidestepping the *rangoli* that adorned the wooden floor.

I went into the kitchen to fetch the drinks and Addi followed.

'So what's it like? Having them here?' she whispered.

'Nightmare. I can't do anything right, not even the chai,' I whispered back. 'And Roy and his father got into an argument last night.'

Addi rolled her eyes. 'When do they leave?'

'Tomorrow, thank God.'

I flung my *dupatta* over a chair and lined up the glasses next to a bowl of salted peanuts on a tray. Scotch for the men, Virgin Marys for the women. Who needs a time machine when you have a mother-in-law?

'How's therapy?' Addi asked, trying to sound casual as she folded the serviettes into little triangles and arranged them on the tray.

'Yeah, good,' I replied, not looking up.

Addi and I danced around this conversation every couple of days. She would ask me about therapy and I'd give her a completely bland response. We both knew that I wasn't going to go into any details after what she'd pulled with James, but like any normal family, we pretended everything was perfect, sticking to the usual 'how's therapy, yeah fantastic' script. It was comforting, in the way that traditions always are.

I put on my bright green oven mitts and pulled out the baking tray with the samosas from the oven.

My phone was buzzing on the counter. Addi reached for it.

'It's . . . Chris? Ooh, he's handsome.'

I smiled. 'And you're newly married. Give me that,' I said, taking off the mitts.

'Hello.'

'Mia, Happy Diwali! I can't believe I'm missing the feast this year,' Chris's voice boomed down the phone.

I laughed. 'Well, I miss you too, Chris.'

'Listen, I'm so sorry to bother you while you're on holiday, but . . .'

I mouthed an apology to Addi and went upstairs to finish the call. There was a problem with the Eastside order – the mills in Turkey had gone on strike and the factory was asking for an extension on the shipment date.

'How much fabric has the factory got in-house?'

'Just under fifty thousand metres.'

I quickly did the maths.

'That should be enough for sixty per cent of the first hit. Ask the factories to go ahead with that and tweak the ratios so we've got more of sizes eight to twelve. In case we do need to get an extension, sizes four, six and fourteen to twenty can follow later.' I paused to think; we couldn't risk a delay on this order. 'Do we have a contact at the mill?'

'Yes.'

'Good. Speak to them and see if we can call in any favours. Pick up all the stock that they have in our fabric. Then ring Monir. He knows all the mills in Turkey. See if we can move the rest of the order to another mill.'

'Okay, sounds good. Thanks, Mia.'

'No problem. And Chris, keep me updated.'

'Addi, do you want to help with the *diyas*?' I asked.

Lighting the *diyas* was Addi's and my favourite bit about Diwali. We always fought over who would get to do the most when we were little, even when all we were allowed to do was line them up along the wall and wait for Mum to come and light them.

'Of course,' Addi said and followed me into the kitchen.

I had soaked all the *diyas* in water overnight and then laid them out earlier that morning. It stops the oil seeping into the clay and makes them last longer, Mum had explained to us that first year. I smiled as Addi and I rolled the wicks and lit them one by one. Diwali had always been exciting in India. The whole house lit up, the streets abuzz with crackers, neighbours and relatives slipping in and out of our living room, laden with sweets and presents.

You were in India because your father died, the voice in my head whispered and I wiped the smile off my face. *Have you forgotten where you come from? India isn't home, Bristol is.*

I shook it off. I hadn't forgotten anything.

'Have you spoken to Mum since you got back?' I asked Addi.

'Uh-huh.'

'Did she mention anything about the house?' I paused. 'Daddy's house, I mean.'

Addi blew out her matchstick and turned to face me. 'Yes, darling, she told me. I'm with her on this one, I'm afraid.'

I took a step back. Addi was supposed to be on my side.

'What? Why?'

'Well, Mum's right. It's costing us too much to keep it.' She took the matchstick from my hand and blew it out. 'We have to let it go, Mia, it's been a long time.'

'No. I can't believe . . . no.' I shook my head. I couldn't get a second mortgage large enough to cover it myself. I needed Addi to co-sign. 'We can invest in it, you and I. Fix it up.'

'I don't think that will be the cleverest idea. Plus James and I have used up all our savings for the new flat.'

'Uncle Bill said . . . the solicitors . . .'

'That's all nonsense. He has no rights here.'

'What about my rights?' I asked.

Addi sighed but said nothing. I looked at the *diyas* we'd just lit, the flames flickering in perfect harmony. They were meant to bring in good luck, joy.

Leave the doors open, Addi had yelled after me that first year, as I ran from room to room checking if the *diyas* were still alight. The good fortune will go away if it can't enter, she had said. Now, years later, Addi was the one closing the door.

'Did you know? Before the wedding?'

Addi's silence told me everything. She had been as much a part of this deception as Roy and my mother. The realization broke me.

'James and I met with the agents yesterday. We've given them the go-ahead. I'm sorry, darling, but the house will be on the market next week.' She hesitated, and then continued when I didn't interject. 'There's something else as well. I'm going to India for a few weeks. James will deal with anything the agency needs, but if the sale does go through while I'm away, we might need you to go and sign the paperwork.'

I heard the front door go. Jovial voices bounced off the stripped-wood floors and breezed past me. Outside in the street someone set off firecrackers. Addi and I looked at each other. Her face was set. This was what I'd been dreading my whole life.

She had locked the door and thrown away the key.

My sister had cast me aside.

ROY

Emily was perched along the bar when I walked in. I pulled up a stool and sat down next to her.

'Hey,' she smiled. She unclasped a clip and shook her hair loose. She was wearing a low-cut black dress. The bartender stared. 'You look tired. Buy you a drink?'

As if she had ever paid for anything in her life. 'No, thanks. I can't stay long.'

'What's wrong?' She leaned over and placed her hand on my leg. I brushed it off. I tried to come up with a way to phrase this right.

'Is this about last night? I'm sorry. I was out and I'd had too much to drink. I was just missing you,' she pouted.

'Ems, I've been thinking,' I started, picking my words carefully. 'With everything else that's happening, we'd be crazy to keep this going.'

She started. 'What are you saying?'

'We're both good people. I think that's what attracted us to each other in the first place. But this . . . this feels wrong.

I'm married. And as much as I enjoy seeing you, I can't keep this up. I feel like I'm living a double life. And the guilt . . . it's crippling. You're leaving in a few weeks anyway, so let's just end it now.'

'You're dumping me?'

'I just don't want anyone to get hurt,' I said, speaking quietly, willing her to do the same.

Needless to say, I didn't succeed.

'You mean you don't want your *wife* to get hurt,' she said, her voice rising. 'What about me?'

A group of tourists on the other side of the room turned, peeling their eyes away from the giant TV screen to look at us. I smiled and shrugged, then put my hand on Emily's to calm her down. What had happened to all her proclamations about keeping this casual?

'You know how much I care about you. But this isn't good for anyone involved.' I paused and made a show of checking my watch.

Emily stood up and put her hands on my chest. She clutched my shirt. 'Can we talk about this?'

I disentangled myself and moved away from her. 'Don't. Please.'

'Are you telling me you feel nothing? That I'm imagining this?'

'You have to understand, Emily. This was a mistake. I know I shouldn't have let it get so far, but I just can't walk around feeling like this anymore. It's killing me,' I said. 'I could lose everything.'

If I could, I would take that last sentence back.

Emily started yelling at me then, screaming, cursing, telling me she didn't care what happened to me. She was behaving like a spoilt little girl. I wanted to smack her into complying. Instead, I listened patiently, I spoke softly, I snapped, I shook her hard. I tried everything I could to calm her down but when she didn't, I turned around and walked away. I had to.

I got on the 18.08 to Crystal Palace. Sat on the window seat, pulled out my phone, sent a text.

As the train chugged along, I felt calmer by the minute, the muscles in my back loosening and relaxing as Emily receded into my past. I leaned back in the seat, at first putting the lightness that I was sensing down to the warmth of the train, until it occurred to me that it was the relief that comes with closure.

Who knew guilt could weigh so much.

MIA

I stepped out of the bedroom and checked my watch again. It was only half six but I could already hear sounds coming from the kitchen. I had planned on cooking breakfast before everyone woke up but it looked like I was too late. Another strike against me, I thought, twisting my hair into a loose bun. I wasn't sure if I cared anymore. My in-laws' opinion of me seemed irrelevant when my own sister had pushed me aside.

I closed the door softly behind me. Roy was still asleep.

I was at the foot of the stairs when their voices became clear enough for me to decipher the words. I stopped. Another overheard argument, from years ago, sprang to mind. I cleared my head and focused on the present.

'You promised you would try,' I heard my mother-in-law say.

'I can't help it if he's so touchy.'

As the voices grew louder, I felt my breathing hasten. I sank down, clutching the banister.

Panic claimed me. I was tingling all over. I looked down at my feet and the floor began to dance.

'*Accha*, what did you expect? You pushed him . . .'

'He's come a long way. I was congratulating him!'

Shaking my head, I gripped the banister harder and closed my eyes. My in-laws' words quickly morphed into something else and images from the past filled my head, circling my skull, pushing against it, each one more aggressive than the other.

Addi and me, playing hide and seek.

Me hiding under the staircase.

Daddy storming into the house.

I tried to shake them away but they wouldn't budge.

The images were accompanied by sounds now. A man and a woman. Screaming. I strained to hear them over the thumping that seemed to be coming from inside me.

'What the fuck is this? I didn't think . . . not a child . . .'

'David, calm down, please. The girls . . .'

'. . . how dare you bring . . .'

'. . . wasn't like that . . .'

All the sounds and voices were scrambled up, blending into one. A hand was pulling me, dragging me out from under the stairs.

'Mia. Mia, are you okay?'

I pushed the voices away. I opened my eyes. My father was crouching in front of me. I shook my head and blinked. I tried again. My mother-in-law was crouching in front of me. My father-in-law was hovering behind her.

'*Kya hua?*'

I forced myself to slow down. I tried to speak.

'Are you ill, *beta?*'

I nodded.

'Go back to bed. *Chalo*, get up.'

Her fingernails dug into my arm.

Before I knew it my mother-in-law was pulling me up and walking me back to my bedroom.

She closed the door behind her. Roy was sitting up in bed, staring at me. I went to the dresser, fished around for my emergency stash of sleeping pills, gulped two down and crawled into bed.

Maybe it had something to do with the sleeping pills or perhaps it was a side effect of the panic itself, but when I woke up several hours later, it felt as though the world had shifted back into focus. I prodded the memory that had been evading me for years and everything about that day started coming back to me, the words clearer, sharper than ever before.

Ready or not, here I come . . .

I could see myself scrunched up in the triangular space under the stairs, knees drawn up to my chin, the door open just a crack so I could jump out and tag Addi as soon as she passed. I could hear the scratching sound coming from behind me and feel the goosebumps on my skin. I was scared of mice but it was only for a hundred seconds, I had reasoned. Time passed but Addi still didn't appear so I decided to count to twenty, just to be safe, and then go and find her. The door slammed and I saw Daddy's legs go into the kitchen. He'd been away for two whole days. I was about to run out and give him a hug, when I heard them shouting. I stayed inside.

'What the fuck is this? I didn't think you were capable of stooping to this level.'

'David, calm down, please . . .'

'Is this what you get up to while I'm out every day working my—'

'Please, the girls . . .'

'Don't you dare bring the girls into this. Tell me, why did you do it? Were you bored? Is that it? Needed a little extra attention?'

'Stop shouting at me! David, please . . . It wasn't like that . . . I'm sorry, okay, I'm sorry I lied to you. Just stop shouting, the girls will—'

'Let them. Let them fucking hear what a manipulative . . .'

It was awful. I remember shrinking further back into the cupboard and knocking something over. Next thing I knew, my mother was pulling me out, screaming at me for hiding in the cupboard when I should have been upstairs doing my homework. Daddy was hovering behind her, his face full of worry. I was crying. I had scraped my elbow. I wanted Daddy to kiss it better and tell me I'm unbreakable, but Mum wouldn't let him.

Then Addi was there, dragging me upstairs and asking me to keep quiet; kissing my elbow and putting on a plaster; reading me a story, her voice getting louder and louder as the voices from downstairs drifted up.

Even as a kid, Addi had always sided with Mum. Look how much *that* cost us.

I thought back to the rest of the day. I had stared out of the window as Daddy got into his car and drove off. Addi kept asking me to come back to the bed and listen to her story.

I could hear Mum crying downstairs. I had heard what she had said to Daddy; how she had begged him, apologizing and telling him she'd stop.

The truth seared through me.

I wondered how long Addi had known.

I hadn't understood then but it all fell into place now.

My mother had been having an affair. Daddy found out and that's why he drove off that day. That's why he was speeding to get back for my party the next day.

I had spent all these years blaming myself when really it was my mother's fault.

She killed him with her lies.

PART TWO

Present Day

London

ROY

Sunday, 6ᵗʰ December

My heart flips in my chest. Emily's face is staring up at me. I haven't seen her like this before. She's wearing a pink T-shirt and star-shaped earrings. Her light blonde hair is tied up in a ponytail. She has no make-up on. She looks young, innocent.

I think of the last time I saw her. I shudder involuntarily.

I feel Mia watching me and I tear my eyes away from Emily's. I force myself to look at Mia.

'Mia, I . . .' I struggle. I don't know how to do this. My eyes dart back to the flyer. *MISSING*, it says in bold red letters.

The police will be back. Soon. Telling Mia myself is my best shot at this. I have to manage this.

'I – I'm sorry,' I try again. 'I've been so stupid. It was nothing. It *meant* nothing.'

Mia's leaning forward in her chair, her arms wrapped around her stomach. She looks like she is in pain, but her eyes don't leave mine for a second.

'Emily and I, we . . . you have to understand, it was a mistake.'

The silence that follows seems to go on forever. Mia looks down, folding into herself.

When she finally speaks, her voice is barely above a whisper. 'You're having an affair.'

'No, that's not what it—'

'Did you sleep with her?'

She looks up when I don't respond. 'How long?'

'Not long.'

She sits up. Her words are slower this time. 'How long?'

'A few weeks.'

'Since the wedding.'

It is more a statement than a question, but I nod anyway.

She stands up and storms into the kitchen. I follow her.

'Why?' she screams.

'I don't know. She was there and I – I messed up.' I hesitate. 'But I ended it. Last month. I've been feeling so guilty, Mia—'

'Stop lying to me! You told the detectives you met her last week.'

'Only because she wouldn't let it go.' I take a step towards her and she recoils, flattening against the fridge. For a moment I think she's afraid of me. 'Mia, please, you have to believe me,' I say. I walk up to her and grip her by her arms. 'I ended it.'

'Get away from me,' she says, pushing me away and striding to the other end of the room.

'We're married!' she screams out all of a sudden, turning to face me.

'I know. I'm sorry.'

There are tears rolling down her cheeks. She brushes them away. Her voice wobbles. 'I've been trying to hold us together, with your – with your parents and your project and all – all the travelling. And you . . .'

'Mia . . .'

'How could you?'

'I don't know what to say. I'm so sorry. I never meant to hurt you.'

'Never meant to hurt me? If you cared about me, you wouldn't have slept with that – that whore!'

'I didn't plan this, Mia. Things with Emily just, sort of, happened,' I shrug.

'*Just happened?* How is that even possible?'

I order myself to stay calm. I take a deep breath and let her carry on. Get it all out.

'Where did you do it?'

The tears have dried up. There is an edge to her voice. I wonder if telling her was a mistake.

'Is she good?'

Relentless.

'Answer me! Is she good?'

'I'm not going to do this,' I say finally.

'Why? You don't kiss and tell?' she spits out.

It's difficult to believe I once loved this woman.

'Did you do it here?'

'No.'

'Just tell me the truth.'

'She never came here.'

'Then where?'

'Stop it, Mia. I told you it's over. We need to focus on—'

'Where did you fuck that bitch?'

'Hotels,' I give in.

'Hotels,' she repeats. I watch the realization creep across her face. My press trips, the welcome-back sex. She takes a step back.

My phone vibrates on the table and we both lunge at it. Mia gets there before I do. She fiddles with it then turns to me.

Thank God I changed the pin.

'What's the code?'

'Excuse me?'

'Tell me your goddamn code, Roy.'

'No.'

'Why not? It's her, isn't it?'

'I don't know who it is, Mia. You have my phone.'

'Do you know where she is?'

'Of course not,' I say. I don't want to lie, but I know she can't take the truth, so I settle for something in between.

She goes back to punching things into my phone and it protests, emitting a long beeping noise.

'Stop it,' I yell and grab my phone off her. There's only so much drama I can take.

'Give it back!'

'No,' I shout back. I can't hold it in anymore. I push her once, hard. She stumbles and falls.

I stoop down till my face is inches away from hers. 'You can't order me around. You want my phone?'

The broken expression from earlier is gone, and her face freezes into something between shock and fear.

'Here,' I say, straightening up and hurling the phone to the other side of the room. It bounces off the wall and across the floor, coming to rest finally in the middle of the room.

I walk over. My phone is still on. Mia's still staring at me.

I pick it up and smash it into the wall, aiming for the same spot again. And again, and again, until it's lying on the floor shattered into three pieces.

I turn around to look at Mia, but she's already gone.

MIA

Sunday, 6th December

Everything blurs. The trees, the road, the cars, the sky. But I keep running anyway.

Why are you so fucking stupid, Mia? You invited her to the wedding. You knew he kissed her and you did nothing. It's your own fucking fault. You should have seen this coming.

Terror tears through me. I keep running. My thoughts trip over themselves.

Roy was cheating on me. He lied to me. *He* broke us. It's not my fault. He did this.

Happy people don't cheat.

Who said that?

That fucking bitch. How dare she go after my husband? Slut. I hope she suffers. She deserves to be dead.

Stop it. It's not her fault. You did this. You destroyed your own marriage.

This is fixable.

He was screwing both of you at the same time.

He said it didn't go on for long.

Not long? It's been three months since your sister's wedding.

It meant nothing, he said.

He's lying. Nothing means nothing. He enjoyed it. He enjoyed her.

Little atom bombs go off in my brain and rain down my cheeks.

Why?

Was she good?

How many times?

Does he love her?

Was she good? Was she better?

Roy would never compare me to her.

Of course he would.

She must be better.

I think I'm crying.

You're pathetic.

A sharp pain rips through my side, but I keep running. It's getting hard to breathe but that doesn't matter. Running is good. Sometimes, if I'm really focused, I can outrun the thoughts.

The wind is screaming.

Where did she come from?

I thought we were happy.

He doesn't love you.

But I love him. I can fix this.

It's too late.

He's all I have left.

Coward.

The pain intensifies. I stop. I bend over and hug myself,

panting. It's all too much. My stomach lurches and even though I know it's coming, the sheer force with which the nausea hits leaves me dizzy. My heart has been torn open yet I am still alive.

How?

I close my eyes and force myself to slow down. I count to ten. I try to tighten my grip on the here and now.

When I look up, somehow, I'm in the park.

There's a bench. I sit on it and focus on the sound of my own breathing, waiting for the panic to loosen its grip. When it finally does, I am fenced by silence.

I can't bear it.

Where is everyone?

I want to scream. I want to be heard, but I am alone.

I'm still here.

I ring Natalie. Voicemail. I remind myself she's on holiday.

I'm the only one who hasn't abandoned you, though God knows you deserve it.

I give up and let the voices fill my head, nudging, prodding, taunting.

Of course she's better.

She's younger, prettier.

You could never be as flexible.

He loves her.

You're disgusting. Did you actually think you were good enough for him?

He's going to leave you.

Night falls before the sun leaves.

ROY

I hear a car screech and walk over to the window. The car speeds past undeterred. Mia's been gone for a couple of hours now and I'm starting to worry. She hasn't taken the car so she must be nearby. I consider going out to look for her but I haven't the faintest idea where she might be. Perhaps she just needs some space. God knows I do.

I pour myself some Scotch and sit down on the sofa. I switch on the TV and skim through the channels. Jack Nicholson flickers to life. He's punching a woman, screaming in her face. Something springs to mind. A memory. Or a memory of a memory, perhaps. I put it on mute. I need a new plan.

I thought I had it all figured out but the police showing up changed everything. I want to speak to you but that is no longer an option. I want to leave but I know that will make me look guilty. I need to wait until this blows over. Then I can finally have what I want. What I know I deserve.

I think about my phone lying destroyed on the kitchen

floor and I cringe. Mia can be so difficult sometimes. I was trying to have a calm, adult conversation but Mia . . . she brings out the worst in me. Yet, I know I'll be the one apologizing when she gets back. I don't want to grovel but tonight, I know I have to. *I didn't mean to . . . I lost control . . . forgive me.*

My father's face flashes in front of me. Eyes on the prize, he used to say.

Eyes on the prize.

MIA

It's about three in the morning. We are in bed. I open my eyes a sliver and look at Roy through my eyelashes. He's lying flat on his back. I curl up on my side, facing him. Slowly, I edge my right hand towards his. I want to reach out and touch him. I want to convince myself that even though he stepped out of our marriage temporarily, he's still the man I married; that he's still *here*. But I can't. There are no more than a few inches between us, yet the distance feels as vast as an ocean.

Roy's eyelids flutter. He flips on his side, away from me.

I bring my hand back and tuck it under my head.

We are both awake yet we feign sleep.

Horizontal bars of sunlight pierce through the window blinds. I realize I must have fallen asleep, exhaustion winning over anxiety just this once. I turn around expecting to find Roy sleeping, but his side of the bed is empty. I get up, brush my teeth and run a bath. I text Mike to let him know I'm taking the day off and then I strip off last night's clothes and sink in, letting the hot water engulf me.

I don't want coffee but I take it anyway. I hold the cup in both hands and take a sip. It scalds my tongue.

'Do you want some toast? Or cereal?'

It's bizarre. My husband has been cheating on me, his mistress is missing and he's standing here, in his favourite pyjamas, casually asking me if I want breakfast. The sheer audacity of it all leaves me reeling and in an instant the despair from last night is coloured with something else.

'That's what you want to talk about? Breakfast?'

'Mia,' he sighs, 'you should eat something.'

'I'm fine,' I say, ignoring the rumble that seems to be coming from my stomach.

He pours some cereal and milk into a bowl and sits down across from me at the table. I can hear the crunch of Kellogg's as he chews on, his eyes evading mine.

'Stop it,' I say.

'Stop what?'

'Avoiding anything hard. Avoiding *this*.' I point to the floor where a few stray fragments of what used to be Roy's phone are shimmering in the sunlight. 'You've done it with your parents for years. And now you're trying to dodge this conversation by, what, pretending to be hungry?'

Roy puts his spoon down and pushes the bowl aside.

'I'm not pretending to be hungry; I am hungry. And last night . . . I'm so sorry, Mia . . . I lost my temper and I shouldn't have . . . I know how hard this must be for you. But you have to understand, it's been hell for me too.' He cradles his head in his hands. 'I never thought this would happen to us.'

Try as I might, I can't keep the resentment out of my voice. 'This didn't happen to us, Roy. You did this.'

He looks at me hopelessly and I sigh.

'I've taken the day off,' I say. I watch him, waiting for the disappointment to cloud his face.

Nothing.

I realize he is a much better liar than I ever knew.

'You can't imagine what it's been like for me. The pressure. *Every day.* From you, from my parents. Sometimes I feel like I can't even breathe without disappointing you.'

I turn to look at him.

'What pressure?'

'To move back. To have a baby. To fucking provide,' he exclaims, standing up and pacing the room. 'It's never-ending, the list of things you want from me. It's like you're all just waiting for me to fail. And I . . . I can't stand it. This is not the life I wanted.'

I stare at him, astonished. I want to scream. *Pressure to provide?* He works a ten-hour week. The three articles he writes every month barely cover his own expenses.

'Roy—'

'When I left home . . . I had this vision of what my life would look like. Dreams. I wanted so much. I used to be free . . . *alive* . . . and now, I'm . . . I don't know how to explain it. It's like I'm trapped.'

'You've got all the freedom in the world! What are you on about?'

'See!' He stops pacing to stare at me and bangs his hands on the kitchen table so hard even the fruit bowl trembles. 'This is exactly what I mean. You never did get it.'

I stare up at the streaks the late afternoon sun is making on the ceiling. My back aches from lying in the same position too long. The voices in my head remind me of all the things I'd done to welcome Roy back from his trips over the past few months. Each act is more repulsive than the last: racing home from work to whip up Roy's favourite meal; surprising him with little presents; waiting for him, dressed up in sexy lingerie. I push them away and try to shake off the disgust that crawls through me.

'You didn't have to come back and sleep with me after you'd been with that – that . . . Why did you do that? Every single time. What were you trying to prove?'

'I wasn't trying to prove anything,' I hear Roy say. 'Not everything is about you, Mia.'

My phone buzzes; it's Mike again. I silence it and close my eyes, retreating into myself.

Pity sex, the voices sneer.

I flinch as Roy switches on the light.

'You know how much this project means to me. But you shot it down. Without a second's thought.'

My eyes follow him as he walks over to the window. It's raining outside. Heavily. It surprises me that I've only just noticed that.

I sigh. 'We can't afford to put all our money into one project.'

'Because I could never earn it back,' Roy mutters.

'I never said that.'

'You didn't have to.'

'Don't twist my wo—'

'What about your father's house, we can afford that?' he says, spinning around to face me.

I get up. I snap.

'Well, it's not happening so I don't see the point in arguing about it now.'

'The point is that you didn't even discuss it with me. You just decided to buy it like it was one of your handbags.'

'The one time I do something without—'

'It was not *one* time. It's everything, all the fucking time. This is not the life I imagined for myself. It's always about what *you* want. Where we live, where we go on holiday, what we eat. You've got the next fifty years planned. Our whole lives! *You* need to know where things are going even before they get started. But I'm not like you. I can't live like that!'

'Oh, come on. I don't do anything without checking with you first. And I plan because I have to! We can't both breeze through life with our fingers crossed, hoping everything will work out. Someone's got to be an adult in this relationship. And you know what, you're right, we *are* different. I don't destroy the people I love.'

'No, you just manipulate them.'

'There's been others?' I ask after we've finished dinner.

Don't be stupid. Of course there have.

I push the voices back inside my head and focus on what Roy's saying.

'Emily . . . that's the first time I've – You have to understand . . . everything that's happened, meeting her, my parents visiting, everything with your family, the wedding . . . I don't think any of it was a coincidence. It had to happen so I could see how far I've come from the life I envisioned for myself.'

'I thought you wanted to be with me. All these years . . . Isn't that why you asked me to marry you?'

'Are you done?'

I wince, and then realize Roy's pointing to my box of noodles. I nod. He picks it up and peers inside. I've barely even touched it.

'I did want to be with you. I just don't think I realized how much I would be giving up,' he says, chucking our boxes in the recycle bin. 'I've always been so scared of hurting you, I haven't been honest and I'm sorry about that. But the truth is, I haven't been happy, Mia.'

'And you think you can have all this . . . *freedom* . . . with Emily?'

'It's not about Emily. I told you.' He speaks slowly, as if

explaining common logic to a child. 'I ended things with her. She was a trigger.'

A trigger.

I think the bullet has lodged itself in my heart.

Over the next few hours, Roy points out all the ways I've disappointed him, cataloguing every sacrifice he's ever made, from having to eat the wrong kind of *dal* to not being able to travel the world. He talks of destiny. He talks of freedom and spirituality and gentleness. Then he tells me I bring out the worst in him.

Try to stay calm; don't overreact, I tell myself. Emily's gone now, so if you can do that, if you can ride this out, we can fix this. Just get all the information and come up with a plan. Fix this.

The voices in my head laugh, mocking me for my naivety. I silence them and I listen to Roy. I listen to him blame me for everything that's ever gone wrong in his life. I listen as he tells me, repeatedly, how refreshing and fun being with Emily was.

That's because she's barely an adult, I want to scream out, but I don't. It's killing me, but I listen.

By the end of it all, I am drained and confused. I remind myself that this is the same man who used to list out all the things he loved about me; who used to turn up outside my office to surprise me; who used to tell *me*, repeatedly, all the ways I made his life better, brighter, infinitely more fun. He loved me once. He's just lost, I realize.

So I tell him I'll change.

I tell him we can go anywhere he wants, live how he wants, where he wants.

I tell him we can save our marriage, turn back time.

I tell him he is my whole life.

It doesn't work.

None of it works.

We scream and we shout.

I cry.

We brood in nuclear silence.

We talk through the night, much like when we first started dating, except we now employ our words to injure each other, each word a carefully contracted dagger, aimed to hit where it will cause the most damage. And once it does, we twist it, deeper and deeper, till there's nothing left. We know each other too well to show mercy.

And yet the accusations and the arguments and the quiet protect us, allowing us to swerve away from the only questions that matter.

Can we make this work?

Do you want to try?

Do you still love me?

Love is the most lethal form of destruction there ever was.

MIA

I am woken by the sound of the phone ringing. Mike.

'Where are you?'

'At home. I told you, I'm not well.'

'What's wrong?'

'I – I'm just run down, I suppose. I—'

'Guess what, I'm run down too but I don't get to sit around at home just because I'm tired. Get in here. There's a problem in Turkey.'

The train jerks to a stop and I'm ambushed by dozens of teenagers on what appears to be a school trip. The carriage fills up within seconds. A middle-aged woman sits down next to me. I glance at her as she takes off her gloves and places them in her handbag. She pulls out her newspaper and there she is, the archetypal victim, young, beautiful and intelligent, with everything to live for. I cannot escape my husband's mistress. The newspapers have found her and she's found me.

I close my eyes and lean my head back against the seat.

I picture Roy with her.

I wonder if they developed their own moves or if he simply recycled ours.

The very thought turns my stomach.

Emily burying her face in the crook of his neck.

Roy kissing her toes before placing her feet on his shoulders.

Roy and Emily lying facing each other, her right leg draped over his left.

Roy whispering into her hair while running a finger along the curve of her hip.

Images flash past me unbidden and I torture myself all the way to the office, watching a film of achingly familiar, but distorted memories. Everything in the film is real. All of it happened. The only difference is that it stars Emily instead of me.

The train staggers to its final stop. I wait till the school group gets off and the carriage is quiet, and then open my eyes. Emily is looking down at me, her unmoving stare burning into me through the slatted grey metal of the luggage rack. I get up and walk towards the door, then turn back, reach up and grab the newspaper. I put it in my handbag for later.

I go straight in to see Mike when I reach the office.

'What is it, Mike?'

'Shipment's late. Sort it out.'

As I walk from Mike's office to mine, all around me

people are busy working, having tea, slagging off Rihanna's new single, arguing over the last Hobnob and it pisses me off. I stop walking and just stand there, somewhere in between the Sourcing and Merchandising desks, but they all just carry on. Can't they see what I'm going through?

Perhaps I have become invisible.

I walk into my office and close the door. Someone's left a pile of paperwork and some swatches for me on my desk. I flick through them and call Chris.

'Chris, what the hell is going on? I thought we were back on track.'

'We were. The shipment is ready.'

'What's the hold-up then?'

'I wasn't sure if you'd want Mike to know . . .' Chris hesitates. 'The factory's forged the test reports.'

It seems cheating is the new normal.

'How do you know?'

'Monir knows the inspection officer.'

'I see. The MDAs?'

'I haven't issued them yet.'

I try to streamline my thoughts. If I don't say anything, we might get away with it. If I come clean, I lose the order and Eastside as a client. Plus the fine for the loss of sales on such a large order would be monumental.

'Who else knows?'

'Just Monir.'

Just Monir. It's a gamble but a minor one compared to everything else in my life. Fuck it. I give in to the convenience of the half-truth.

'Issue the MDAs, Chris.'

'Mia, are you sure? If they figure it out . . .'

'Just do it, please,' I say and hang up.

I spend the next few hours staring into my computer, making sure I look focused and put-together even as the edges of my life start to fray.

I last till midday.

When I see Mike walk out of his office at lunch hour, I get up too. I scrawl a message on a Post-it, leave it on his desk and walk out.

The first thing I notice is the BMW parked outside our house. It's been crammed into a space too small for it, the rear wheels sticking out at an angle, yet along the street there are plenty of empty, larger spaces.

I slip my key into the front door and go inside.

I'm about to call out to Roy when I hear voices. I lower my handbag onto the floor, slip off my shoes and tiptoe into the living room. The two detectives from last week are in there with Roy. I step back into the hallway, unseen. I flatten myself against the wall and disappear into the shadows.

If anything, I'm an expert in invisibility.

'. . . there's more to your relationship than you let on the last time we spoke. Am I right?' DI Robins is saying.

There's a long pause and then I hear Roy speak.

The truth. Finally.

At least I hope so.

ROY

'Yes . . . Emily and I had an affair earlier this year. When you were here last . . . my wife . . . she didn't know. I didn't want to lie, but . . .'

Robins is sitting on the sofa across from me. 'I understand, it's a delicate matter,' she says, almost too breezily. 'You were just trying to protect your wife.'

I nod. 'I told her after you left.'

'It's good to come clean,' Robins says.

Is it? I want to ask. I notice the wedding band on her finger, as inconspicuous as her tone. No engagement ring, I note. I wonder if she has children.

'So this affair, how long did it last?' the other officer, Rob Wilson, asks from his current position by the window. He's constantly moving; he must have done ten laps around the room by now.

'About seven or eight weeks. We met in India in September, at a shoot, and things just happened. I ended it last month.'

'Why? Your wife had no idea, right?' Wilson asks, walking towards the fireplace. Even as he perches his elbow on the mantelpiece and leans back, his gaze travels the room, bouncing from one object to the next. It feels as though he's taking stock, ready to arrest me should anything else go missing.

I direct my reply to Robins. Suddenly she doesn't seem so bad. 'No, but I couldn't do it. The lies, the guilt . . . I . . . it just felt wrong. I never wanted anyone to get hurt.'

Robins nods. 'How did Emily feel about your decision?'

'She wasn't happy.'

'She wanted to carry on the affair?'

'She didn't see why it had to end.'

Robins frowns. She looks at Wilson. 'Isn't she meant to be leaving for Australia soon?'

Wilson nods slowly. 'Just after Christmas, in three weeks.'

'That's what I said. I tried to reason with her.'

'Break-ups can be hard. I can imagine how angry you must have been.'

'I . . . well, yes. Emily and I, we were supposed to be casual. No strings.'

'You broke up with her last week?' Wilson asks.

'No, I told you, last month. November.'

Robins checks her folder. 'But you met her last week?'

I nod. 'Emily took it pretty hard. When she reached out last week, I agreed to see her one last time.'

Robins leans forward, elbows on knees, and looks me in the eye. 'How did that go?'

I look away. I think back to the last time I saw her: her pulse throbbing beneath my hands, the colour draining out of her face, her fingers clawing at me. My hand goes automatically to the small bruise behind my ear. I shake my head slowly and look at Robins with my best how-did-this-happen face. 'She was calmer. She said she was looking forward to Sydney. She wanted us to stay in touch. She looked fine, happy.'

'Emily asked to meet you?'

'She begged me to.' I know the story I'm trying to spin. The responsible married man who realizes he made a mistake and tries to put things right; the pushy young woman who tries to cling on to a fleeting affair but can't. The only logical ending is that she decided to run away, get away from it all. She'll turn up once she realizes she needs to move on. She just needs some time to figure it all out. Not the whole truth but not a million miles from it either.

'This was on Friday?'

'No, *Wednesday*. At the pub. In Archway.' I speak slowly. They are both a bit slow for CID detectives.

'Ah, right. Sorry, I keep getting my dates mixed up. My husband keeps telling me I've got Alzheimer's.' She attempts a fake laugh.

Or perhaps that's what they want me to think.

'You remember *that*,' Wilson says, rolling his eyes. 'Have you been in touch with Emily since you last saw her?'

'No,' I lie. 'Look, we've been over this before . . .'

'I know, I'm sorry,' Robins says. 'But like you said, you weren't entirely honest with us last time.'

'Well, I've told you everything there is to tell now. So if there isn't anything else . . .'

Wilson looks at Robins. An almost imperceptible nod and he takes over.

'Where were you on Friday, Mr Kapoor?' Wilson asks, sitting down on the sofa next to Robins.

I look at Robins but her face is unreadable. I feel my confidence start to flounder.

'Friday?' I pretend to think for a minute, and then add, 'I had a breakfast meeting in town.'

'Where?' Wilson interrupts.

It hits me that they're looking at my story the wrong way around. They're seeing a vulnerable young woman who tries to cling on to an ill-fated affair and a married man who realizes he has everything to lose, but can't so he gets rid of her. This one's not a million miles from the truth either.

'Notes, near Charing Cross.'

Robins scribbles in her folder and nods at me to carry on.

I hesitate for a moment but I have no option but to tell them this next part truthfully. They will find out eventually and if I tell them myself, perhaps I can steer the story my way. 'I came back home, sent some emails, had lunch, then drove down to Brighton to see a friend.'

Robins' head jolts up from her folder. I know exactly what she's thinking.

'That's a long way to go for a friend,' Wilson smirks. 'What time did you leave your house?'

'I'm not sure . . . must be around six p.m.'

'And you got back . . . ?'

'I stayed over. I came home on Saturday afternoon.'

Robins and Wilson exchange a look before he hammers on. 'I see.' He turns to Robins. 'Seaford is, what, twelve miles from Brighton?'

Robins nods. 'Lovely little town for a day trip,' she says, 'so much quieter.'

'Look, I'm trying to help you guys out, but this is starting to feel like an interrogation. What's going on? Do I need to be worried?'

'Not at all. You've been so helpful. But you know what it's like in these cases, Siddhant,' Robins says. She pronounces my birth name wrong. 'May I call you Siddhant?'

'Roy,' I correct her.

She keeps her eyes on me a second too long.

'Okay, so, Roy, as I was saying, you know what it's like in these cases. The first port of call is always the husband or the boyfriend. It's slightly more complicated, with you being married and all. So we just need to cross you off our list.'

I try to figure out how I'm expected to react in this scenario. I can think of no precedent for a married man whose ex-girlfriend is missing. I decide to go with the panicked boyfriend response.

'Emily is missing. *Missing!* What are you actually doing to find her? Have you got any leads?'

'You know we can't discuss that,' Robins says, putting

me back in my place with a sweet smile: married ex-boyfriend.

I sigh. 'Am I under caution?'

'No, of course not. And like I said, you're under no legal obligation to talk to us. If you want a solicitor—'

'No, I don't, thanks.' I'm not falling for *that*. A confession would be just as incriminating.

'Okay. Let's just go back to Friday for a minute, then. Did you stay at your friend's house in Brighton?'

'I stayed at a hotel.'

Wilson raises his eyebrows.

'Grand Albion,' I add.

'Fancy,' he mutters as Robins shoots him a look and puts *him* in his place. It's obvious who is running the show here.

'What time did you check in?'

I feel a dull ache in the centre of my chest. 'About ten p.m.'

'And you checked out at?'

'Just before midday.'

'Did you leave the hotel between ten p.m. and midday Saturday?'

'No.'

'Any visitors?'

I look at her. My heartbeat quickens.

'Roy,' Robins repeats, 'did you have any visitors?'

I realize this is it. If I don't say something now, I'll have no alibi.

'Yes, one. Celia Brown.'

Robins looks at me, her face itself a question mark.

I take a breath. I pull myself together.

It's time for act two.

'My girlfriend.'

MIA

Sometimes I feel like I'm in a film. I see myself from the outside, an invisible critic floating above the film-me. I hear Roy speak and I dissociate. I see my legs buckle, my arm stick out in the dark, groping for something to hold on to. I watch as I lean on the radiator in the hall, my face contorting with pain and anger while the hot metal sears through my tights.

Robins' voice, louder than before, snaps me out of it.

'Girlfriend?' she says.

I don't know what to think anymore.

Roy speaks. 'I met Celia a few weeks ago. We . . . we fell in love. I was with her on Friday.'

Was it that simple?

'Right, let me wrap my head around this,' the man says. 'You've been sleeping with one woman, whilst married to another *and* in love with a third?'

There's a moment of complete silence, then Robins speaks.

'Was Miss . . .' She pauses. 'Celia with you all night?'

'Yes. She arrived about forty-five minutes after I checked in. She . . . umm . . . stayed the night. In the morning, we ordered breakfast, must be around nine a.m. She left shortly afterwards.'

'I see,' she says. 'Could you help us with her details? Please.'

'Sure.'

Another long pause. I picture Roy writing down this woman's details in his schoolboy handwriting, his DNA embedded in every neatly etched letter.

'I'll need her full postal address as well.'

'I – I haven't got it.'

'You say you're in love with this woman but you don't know where she lives?' the man asks.

Roy's reply comes a beat too soon. I can almost picture him, defiant, head cocked to one side, meeting the detective's gaze squarely. 'She lives in Brighton.'

'Why would you go to a hotel then?'

'Her husband . . .' Roy trails off.

'Of course,' the man snorts, loud enough that I can hear it outside. Or perhaps it's all so ludicrous that I fill the pause with an imaginary snort.

I hear Robins speak. 'Does Ms Brown have a job?'

'She's a dancer. Freelance.'

An excruciatingly long pause, and then Roy speaks. 'Will you be contacting her?'

'Is that a problem?'

'No, no. I just . . . perhaps you could be discreet. Like I said, her husband . . .'

'You don't need to worry about discretion.'

By the time I realize the conversation is over, it's too late for me to run up without being seen. So I stand there and act as if I've just come in.

The detectives come through with Roy and from the look on their faces it's obvious.

No one buys it.

MIA

Tuesday, 8th December

I sit on the bottom step and stare at the back of his head, my husband's head, as he shows the detectives out. We used to joke that we could step inside each other's brains and pluck out entire sentences before the thoughts could even complete themselves.

These days even the things he says out loud baffle me. Roy moves slightly and I look away.

The newspaper sticking out of my bag catches my eye. I pull it out and read through the article again, properly this time.

POLICE EXPAND SEARCH FOR MISSING LONDON STUDENT

A large-scale search operation has been launched for twenty-one-year-old journalism student Emily Barnett, who has been missing for three days. Emily, who graduated from King's College, London, earlier this year was reported missing on Saturday evening, after failing to attend her brother's engagement party. Miss Barnett is described as 5ft 8ins tall with brown eyes and long blonde hair.

More than a hundred people, including police officers and coastguard staff, as well as specialist dog units and search and rescue helicopters, have been searching for Miss Barnett after staff from the Seaford Head Hotel in East Sussex confirmed last night that she was a guest at the hotel. Miss Barnett checked in on Friday evening and was last seen at the hotel restaurant around 9 p.m. on the same night. Miss Barnett is believed to have been alone.

With its limestone cliffs, Seaford is infamous for being the suicide hotspot of the UK. The first searches were concentrated in the cove area until midnight on Sunday and then resumed all day on Monday amidst speculation that Miss Barnett's case is being treated as high priority due to widespread public interest. Miss Barnett's brother, Daniel Barnett, head of the London-based PR firm Wolfe & Barnett, launched the #FindEmily social media campaign on Sunday to appeal for any information on Miss Barnett's whereabouts. It is understood that an anonymous call to the campaign tip line led the police to Seaford.

The police have not yet confirmed if Emily's disappearance is being treated as suspicious.

By the time I finish reading I am shaking all over. I can feel my edges getting softer, slipping away as the darkness begins to descend. A single word anchors me.

Seaford.

I force myself to think about everything that happened the other day. Not my usual sugar-coated version of events, but the real, stubborn truth. Roy shoved me and smashed his phone to pieces. I force myself to consider what might have happened if he didn't have the phone to hand.

A memory from years ago, still sharp, resurfaces. I'd come home late from a party. Roy was furious because I had forgotten to text him. He said that he had been worried, that I shouldn't have been so irresponsible. But I was with George, you knew I was safe, I said. Things got out of hand. He wept. He promised it would never happen again. I believed him. I convinced myself that any man would lose his temper if his wife stayed out all night; that a single push didn't constitute abuse. I called in sick the next morning.

I am amazed at my own gullibility.

The sound of the door closing jolts me back to the present.

I've spent the past few days trying to bargain my way back into my marriage, convincing myself I can make it work. I've been telling myself Roy's words only hurt so much because they are true, that his guilt only feels superficial because I'm being unrealistic. I've been blaming myself, bending over backwards to try and see things from Roy's point of view. I've been blaming Emily when clearly the only one to blame here is Roy.

I wonder if Emily was as naive as I was.

I think of the little piece of paper tucked in my wallet. I can't pretend it's irrelevant, not anymore.

Roy's been lying to me and to the detectives. And I've had enough of it.

ROY

Tuesday, 8th December

I close the door and lean my head against it. That did not go well.

I turn around to see Mia going up the stairs. Snooping again. What do I need to do to get some privacy in my own home?

'Mia.'

She doesn't turn. I follow her up to the landing.

'Mia.'

'Leave me alone,' she says, her back to me.

She walks the three paces to our bedroom and I go after her. I grab her shoulder and spin her around, flattening her against the wall. She looks away.

'Look at me. Mia, look at me.'

'What?'

'I didn't want to hide this. I was going to tell you.'

'How noble of you. Is this new girlfriend real or yet another one of your elaborate lies?'

'Of course she's real. Why would I lie?'

'For an alibi.'

'I don't need an alibi. I haven't done anything wrong.'

'I know where you really were, Roy. You need an alibi. And who knows what lengths you'd go to to get one? I'd have to be stupid to believe anything you say anymore.'

'You're being crazy.'

'Show me a picture.'

'No.'

'Because she doesn't exist.'

'Because I care about her,' I say. I relax my grip on her. I soften my voice. 'And I don't want to cause you any more pain. Our marriage means something to me.'

'Yeah, right,' she smirks.

'Will you listen to me for once?'

'Why? Did you think of something else that you want? Shall I placate your mother? Or fund your next trip around the world? Or bend over so you can screw me?' she spits out. She closes her eyes, lets out a breath, and then opens them again. 'What do you want from me?' she says. The look she gives me is chilling.

I let her go. I step back. What happened to the carefree, funny, gorgeous woman I married? 'That's just it. I don't want anything from you.'

'Because there's nothing left for you to take,' she mutters, her retort lost in a puff of air. She turns around and walks into the bedroom.

'What did you say?'

'Nothing,' she says, flicking on the light.

'What did you say?'

'I said there's nothing left for you to take,' she says, spinning around to face me. She lets her bag drop to the floor, its contents spilling out with a clatter.

'What have *I* taken from *you*, Mia?'

'Everything,' she screams. 'You've taken *everything* from me. I've spent years putting myself second, propping you up, applauding your pathetic career, paying for you, lying for—'

'See this, this right here is why it's so difficult being with you. You're so . . . petty. All you care about is money, status—'

'Yes, yes, I've heard that before. You want a simple life. You want to travel. You want to give back to the world. Tell me, Roy, how exactly do you intend to do any of that without money? Actually, let's be more specific, how exactly do you intend to do that without *my* money? I mean, you aren't exactly the type to rough it out. You work on more submissions than commissions. You're still holding a grudge about having to pay for your own tuition. You can't handle so much as an auto ride in India and you plan to, what, backpack around the world?'

'How dare you—'

'All these years, it's been your career, your parents, your plans. You. You. You. That's all this marriage has been about. What about me?' She collapses on the bed. 'What about me, Roy? All I ever did was love you. And you – you used me. You *broke* us!'

She looks up at me, tears pooling in her eyes. She looks so vulnerable that for a moment, my anger subsides. I am reminded of the woman I fell in love with. She did love me. Probably still does, in her own twisted way. I can't fault her for that.

'How could you do this to me, Roy?'

It doesn't matter who I fell in love with, this is who I married – an angry, jealous, bitter woman. I remind myself that I still need her, but the words slip out before I can stop them.

'I had an affair, yes, but only because being with you is so fucking painful. Can't you see that?'

'Don't you dare try to pin this on me. We were happy. And then you fucked up. You did something you couldn't come back from and now you're trying to convince yourself it wasn't your fault.'

'Oh, this is rich coming from you.'

'What's that supposed to mean?'

'You manage to convince yourself you're the victim in every situation. The righteous little girl wronged by the whole world. Do you have any idea what all I've been forced to do for—'

'Screw you, Roy. You couldn't even stand by me the one time I needed you! Daddy's house – you could have—'

'Enough about that fucking house! Open your eyes, Mia. Don't you get it? Think about how frail your mother looked at the wedding. She's ill. She needs the money. That's why—'

'Shut up.'

'—Aditi's in India. That's why they're selling—'

'Shut up!'

'—the place. She needs you and you're too stubborn to even see it. It's a good thing your father isn't here to see how selfish his *angel* turned—'

'Shut the fuck up!' Mia screams. She gets up and opens the wardrobe. She pulls out a duffel bag and starts throwing things in it.

'What the hell do you think you're doing?'

She walks around the room, picking things up and shoving them in the bag.

'Will you stop for one second!' I grab her elbow but she shrugs me off.

'Mia!'

'No, I'm done. I'm done believing you and I'm done lying for you.'

She stops when the bag is full. 'I'm done.'

'I'm your husband.'

'Yes,' she says. She thrusts the bag at me. 'But this is my house. Get out.'

MIA

Tuesday, 8th December

I wait for the sound of angry footsteps, for Roy to storm back in and demand I open the door, but the house is silent.

Do you know what you've done?

He isn't coming back.

Ever.

Good.

I reach for my phone and ring the only person I know who will still be on my side.

'Georgie,' I whisper.

I peer at the mirror in the bathroom. The face that stares back at me isn't my own. I splash some water on it and grip the sink.

I told you this would happen. Tighter. *You may have asked him to leave the house today, but he left you long ago.* Tighter. *Because you're disgusting. Weak.* I watch my knuckles go white and then I let go. I step back. It doesn't matter any-more.

Ringing George made it official. My marriage is over.

The bed feels bigger. I've been tossing and turning all night, trying to find the truth that must lie somewhere between Roy's side and mine. It's still dark outside but I get up and go to the wardrobe. I kneel down and reach for the Chloe handbag, plunging my hand into the soft leather, fishing around till my fingers graze the cold metal. I close my fist around it and sit like that for a minute, relishing its weight and arrogance. I'm not prepared to pull it out yet.

Roy may not believe in consequences, but I do.

I know it will destroy me. It *did* destroy me. But its heady power is seductive. It offers oblivion.

I don't want to be weak anymore. I pull it out.

I get up and change into a pair of jeans. I put on a sweat-shirt.

I can't escape the darkness. I might as well own it.

ROY

Wednesday, 9th December

I wake up in a seedy hotel room around the corner from my perfectly lovely house. It's still early and my head is still spinning, a nasty hangover pressing down on my skull.

I know the police will be back – maybe not today, but soon. Why bother looking elsewhere when everyone knows it's always the boyfriend? First port of call, Robins had said.

I check my brand new iPhone: dead. I plug it in and consider ringing Mia but decide against it. I had already left her a message last night letting her know where I was, so she could be the one to apologize for once.

I switch on the light and survey my surroundings. The patterned wallpaper – this hotel is ancient enough for wallpaper – is faded and peeling off in patches. The carpet that looked merely ill-advised last night now reveals itself as filthy. The TV is an old box, much akin to what I had in my room as a kid. There's a draught coming in from the window and the door looks like a child could kick it open.

This room is nothing like the ones I review. It isn't just basic; it's as if the hotel is *trying* to give its guests the opposite of a luxury experience.

It's like being in prison.

I spot the mini-bar under the luggage rack and open it. It's empty save for a half-drunk bottle of water. So this is what I paid the overweight man at the reception eighty quid for. Peak season, he said when I objected. Yeah, right. The hotel is empty. No one would know if I died in here.

I was in the middle of an argument with him when my phone rang. It was George. My relief was entirely unwarranted.

'Hi, George. Sorry, dude, I haven't been able to get back to you on the schedule. Things have been manic around here.'

I noticed the whisky in my words and paused, waiting for George's heavy voice to fill my ear, but he didn't say anything.

'George?'

'Did you hurt her?'

His words, when they came, were quiet. He knew.

'No! I didn't touch Emily. How can you even ask me such—'

'Mia.'

'Of course I didn't.'

His voice got closer. The receptionist was staring at me. I threw the money at him and picked up the keys.

'Stay away from her, Roy. I mean it. I won't let you hurt her.'

'She's my w—'

'And as for the documentary, don't bother getting back to me.'

Even as I recall the conversation for the umpteenth time, I am filled with rage. I want to strangle my wife. It's typical of her to look for a sly route to get back at me. What better way than to use her old boyfriend to do the job.

I find the plastic-covered remote in the bedside drawer and press on the red button a few times till the TV crackles to life. I flick through the channels till I come to Sky News. Emily's face fills the screen. Thanks to her brother, she is now the leading news story. It seems she's finally getting the attention she was hungry for; too bad she isn't here to enjoy it.

The reporter is saying the police have several new lines of enquiry. I feel my breathing quicken. They've found her scarf. I'm still staring at the screen when I notice the door to my room is rattling.

I get up and make my way over to the other side of the room, the loud banging on the door a mere whisper compared to the beat my heart is drumming.

MIA

I am waiting.

Waiting for the high to kick in.

Waiting for the guilt to surface.

Waiting for the police to return.

Waiting for the tears to come.

When Daddy died, almost instantly the house was full of people. First came the police, bearing the news, then Daddy's family, bearing sorrow, and then the constant stream of friends, neighbours and acquaintances, bearing food. All unwanted but essential all the same, each of them going out of their way to help us. Where are they now? Where are the casseroles and lasagnes they threw at us?

I look around me; I'm sitting in chaos of my own making.

What have you done?

What are you doing?

I am sitting down but it feels like I've stood up too

quickly. My legs are tingling. I have no grip on time anymore. The numbness is my only comfort.

I am waiting, waiting, waiting.

There's no one here.

I can wait forever.

I am a connoisseur of being left behind.

ROY

My first thought when I'm brought in is that the lights are too bright. The second is that the room is too cold. I look around as best as I can while keeping my head still, trying to determine the source of the draught but there are no windows. I glance at the blindingly white walls, blending into the ceiling. The room is meant to be anonymous, I conclude. It will take on whatever mood the table at its centre dictates.

I hear the door open behind me and I resist the urge to steal a look. Hushed voices, the dull thud of the door closing and then the screech of the chairs on the tiled floor as Robins and Wilson sit down across from me.

'Thanks for coming in,' Robins begins. Her voice is unusually sharp.

'Of course,' I reply. An invitation from the police is not one you can decline.

'You do not have to say anything. But it may harm your defence if you do not mention, when questioned, something which you later rely on in court. Anything you do say may be given in evidence,' she drones on. She reminds me that I am not under arrest and asks me again if I'd like a solicitor. I say no and then it begins.

'Roy, don't you think it's about time you started being honest with us?' Robins asks half an hour later.

'I *have* been honest.'

'Right, well, maybe we've got it wrong then,' she says, holding up her hands, smiling.

I caution myself. That smile has fooled me before.

'Let's run through your last meeting with Emily once more, shall we?' she says, tapping her notebook. She flicks it open and leans back in her chair.

I glance at her and then at Wilson as if to say we've had this conversation before, but she carries on.

'How was Emily's demeanour when you met her?'

'Fine. Normal.'

'Did you speak to her after that?'

'No.'

'So you had no contact with her after Wednesday, December the second at all?'

'No,' I say without batting an eyelid.

'Why did she ask to meet you on Wednesday?'

'I don't know. To chat, I suppose, clear the air. She was – is leaving for Australia soon. She said she didn't want us to end things badly.'

Robins leans forward and looks me in the eye. Wilson still hasn't said a word. 'See, here's what's bothering me, Roy. A few people have mentioned that Emily was very stressed in the days before she disappeared. They said she seemed distressed, manic almost. Yet here you are, saying she was perfectly fine just two days before she was last seen. Seems . . . odd.'

I weigh my words, reminding myself that they have nothing concrete to go on. 'Well, she seemed fine when she met me. I can't comment on her behaviour with others.'

'She told a friend she was scared. She said she had done something that the man she was seeing wouldn't like. What did she do, Roy?'

'I have no idea. I can't imagine why Emily would say something like that.'

'Did she get too attached? Threaten to tell your wife, perhaps?'

'No! I told you, I ended things because I was afraid someone would get hurt.'

'Well, clearly someone did,' Wilson mutters.

Robins shoots him a look and he slumps back. She carries on. 'Emily said her boyfriend had an unpredictable temper. She was worried what he – *you* might do. Why would she say that?'

'I don't know. Maybe she meant someone else.'

'Are you saying Emily had another boyfriend?'

'She was popular.'

Robins takes in a breath and leans back. 'Are you sure there's nothing else you want to tell us?'

I look at the scratched surface of the desk. I wonder how many people have been interviewed in this room. I wonder how many of them were guilty.

I wonder how many of them were stupid.

When I look up both Robins and Wilson are staring at me. I breathe in the stale air and brace myself.

'No, that's everything. I've been as helpful as I could and now I'd like to leave.'

I step out of the station five minutes later and make the call I should have made to begin with.

MIA

Wednesday, 9th December

I push myself off the floor. It takes me a second to find my balance and then I go into the kitchen. I fill up a glass with tap water and gulp it down, wiping away the meandering trail it traces around my mouth and chin with the back of my hand. I leave the glass on the counter and go back into the living room. I slump on the sofa and survey the room. It's devastated: dirty dishes and wine bottles nestled amongst the cushions on the floor, a cover-less duvet on the sofa, takeaway boxes littered across the room. My gaze settles on the metal case on the coffee table.

Your mother wouldn't approve of this.

She lost her right to judge me when she broke up our family.

Haven't you just done the exact same thing?

I inhale.

I am choked with guilt.

Marriage is meant to be forever.

I exhale.

I am bursting with relief.

It doesn't hurt anymore.

It will.

I know I should take a shower, eat, ring Natalie. Do something. But I am frozen.

Tomorrow, I tell myself.

Tomorrow.

Today I will wallow.

Today it is allowed.

I'll be better tomorrow.

You'll never get better.

I crawl over to the coffee table and roll another joint.

A dense fog is rising up through me. It spirals upwards, then jerks to a stop. I close my eyes. I risk a breath and it starts again. Down. Up. Down. Stop. Again. It whirls around, pulsing, climbing through me, till it reaches my head, and then the spirals get tighter; they coil around my brain, each loop tenser, pushing against my skull, tighter, tighter, tighter.

Daddy.

And then there is blackness.

Time folds into itself. Seconds become days. Years become hours. Flashes of memories layer over one another, merging with fragments of my present and imagined snippets from my future until I can no longer tell them apart.

Marry me. Roy in the lavender fields, holding two glasses of Prosecco.

You're beautiful. Mum pleating my *sari* and folding it into my waistband.

I'm pregnant. Me crouching over the toilet.

I win. Addi running past me to the swings.

Be brave, like the princess. Daddy tucking me in at bedtime.

You disgust me. Roy's hand, curled up into a fist.

You have to stop doing this to yourself. Addi kneeling by my bed.

Some things can't be fixed. Chris weeping.

It's all destined. James drunk, slurring.

You fuck everything up. Mike screaming.

You're nothing compared to her. Roy sniggering.

My head spins.

I still myself. I focus. I try to pry the truth away from my stories. Mum. Emily. Daddy. Dead. Roy. Celia. Addi. Real?

I look down. The floor dances.

I look up. The ceiling dives.

Nothing makes sense.

I am broken and I must be fixed. I pop another pill.

You're unbreakable. Daddy.

Daddy would have fixed this. He should have been here. He *could* have been here. My fury oscillates between Roy and my mother.

Her infidelity stripped me of my childhood.

His infidelity robbed me of my future.

I cannot rebuild either.

*

Natalie leans back in her chair when I finish speaking.

'It sounds like a lot has happened since we last met. How are you feeling?'

I look down at my hands. 'Angry. Scared. Guilty,' I say. I've told her everything: the police, Emily, Celia, my mother's affair, Roy's parents visiting, Addi leaving, Mike, work, the Eastside order, everything.

Except the drugs, that is. That I keep to myself. I wonder if she can tell my head is still swimming.

She nods. 'I can imagine how difficult these last few weeks have been for you. But you've made a big leap, Mia. Standing up to your family and your husband, that took immense courage. You must congratulate yourself on that.'

I nod my agreement even though it doesn't make sense. She wants me to congratulate myself on throwing my marriage away?

'All the same, I want to make sure you've thought this through,' she continues.

'Meaning?'

'Well, these are some big life choices that you've made. Have you considered what happens next? Are you thinking about divorce?'

'No! That's not what – I – I'm not a quitter.'

'I know.'

'This is my marriage we're talking about.'

She nods.

'Maybe I can still fix this.'

She doesn't say anything.

'He's just lost. Maybe this time apart will remind him he loves me. You said yourself we could fix this.'

'I did, but—'

'But you weren't here. You said we'd work on things together, but you weren't even here.' I close my eyes. Fear snaps them open again. 'What if they arrest him?'

'I'm sorry you had to go through this alone and, in the future, I'd be happy to put you in touch with a colleague who can help. But for now, I'd like us to focus—'

'Are you going on holiday again?'

'I'm sorry?'

'What do you mean in the future?'

'Well, I was hoping we could spend the last few minutes of our session discussing this, but we may as well talk about it now,' she says. A quick pause, her eyes dart to the clock and then, 'I'm afraid I won't be able to carry on seeing you anymore.'

I stare at her, stunned.

'There was a personal situation that came up while I was away and I'm having to move abroad temporarily.'

'When?'

'In a few days. Before Christmas. I'm wrapping up all my sessions this week. Now I know this feels sudden and I want you to know this has absolutely nothing to do with you. I've put together a list of some excellent therapists that I can refer you to. We can discuss some options now . . .'

This is a waste of time. Another person I was relying on, gone. I don't want another therapist; I want another joint. 'That's okay. I don't need a therapist right now.'

'I understand you're upset but I think you should consider—'

'No, it's fine,' I say, reaching into my bag and pulling out my wallet. I leave her fee on the table and stand up.

I'm already at the door by the time she gets up. 'Mia, we need to phase out therapy in a responsible—'

I step out and close the door behind me. I don't need anyone. They all leave anyway.

ROY

Thursday, 10th December

I am not surprised they are here. I am surprised they are here so soon.

I step aside to let them in and watch the hotel room shrink.

'I told you, you didn't need to come.'

'Of course we needed to come. You're being accused of murder,' Ma says, putting her handbag down on the bed and taking in the entire room with a single disgusted glance. My father settles into the chair by the window.

'Calm down, Ma. No one's accusing me of anything.'

Yet.

'Is it true? You were having an affair with that girl?'

I nod. I stare at my feet.

'How old is she?' my father asks.

'What difference does that make?'

'It makes all the difference in the world, son. Did you learn nothing working in the media?'

He could never pass up an opportunity to show me my place.

Ma swoops in before I can say anything. 'This is not the time to argue, *ji*. *Lawyer ko phone karo.* This is our son.'

Within minutes I have an appointment with a criminal defence solicitor. The best, and most expensive, one in town, I'm told.

I also have a suite at the Hilton. Connected to the one my parents are in.

I give in and ring Mia but she doesn't answer. I leave her a voicemail, and then send her a text as well. There isn't anything left for me to do.

I sit down and let my mother fuss over me as my father resumes control over my life.

MIA

Thursday, 10th December

A couple of weeks ago, Roy went to Dublin on a press trip. I was in meetings in Leicester all day so he asked me not to pick him up at the airport.

I was in bed with a book and a pizza when he got home.

'You're late,' I called out.

Roy appeared in the doorway moments later, looking haggard, unshaven and incredibly handsome.

'I know. There was a mad queue for taxis,' he said, slipping off his trousers and climbing into bed. 'Is it too late now to say sorry?'

'Cos you're missing more than my body? Bieber? Seriously? Who have you been hanging out with!'

'What do you mean?' he said, tickling me and almost knocking the takeaway box over.

He had gone on to demolish the pizza.

He must have been with Emily that weekend. Or perhaps Celia, if she exists. And I had welcomed him home like the pitiful, desperate wife that I seem to have become.

I know this, yet I want to hit rewind and jolt myself back to that night, to any night, when I could take my marriage for granted.

I sit down on the floor and try to find something to focus on, but everything in the room taunts me, reminding me I can never really win. I may have kicked him out but I am still the one left hurting.

Divorced before thirty. Pathetic.

Perhaps I made a mistake.

Or perhaps I made up my mind but my heart doesn't want to comply.

My phone buzzes. It's Roy again.

It would be so easy to let him come back. He would apologize, I would forgive him and we'd go back to how we were before all this. Safe. Happy. Loved.

But every text, email, voicemail Roy has left me since that day says one thing and one thing only – we need to stay together till this blows over. He doesn't want me, not really.

I let the call go to voicemail.

I try to appeal to the feminist in me: You made a decision and now you need to stop waiting. You need to stop wanting him back. You can't make him love you.

Why would he?

I lie back on the floor and stare at the ceiling. I push my earphones in and click on to Spotify, scrolling till I find Amy Winehouse. The more I think about it, the more real it seems.

I had thought with Emily gone, we had a chance. But

how could I have known about Celia? If she's real, he's clearly in love with her. If she isn't, he's clearly ready to leave me.

I hit play.

Not one woman, but two.

He must have been desperate to get away.

The music pounds through me.

The lyrics clutch on to my heart.

Because suddenly everything that is sad is relevant.

ROY

His name is Alistair Stanton of Stanton & Kent and he's nothing like I expect him to be.

When my father told me his friend at Cambridge Law said Stanton was the best in the business, I expected someone brusque, loud and ruthless. I was picturing the male version of Annalise Keating. I had presumed he too, like Annalise, would come with an entourage. But life isn't an episode of *How to Get Away With Murder*.

Though it wouldn't hurt if it were.

In his early forties, not overweight but with a slight pudginess around the middle, Stanton is dressed in an expensive, but ill-fitting grey suit, no tie. He's clean-shaven; his hair is cut short and brushed back, a few hairs standing up this way and that. His watch is as discreet as the dull gold wedding band on his finger.

I was a bit taken aback when he suggested we meet at the hotel instead of in his office but I realize quickly it's all just a part of his carefully curated facade; he wants to put me at ease, lower my defences. Despite myself, I am impressed.

'I prefer to speak with my clients confidentially, Mr Kapoor, so if you don't mind . . .' Stanton trails off.

My father gives Stanton a dangerous look and I'm sure he is about to object, but he gets up and walks off with a curt nod, closing the door behind him.

I like him already.

'We can meet at my office the next time. You'll love the space; it's on the eighteenth floor overlooking the Thames. Stunning view and the light . . .' He pauses, eyes wide, and shakes his head, as if we are discussing the latest hotspot in London.

'Sounds wonderful,' I say, matching my expression to his. I wonder if he'll be charging my father for this random conversation.

I hear the door click and watch his face change.

'Roy, I wish you'd called me before speaking to the police but what's done is done. As of now, I think we can assume that you're the prime suspect. There may be others, but the number of times they've interviewed you suggests they're looking at you' – he pauses – 'closely.'

I nod. I had figured as much.

'The only reason they haven't made an arrest yet is because they can't afford to make a mistake, what with all the media interest in Emily's case. On the other hand, every day they don't take action is a strike against them. So we need to be prepared for an arrest. It may not be immediate, but they need to show the public they have this under control as soon as practicable.'

'But what would they arrest me for? It's not like they've found her body.'

'They don't need to. All they need is a motive and reasonable doubt.'

My eyes widen and he pauses to explain.

'It's rare, but there have been instances in the past of murder trials without a body and Emily's been missing long enough now . . . In such cases, the purpose of an arrest is usually to provoke a confession. They can't charge you unless they have enough evidence.'

'Now, I'm not saying that that this will happen,' he continues. 'But it is my job to prepare you for all possibilities.'

He's working on the assumption that she's dead but he still hasn't asked me if I killed her.

He looks like he's about to ask me a question, then shakes his head. 'Let's start at the beginning, shall we? I need you to be completely honest with me. I can't help you unless I know everything you know. Sound reasonable?'

'Absolutely,' I say.

And then I tell him as much as I can.

I begin, of course, with you.

I tell Alistair – he asks me to call him Alistair – about how we first met. I tell him about what you said at the Eurostar terminal, how angry you were when you saw me with your notebook. I feel guilty when I tell him how we spoke about the universe conspiring to make us run into each other again and again. Is it strange that simply recounting our conversations to Alistair fills me with more guilt than cheating on Mia ever did? That my loyalties are tied so deeply to you, it makes my marriage and every other relationship feel like a sham? I suppose it is a matter of love.

Or the lack thereof.

I tell Alistair about that time at the National Gallery. I'd walked in to find you standing in front of the Constable piece, unmoving. You were so lost in the painting you barely even noticed when I came and stood next to you. Neither of us said a word. We didn't need to. We walked through the exhibit rooms, weaving our way through the tourists and the art students. I remember looking at you from the corner of my eye and noticing how drawn you looked. Your fingers grazed mine and my gaze travelled down to your hand automatically. You'd taken your ring off. There's so much that happened in that one instant, but what I felt most of all was relief. For you. You caught my eye, you shook your head, and my heart sank. My eye travelled to your other bandaged hand. You would tell me later that that was the day Dave found your phone.

As we approached the exit, we fell out of step just as quietly, without any drawn-out goodbyes or promises of future meetings. We never needed any of that, but something changed between us that day. It was the start of our private world, and without a word we both acknowledged we wanted the same thing – each other.

Alistair asks me a question and I pull myself back to the present. He wants to know if you'll testify for me should we go to trial. Of course, I say, without a moment's thought. You'd do anything for me and I for you. We know that now.

'How were things with Emily at this stage?'

'Complicated. She would ring me every night, sometimes eight, ten times in an hour. She wanted to see me all the time, she wanted me to meet her friends . . . She wanted a relationship and I couldn't give her that.'

'Did Emily know about Celia?'

'No, I didn't think it would do any good to tell her. And frankly, there wasn't much to tell at that point. Celia and I . . . there was nothing physical until after Emily.'

'I see.' He nods, not unsympathetically. 'Was your wife aware of anything at this point?'

'No, she only found out last week.'

'Okay, let's go over the timeline once again. When we spoke on the phone, you mentioned you had a meeting in town on the morning of the fourth; you spent the afternoon at home and then drove straight to your hotel in Brighton, where you met Celia. You spent the night at the hotel and then drove back to London midday Saturday. Is that correct?'

'That's what I told the detectives.'

If Alistair is surprised, he doesn't show it. 'Is that the truth?'

'It is, but I – I made a stop on the way.'

'Where?'

'Seaford. I went to see Emily.'

'Emily rang me when I was on my way to Brighton. I had been fielding calls from her for weeks, but that day, she must have called me twenty times in an hour. She was upset. She wanted to see me. I told her I'd see her on Monday but she kept insisting we meet straightaway. She was crying, practically howling on the phone, so I agreed. I picked her up on the High Street and we drove to Seaford Head.'

'Why Seaford?'

'She was going to spend the weekend at her parents' place in Sussex and I was already on my way to Brighton, so . . .'

'I see.' He flicks through his notes. 'What did she want to talk about?'

'Getting back together. She wanted me to leave Mia. I refused. We spoke about it and then I dropped her to her hotel and drove to Brighton. I didn't see her again,' I say.

Yet another one of the half-truths that my life is built upon.

'What happens now?' I ask after Alistair's finished with his questions, his notebook overflowing with snatches of my life.

'Well, to begin with, I'd like to speak with Celia. If the

police have already been to see her, I need to know what she's said to them and prepare her for any future interviews. Would you be able to set up a meeting or shall I have one of my associates call her?'

'No, I'll do it.'

'Excellent.'

'Anything else?'

'Yes, your wife. What are the chances of her agreeing to let you move back in?'

'I've been trying to speak to her but she refuses to take my calls.'

'Can you convince her? Having her on your side would be extremely beneficial. If she's supportive and forgiving in the face of an affair, well, there's little reason for you to harm Emily.'

I flinch but I don't correct him. He stresses the importance of a character witness, and then coaches me on what to say to Mia. I want to tell him to stop, I know exactly what I need to say, what buttons to push, but I just listen. *Apologize for the affairs. Stress the importance of the marriage. Remind her why she married you.* I nod along. I have tried everything, but I'll try again.

'Meanwhile, I'll have my associates dig around, see if we can find any other potential suspects,' he continues.

I tell Alistair about that first time in the park. I'd asked Emily afterwards if she wanted me to accompany her to a pharmacy. I had presumed she would need emergency contraception. But she simply shook her head and told me she was on the pill. Alistair perks up instantly and the flicker of annoyance I felt that day distills into a single strand of hope. Emily might have given me the perfect way out of this.

Another boyfriend. Another suspect.

On Friday, 11 December at 01.33 p.m.,
Roy Kapoor <roy_kapoor@me.com> wrote:

Dear Mia,

I know that you've been deeply hurt by me and I am really sorry for that. I can't even begin to imagine the pain you're going through. But perhaps this had to happen for us to reach a happier, more honest place.

There is a lot for us to talk about and I'd like to have a heart-to-heart conversation with you like two grown adults – nothing but the truth, I promise.

Mia, I know I've made some terrible mistakes but I am still the man you married. I am hoping that you will find it in your heart to meet me so we can begin repairing the damage that has been caused and find a way out of this. It's my home too, and anyone else in my position would force their way back into it, but I know that you need space, so as much as I hate being in a hotel with my parents, I won't do that.

I'm staying at the Hilton in Canary Wharf. I will meet you anywhere you say but honestly, all I want right now is to come home to you. Let me make it up to you, please.

Yours,
Roy

MIA

Roy's email touches something in me. I've been waiting for
him to apologize properly but it occurs to me that I haven't
given him the chance to do that. Moreover, didn't I have a
part to play in everything that happened that night as well?
I said things that I knew would push him over the edge, as
if by testing the limits of our marriage I could somehow
pull it back together. What I hadn't realized was how close
to the tipping point we already were.

When Roy calls, an hour later, I give in.

'Hello.'

'Hello? Mia?'

His voice takes my breath away. I know instantly that I
made a mistake. I'm not ready for this conversation.

'Yes.'

'I . . . wow . . . thanks for answering. I, um, just wanted
us to talk.'

'Okay. Talk.' I force myself to sound curt even as I try to
blink the tears away.

'Oh, right, okay. Well, first, I think I want to say I am extremely sorry about how everything has unfolded. I know I've hurt you. You must be in shock right now and heartbroken and . . . and I'm very sorry for the pain that I've caused.'

Tears course down my face. I place a hand over my mouth and inhale deeply. I remind myself that I don't want him back. I shouldn't want him back.

'Hello?'

'Just tell me one thing,' I say after I have steadied myself.

'Anything.'

'Did you do it? Did you hurt Emily?'

'No, of course not. They haven't even found—'

'So Celia?'

I hear him sigh. 'Everything with Celia is real. I do . . . I was with her. And . . .' He pauses. I picture him furrowing his brow, searching for the right words. 'I know I've said this before, but I do think everything that's happened so far, Emily, Celia, it was all for a reason. I think the universe was just trying to join the dots. It was saying . . . this is everything you've been wanting, missing in your life: Celia. And this is what you already have: Mia.'

The shred of hope I'd been hanging on to dissipates.

My heart stills.

'And it's been put on me to make a choice,' he continues.

A beat.

A choice? Choose me, I want to scream. Choose me!

'And I know you've been hurt in the process, badly, but I think . . . I think sometimes things have to fall apart entirely before we can start rebuilding something better . . . more authentic. And so I know whatever I decide, whatever *we* decide, it will be for the best. I'm trying to be as honest as I can. I just want us to be happy, Mia,' he finishes. 'What are you thinking?'

'I'm not thinking.'

'I'd like us to try to make it work.'

Yes, I think.

'Why?' I say.

'Huh?'

'Why do you want to try?'

'This situation has been a nightmare. I mean, I hate to blame the situation, but it has been difficult, it still is, and I'm hoping I can get out of it and find a way to be happy again.'

'With you,' he adds. Afterthought.

'Did a lawyer write this down for you?'

'No, he didn't. The police, everything with Emily, all of that, that's another issue. My main concern is our marriage and I need to be at home so we can start talking about us.'

His voice gives it away. He's terrified. For the first time, I allow myself to seriously consider what happened to Emily that night.

'If you're in love with someone else, why would you want to be with me?'

He pauses. He measures his words. He breaks my heart all over again.

'Because love isn't everything,' he says.

ROY

'Didn't work?'

I jump at my father's voice behind me. 'She's just upset.'

'She's smart.'

'Well, it's none of your business. And I'd appreciate some privacy.'

He smirks. 'Sure, son. Just don't get used to it. I hear they like everything out in the open in prison.' He walks back into the living room and I follow. I've had enough of his snide comments.

'What is your problem?' I demand.

'You mean aside from the fact that I've had to drop everything and come to London because my son has been impulsive again?'

'What the hell is that supposed to mean?'

'Don't use that language with me,' he says and I look down. 'And you know exactly what I mean.'

'I was a child!'

'Which is why I protected you. But you are not a child anymore and this is not India.'

MIA

I avoid making eye contact with anyone on the train. A few people stare at me then move away. I can't blame them. I keep my head bent low and stand to one side.

I know I don't look great.

I know they can tell that my life is falling apart.

I just don't know what to do about it.

I feel a hand cup my bottom as the train pulls to a stop and I am swept towards the door. I spin around, more out of instinct than actual desire to yell at the man trying to grab me. But before I can say anything, I feel that hand again, this time on my thigh. I look down. A little girl looks up at me and smiles, all rainbows and unicorns. 'Excuse me, lady,' she says. My eyes fill with fresh tears as I step aside to let her skip past, her mother hustling to keep up with her.

A blast of icy air hits me as soon as I step out of the station. I pull my scarf tighter and start walking towards the office. I don't want to go in but I can't sit around at home anymore. I feel calm, the weed slowing me down and giving me the veneer of confidence.

I stop to pick up breakfast on my way and as an after-thought pick up a coffee for Mike. He'll be fuming after my no-show on Friday.

The office is quiet when I walk in just after nine, every-one already at their desks, heads bent low over laptops. It feels odd until I remember it's Christmas bonus time.

I nip into Mike's office to give him his coffee but he isn't there. I sidestep the boxes and files that litter the floor and leave the cup on his desk with a Post-it before walking over to my own office.

I have barely taken off my coat when Yvonne rings to let me know Harvey wants to see me. He probably wants to go over the planned bonuses for my team, I figure. I gulp my double espresso down and slip a couple of mints in my mouth. I take my work phone with me, scrolling through a week's worth of emails as I wait for the lift: office Christ-mas party menu, holiday greetings, QC reports, cat videos, sample pictures, costings. Nothing urgent. By the time I step into Harvey's office, I'm alert, the coffee having done its job, and I've caught up with everything. It's only after I sit down that I notice Mike in the corner.

So that's what this is about.

I put on a weak smile, and launch into my speech.

'Harvey, I'm sorry I've been in and out of the office last week. I'm sure you don't want me to go into the details, but I've been having some gynecological problems that left me rather worn—'

'Mia, something disturbing has come to light about the Eastside order,' Harvey begins, talking over me.

I pause and wait for him to continue. I wonder how much he knows.

'It seems the factory forged the test results. The shipment is in breach of REACH regulations and I believe there are some concerns about child labour.'

I look at Mike. He carries on staring out of the window.

'That's impossible. Are you sure?'

He holds up a hand and I shut up.

'The fabric hasn't cleared the SVHCs test, so I was quite shocked to see we had issued the MDAs last week. Mike's managed to liaise with the port authorities and had the shipment held in Turkey until we can get to the bottom of the situation. Were you aware of this?'

'Of course not, I had no idea.'

'Did you check the test reports?'

'I did.'

Mike scoffs from his position by the window. Harvey silences him with a look.

'Mia, I wish I didn't have to ask you this . . . but we've had an anonymous report that you were made aware of the situation and you authorized the shipment regardless. Is this true?'

'Who said that?'

'That's irrelevant. Is it true?'

'I heard there was an issue with the reports but I presumed it was something minor, a low score on the wash test or the dimensional stability. I wasn't aware it had anything to do with REACH or working conditions.

'Harvey, we've overlooked issues like this in the past. Hardly any of our orders achieve a hundred per cent compliance,' I continue when Harvey doesn't react.

'This isn't a simple compliance issue, Mia. This goes beyond your level of authority. You should have brought this to me or Mike.'

'I'm sorry, Harvey. Like I said, I wasn't aware of the details. I made a call. Eastside has a very stringent cancellation policy and I didn't—'

'I don't think you understand the seriousness of this. Bringing in products that breach REACH regulations is illegal. Add to that the child labour situation . . .' He shakes his head and leans back. There's a disappointment in his face that I've never seen before.

'By acting on behalf of the company, you've jeopardized the entire business. We could get sued, not to mention the PR nightmare that will ensue if this comes out. Eastside has already threatened to take us off the approved supplier list and if that happens, other retailers will follow their lead,' he goes on.

'I can ring Jo and try to do some damage control. We can tell her we found—'

'That won't be necessary. Mike's meeting with their head of sourcing later today.'

It doesn't add up. The head of sourcing hates Mike, that's why I took over the account in the first place.

'You've been a valuable member of staff here, Mia, but

this is not something the board can overlook. It would be best if you resign, perhaps take some time to recover from your illness, and then when you're ready, I'd be happy to give you a letter of reference.'

I look at him, astonished.

Before I can say anything else, Yvonne appears out of nowhere and ushers me into a conference room. She tells me that the business is willing to offer me three months' severance pay, a nod to my contribution over the years, and then promptly produces a document for me to sign. I skim through it. Confidentiality agreement.

I sign the papers wordlessly. It is fitting when everything else in my life is falling apart that my career should too.

She informs me that I am to turn in my laptop, key card and phone. After that, I'm free to go.

Downstairs, I notice Chris sitting at his old desk. He gets up and follows me to my office but I shut the door before he can come in. It is humiliating enough as it is, I don't need an audience.

It's only as I'm packing up my things that the jigsaw starts to piece itself together. The boxes in Mike's office. The confidentiality agreement. The generous severance package. I inhale sharply. Mike played me, securing the seat on the board and getting rid of me in one move. And Chris helped him do it.

Chris. After everything I've done for him. All for what, a promotion?

I consider going back to see Harvey, explaining to him what was really going on. But it feels pointless.

No one even looks up when I walk out of my office.

I glance into Mike's office on my way out. He's smiling to himself, sipping the coffee I bought him not thirty minutes ago.

ROY

I look up every time the door opens. You should have been here over an hour ago. I try ringing but your phone goes straight to voicemail. There's a light dusting of snow outside. Perhaps there were delays on the train; wouldn't be the first time. I consider getting another coffee but I'm not sure I can handle it. I'm wound up enough already. I check my watch; it's half eleven. Alistair won't arrive till midday so we should still have a few minutes to ourselves before the meeting.

I wouldn't go so far as to call this our usual spot – we didn't have one – but I've found myself clinging to anything familiar this week, so when Alistair said he would be in Islington this morning, I had suggested we meet here. I'd planned on getting us the same table, the one in the corner, tucked behind the column, but in the three weeks since we were last here, they've moved it and put a Christmas tree there instead.

I remember how you scanned the room, before moving your fingers in the most discreet of waves as you walked in that day. You took your time crossing the room, your hips swaying as you threaded your way through the narrow spaces between the chairs. I wasn't able to look away, the natural grace in your movements utterly enchanting. You slipped into the chair across from me and gave me a watery smile.

'This is a nice spot,' you said, placing your bag on the floor while your eyes darted across the room.

It was mid-afternoon on a Tuesday and other than an old couple on the far right, and us, the cafe was empty. I caught your gaze. 'Hey, I checked. It's fine. Shall I get you a coffee?'

'In a bit,' you said, relaxing into the chair after another, final sweep of the room. 'How are you?'

By this point, we had been meeting nearly every day for two weeks. We had not yet kissed but there was an intimacy that had developed between us quite naturally. Even so, when I reached for your hand under the table, the feeling that rushed through me was intense, beginning where our fingers met and sending shock waves through my entire body.

It was the week after I had broken up with Emily. My parents had just left; Mia was spending most of her time at work. I was feeling hopeful. I was feeling like, perhaps, we might have a shot at this for real. I told you that and you nodded.

'It doesn't feel like a coincidence, does it?' you asked.

'What?'

'Everything. Us. It feels as if the universe is joining the dots, bringing us together like this.'

I nodded. You let go of my hand and drew your chair in closer. My knees found yours. 'It's so strange. I've never felt more myself than I have over the past few weeks. And I feel like everything I've ever wanted, all that I'd given up on, it's within arm's reach once again.'

You smiled and leaned forward. At some point your hand found my leg and your thumb started circling my knee. Lightly at first, the pressure increasing gradually, climbing up my leg until I couldn't bear it anymore. I had the urge to kiss you but I didn't, I couldn't, not even in an empty cafe where the only other customers were an old and probably half-blind couple.

Just thinking about it now leaves me tingling, the memory strumming all the desire and frustration that's been festering within me for days. There is a gauze-like fragility to it, and I worry that even thinking about it too much will rip the memory to shreds.

Though I saw you little more than a week ago, it feels like an eternity. The things we spoke about that night, the decisions we made, they've been dictating my every move since and I wonder if it's been the same for you as well; if, like me, you keep finding your thoughts circling back to that last morning we spent together, our thoughts, and our bodies wrapped around each other.

The door opens and a rush of cold air sweeps through. I consider ringing you again but decide against it. I know how difficult things have been for you these past few weeks. You would be here if you could. I wonder if Dave's still at home; perhaps that's why you're late. I remember how relieved I was when you told me he was at work when the police came.

I notice a newspaper on the table next to mine and lean over to pick it up. The police arrested two twenty-three-year-old men for questioning last night. Their names haven't been released but when have details like that stopped the papers? The front page is devoted entirely to Emily: pictures of her drinking, dancing, smoking; each picture is just a little more lascivious than the last, with more cleavage and a different guy, all splayed out under the headline, 'Who were the men in Emily's life?'

I wonder if it is down to Alistair. I fold the paper and put it back, just in time to see Alistair walk in. He's early and you're late.

'Is Ms Brown on her way yet?' he says when the necessary pleasantries have been exchanged.

'Yes, she should be here any minute.'

'Excellent.' He makes a show of checking his watch. 'It's not ideal that she's spoken with the police already but I'd still like to prepare her, and you, for any future interviews. Not the best alibi, but having your stories nailed should help.'

'Sure, sounds good.'

'Have you managed to speak with your wife yet?'

'Yes, but it didn't go too well. I have written to her again but . . .' I trail off.

'Perhaps it's time to take a different route. I can send someone in.'

'She may not respond well to a stranger.'

'I don't know that we have much of an option, Roy. Tell you what, we'll give it another day or two, see if she comes around. If not, I'll reach out to her. The attention seems to have shifted from you right now, but I want you back in your house within the week,' he says.

We sit there chatting about Christmas presents and ski trips, Alistair checking his watch every five minutes, until the coffee and cake orders on neighbouring tables graduate to pastas and salads. I try to ring you a couple of times but it goes to voicemail every time. I give up eventually.

'I don't know where she is. Celia and I spoke this morning and she told me she was coming. It must be something unavoidable or she'd be here by now.'

'Don't worry, these things happen. Not ideal, but hey, what can you do? Let's set up another date and we can try this again. And let's meet at my office next time,' he says, smiling as he gets up and shrugs on his coat.

I order another coffee and I watch from the window as Alistair leaves, catching a last glimpse of his salt and pepper hair, before he disappears seamlessly into the crowd.

I make my coffee last another hour. I look up every time the door opens. But I already know you won't be coming.

MIA

Tuesday, 15ᵗʰ December

When we first got together, Roy and I would spend hours coming up with hypothetical scenarios: should one of us die, of a rare cure-yet-to-be-discovered chronic illness, which one of us would suffer more, the one who died or the one left behind? If one of us were forced to commit a crime, how far would the innocent partner go to protect the guilty one? In a natural disaster, should we have to choose between saving a parent's life and saving our partner, whom would we pick? The scenarios were endless, each more heinous than the other, designed to establish one simple truth: we weren't merely in love; we *were* love.

I run through my last conversation with Roy. I almost convince myself that that is what this is, just another scenario that Roy is playing out with the sole purpose of testing my love for him, and for a moment I am relieved. I am waiting for Roy to pop in and yell, 'Gotcha!' I can taste his wet kiss on my lips. I can sense the warm crush of his arms closing around me. I can feel the tickle of his words in my ear as he whispers and insists that no, he won, he loves me more. I feel a smile begin to form and then the new truth hits me, triumphant in its cruelty.

My heart plummets.

I kicked him out.

I gave up on us.

If this is a test, I have no doubt failed.

Sleep comes to me easily. A deep, marijuana-induced slumber that plunges me into blank space. No dreams, no thoughts, no panic. My phone is ringing. I feel for it in my bed but it goes to voicemail by the time I find it. I click on the notification and press the phone to my ear.

Addi's voice pushes through. Her voice wobbles, rattling me.

After Daddy, Mum was either working or ill and, over time, the relatives and friends that had once crowded our lives in India started to fade away. They were always perfectly lovely, but from a distance, the tragedy of a broken family as infectious as a bad bout of chicken pox. Most days, Addi and I were left to ourselves and, over the years, her stability became my foundation. We'd come home from school, Addi would put together some sandwiches for lunch, and then she would help me plait my hair so I could go for my dance class or go and play with my friends, depending on the timetable pinned above my desk. When I got back, there would usually be a glass of cold coffee or mango shake waiting for me to gulp down. She would then prepare a snack, a bowl of Maggi or some *bhel*, and we'd both snuggle up on the sofa, watching reruns of *Bewitched* until Mum got home. We had picked our roles easily. Addi, a full seven years older, got to play the parent. I had to be the little girl for her to look after. I wonder how long I told myself this; how long I hid behind my cowardice masked as role play.

I watch as the thought turns on itself and I find myself wondering how long Addi used role play to hide the truth about my mother.

I thought Addi had been the one pulling me into the light, when in reality she was simply shielding the darkness. I play the voicemail again.

'Mia, it's me. Listen, I know things have been hard for you so I didn't want to say anything but this is getting too much now. Mum's really upset. You need to return her calls. She . . . she needs you, Mia. We both do. Call me back, please.'

I knew this was coming. I haven't spoken to Mum in months now. Of course she would ask Addi to step in.

Addi answers on the first ring. Even through the mist that clouds my brain, I can hear the worry in her voice. I wonder if she can hear the anger in mine.

'I got your message.'

'Yes, Mia, I was thinking, maybe over Christmas, you and Roy can come to India—'

'No.'

'Sorry?'

'I'm not coming.'

'Mia, Mum needs us. She's—'

'Sick? Roy told me. She's always sick.'

'Mia—'

'You've been lying to me, both of you. For years. I remembered, Addi. All of it.'

'What are you talking about?'

'Mum and Dad! There was someone else, wasn't there? That day, before Dad left, I was hiding under the stairs and . . . I could hear them.'

Silence. I go on, desperate. I'm hoping Addi will tell me that I imagined all of it; that this was yet another one of the lies my brain invented.

'Daddy was yelling and Mum kept asking him to calm down. You knew.' I pause, trying to keep the wobble out of my voice. 'You knew and you never told me. Why?'

'Oh Mia.'

'Just tell me.'

'You're right, darling, there was. Mum didn't want us to know, especially after the accident. She wanted to—'

'I don't care what she wants! She made Daddy leave and he died. *He died*.'

'I know, darling. I'm sorry but—'

'I don't care.'

'Mia, listen to me. What happened that day . . . it was a terrible accident. And I know how much you miss Daddy. I do too, every day. But, darling, please, we won't get this time with Mum again. She needs us with her.'

'She's always ill. She'll have her medicines and she'll be fine.'

'Mia.'

The quiet in Addi's voice stills me.

'It's melanoma, darling, stage four. She's having chemo but . . .'

My head instantly goes to Grandma. She died when I was little. The cancer hit her out of nowhere and she was gone within a few months.

'How long?'

'Six months, eight if the chemo works. You need to come and see her, Mia.'

ROY

I climb out of bed and go straight to my phone – my *other* phone. I know I'm not supposed to, but my fingers fly over the familiar pattern as if by their own accord. It's nine forty-five; Dave would have left for work. I press the phone to my ear. Voicemail. I send you a text. I am about to delete it from my sent messages when I realize I don't have to do that anymore. I leave the text on my phone and jump into the shower, my mind still on you.

Our time together was so limited, I don't know what it is that I am yearning for exactly. All I know is that I want you.

I hurry out of the shower and pick up my phone, droplets of water trickling down my fingers and onto the cheap rubberized keypad. It hasn't buzzed and there's no new notification but I look in the inbox just in case. Nothing.

I get dressed and go into the living room that connects my parents' suite to mine. My mother's sitting on the sofa, reading. She puts her book down when she sees me.

'Ma, I'm going for a walk. Won't be long.'

'Wait, I'll come with you,' she says, getting up.

'No, you don't –' I begin, but she's already putting on her coat. I sigh. 'Don't forget your gloves.'

'Are you working on anything at the minute? Any assignments?' Ma asks, wrapping both hands around her coffee cup.

'A piece on Morocco for *Wanderlust*.'

'Oh, when did you go there?'

'October.'

'Any new trips coming up?'

'Everything slows down in the lead-up to Christmas. I'll look for stuff in the new year.'

'What about the videos you were doing with that man, George, was it?'

'That's on hold for now. It's . . . he's Mia's friend.'

'I see. Have you spoken to her again?'

'No.'

Businessmen and bankers in smart suits rush past us as we cross the footbridge to Canary Wharf. The wind hits me in the eyes and I turn my head downwards.

'Why don't you go and see her? You still have your keys, don't you?'

'Alistair asked me to be diplomatic.'

'She'll come around. She's just confused.'

I'm not so sure but I nod anyway.

We walk in silence for a few minutes, stopping when we

get to a bench by the riverside. We throw our empty cups in the bin next to it and sit down.

The Thames crashes into the bank in front of us, its waters dark and murky. It isn't dirty, a friend told me my first week in London. It's a tidal river, he explained, so the sediment never gets the time to settle, it keeps getting swept up to the surface.

A few seconds of silence, and then my mother speaks again. 'Is it true, what they're saying about that girl? Was she . . . disturbed?'

I nod, keeping my eyes fixed on the water.

Emily has dominated every news channel and front page for the last week, every aspect of her personality pored over and dissected into nuggets of scandalous information for people to chew on, savour and spit out once they're done judging her. Despite everything, I find myself feeling sorry for her. After the slut-shaming last week, it's now time to attack her mental health. Two of her friends, her *best* friends, have spoken about Emily's struggle with manic depression: detailed accounts of mood swings, of entire weeks that she would refuse to come out of her room, the obsessive chatter about death and suicide. I consider it, and then shake the image away. Emily wasn't suicidal.

'Did you know?' Ma asks.

'I knew she was depressed. I didn't know about the pills or the self-harm.'

'It seems she spent a few months at an institute.'

'Yes.'

The two men arrested earlier this week have now been

released, with no charges. Sky News ran a one-hour special on mental health services in the UK last night. The host explicitly stated that the feature would not focus on any specific cases, it was about awareness, yet every expert on the panel kept alluding to Emily's case to make a point. ITV and BBC are following suit, with prime-time shows being advertised for the weekend. Even as the networks use Emily to win the ratings war, I can see the narrative turn on itself. Perceptions are shifting. Sky's expert psychologist deemed self-harm the first step towards suicide; he called it a way to test the waters before plunging in, an almost literal analogy for what the media has decided happened to Emily.

Clifftop suicide.

The easiest way to go.

A tragic end to a lifelong struggle.

Does saying anything with enough conviction make it true, my love?

MIA

Tuesday, 15th December

I sleep. My phone rings. Someone knocks on the door, lightly at first, more persistently after a few minutes – probably just Jehovah's Witnesses – and then the knocking stops, the footsteps recede. Noises float up from the street, muffled through the double-glazed window. Mothers on the school run. Delivery men chatting in the street. I push them all away and I sleep. Fitfully, dreamlessly, lustily. As long as I am sleeping nothing else can go wrong. When sleep refuses to come, I still myself. I breathe deeply. I count. I silence my mind. When none of that works, I pretend.

Fake it till you make it.

I try.

I try.

Who comes up with this shit? I don't make it. I toss and I turn. The Fray's lyrics spring to mind: *between the lines of fear and blame.* My phone rings and rings. I wonder how the battery lasts so long. I stare at shadows on the ceiling and watch the hours pass by. I can't remember when I last ate. The bottle of water by my bed, *our bed*, is empty. I want nothing.

I am nothing.

I hear the jingle of an ice cream truck outside. In December? Strange. Something tugs at my brain. A memory. A summer afternoon. I'm perhaps five or six. Mummy's yelling. I run upstairs and climb into my bed and under the duvet. It isn't long before the tears come, all hot and angry. I start wailing. I know that if I cry loudly enough someone will come for me. I feel a weight settle on my bed and my sobs get louder. I try to figure out who it is.

'Oh dear, what a large mountain. Or is it a cave? I think I might climb it.'

Daddy.

'But wait. I think I can hear something. Could it be that someone's trapped inside?'

He's trying to play our game. But I don't want to.

'Hello?'

I keep crying.

'It looks like there's no one here. Oh well, maybe I'll climb the mountain later.'

He moves as if to get up.

'Help.'

'What was that? Did I hear something?'

'Help,' I say, more loudly.

'Oh dear. There is someone trapped here indeed. I think it's a little cat.'

Despite myself I giggle. He's so silly. I'm not a cat!

'Wait there, little kitty. I'll rescue you in a jiffy-tiffy.' He starts poking and prodding through my duvet-cave, making drilling noises. 'Almost there, little kitty. Just you wait.'

One big, loud drill and he slowly peels the duvet away from me.

'Oh my God! It's not a cat, it's a beautiful princess!'

He cups my face with both hands and bends down so our foreheads are nearly touching. 'Will you marry me, princess?'

'No,' I say. I giggle.

He sits up and puts a hand on his heart. 'Oh, but why not, dear princess?'

I sit up too. 'Because you're my daddy. And you're married to my mummy.'

He gasps. 'Oh lord. What a clever little princess you are.' He scoops me up and plonks me on his knee in one easy motion.

'Daddy.' I wrap my arms around his neck and plant a kiss on his cheek.

He looks at me for a minute then pushes my hair back from my face. 'You mustn't get so angry, sweetheart. Even Mummy and Daddy make mistakes sometimes. So you must learn to forgive. If you stay angry, how . . . will . . . we . . . have . . .' – he pauses – '. . . so . . . much . . . fun,' he adds, tickling me until both of us collapse on the bed in a fit of laughter. When my breathing goes back to normal, I close my eyes and snuggle up to him, reaching my arm as far around him as it will go.

We stay like that for a few minutes, then he whispers, his voice at once hoarse and honeyed, 'Now, did I hear my princess say she wanted some ice cream?'

I feel a smile creep up my face. I open my eyes, expecting to find Daddy lying next to me, my Barbie duvet crumpled beneath him, the air thick with the sound of him breathing through his permanently blocked nose.

But the duvet on this bed is white and the only sound is the incessant ringing of my phone. I pull a pillow over my head and shut my eyes.

I want to go back.

I drift in and out of sleep and when I come to again, the shadows on the ceiling tell me it is still afternoon.

Almost imperceptibly, my head begins to clear, the swirling stops and objects from my life start shifting back into focus.

The bag of weed on the dresser lures me but I am too lazy to get up. The light is still gauzy and it lets me believe that I can stay like this, safe, at least a little while longer.

How wrong I am.

My thoughts flit between my mother and Roy. I can't believe how screwed up everything is. I replay my last conversation with Mum at the wedding, and all her texts and voicemails since then. It hits me all at once. The desperation, the fragility, the insistence that I try to understand. She's dying.

She's dying.

I sit up with a jolt. My mother is dying.

This time next year, I won't have anyone pestering me to fly home for every long weekend. No one will be planning the menu for every meal I'll eat at home weeks in advance or ringing me to check if my flight's landed halfway across the world when I fly back. No one will cup my face and peer at the dark circles under my eyes, worrying about how hard I work and how little I sleep. Or offer to slather my hair with coconut oil because the ends look dry. But most of all, I realize, there will be no one for me to be angry with.

The realization shakes me.

Because if I can't be angry with my mother, where does that leave me?

Tears prick my eyes and I blink them away. Daddy told me, all those years ago, that I had to let go of my anger and forgive if I wanted a shot at being happy. I wonder if I've somehow got to twenty-nine without learning how to do either.

Unless, of course, it came to Roy. With Roy, everything was forgiven, instantly and without apology. I cringe as I think about his emails and the doubts that cloud my brain every time he reaches out. My own double standards humiliate me. Am I really so petty that I can't forgive my mother an affair she had more than two decades ago? Am I so stubborn in my belief that she caused Daddy's accident that I can't see that he was prone to senseless rages himself? That he always was a reckless driver? I question myself incessantly, mercilessly, till there is nowhere left for me to hide.

I run through my scrapbook of memories. I force myself to examine everything, holding each memory, feeling its weight, turning it around, smoothing out its edges until I can see the past for what it truly was: a happy childhood, a troubled marriage and an unfortunate accident. And then I realize something else.

I may have only just pieced it together about the affair but I have been angry with my mother for years. After Daddy died, I pushed her away, bit by bit, until our relationship was little more than a shell of what it used to be. Every happy memory with my mother was tainted with guilt over my father. She was always there for me; she was the one plaiting my hair, whipping up snacks, curling up on the sofa with Addi and me. But for every time I forgot to miss Daddy, I purposely erased her from my memories, to even out the scales.

I punished her for living. For breathing when he had ceased to.

In wanting my father back, I kept pushing my mother away and now that she is dying, I want her back. Her single mistake from years ago doesn't matter anymore. She's spent her entire life alone; she's punished herself enough. It's time I stopped punishing her too.

I get out of bed and go to my dresser. Roy was right. I have been playing the victim.

I take the metal case into the bathroom.

One last joint. You need the relief.

This isn't just about me anymore. I flush the pills down the toilet.

Stop!

I strip off my shorts and T-shirt and step into the shower, taking the little zip-lock bag with me. I flip the bag upside down and shake it out quickly before I can change my mind. I know that I have a window of less than a minute before the urge overtakes me.

I turn on the shower and watch the dark green residue swish and swirl, till it's all swept away.

Idiot.

Then I step into the stream of hot water.

Intense.

Scalding.

Cleansing.

ROY

Tuesday, 15ᵗʰ December

We pass by a couple walking their dogs on our way back. Ma smiles at them and they stop to let her pet the beasts. I step away.

'You don't like dogs?' the man asks me. He's in a neon and black North Face jacket and compression leggings. Hideous.

'I had a bad experience growing up.'

Ma straightens up and lets them pass. 'Maybe it's time to give them another chance. You know what they say, man's best friend.'

She wraps her gloved fingers around my hand and gives it a squeeze. 'You could use a friend, *beta*.'

We walk on to the hotel in silence.

When I was eleven, I did have a friend. A best friend. Sahil Bansal. We were on the same bus route and in the same year in school. We sat next to each other in class, played on the same junior football team, shared our tiffins during lunch break and played pranks on our juniors on the bus ride home. We'd walk together till the end of the road, where Sahil would turn right, to go into his block of DDA flats, and I would go left into the gated private colony in which my father owned a bungalow.

Ma worked full time throughout my childhood so lunch would always be prepared by the help, a never-ending line-up of middle-aged, stocky women with lilting Bengali accents. There were so many of them, their names started to blur.

After lunch, which was usually fish and rice, I would pick up my backpack and walk over to Sahil's. We would finish our homework together – Mrs Bansal was strict about that – and then go to the council park for a few hours. We'd usually take Sahil's football or our bikes or, sometimes, if Mrs Bansal asked us to, we would take the Lab, Max, for a walk.

I never liked Max, but Sahil did so I didn't have an option but to get used to him.

On the Friday before the summer holidays, Sahil didn't come to school. I knew he wasn't going on holiday that year so I figured he was sick. I finished lunch and ran to Sahil's place, panting when I got to the top of the building. We were going to my grandparents' house in Ooty the next day and I wanted to see Sahil before I left. I pressed the doorbell and leaned my head on the cool wooden door.

I waited. I pressed the buzzer again, keeping my finger on it for a full minute.

Max started barking at me from his wire kennel on the

landing outside. Mrs Bansal didn't like him being in the flat unsupervised, said he made too much of a mess.

I leaned over his kennel and peered into the flat from the kitchen window. It didn't look like anyone was in.

Max kept barking. I didn't like him but even I could see he was unhappy about being left alone.

I decided to take him for a walk.

Wherever the Bansals were, they would be back in a few hours and Mrs Bansal would be very happy with me for taking care of Max.

I unlocked the kennel door and he stared at me.

'Come on, Max, let's go for a walk,' I said and started walking down the stairs, expecting him to follow, but he didn't move an inch. The stupid dog wanted to stay in that horrible wire cage. I bent down and lifted him out of it. I set him down at the top of the stairs and whistled to him to follow. But once again he refused to move.

It was roasting on the top floor. My T-shirt was stuck to my back. I hated that building. The stairs were narrow and they always stank of piss. The wooden banister was cracked and rotting. Mrs Bansal told us never to touch it because it had leeches and splinters.

I turned to the dog and clapped. I whistled. I clicked but he refused to move. I considered carrying him all the way down but even though he was only little, he was too heavy for three flights of stairs.

I grabbed his collar – the Bansals never used a lead – and pulled him down behind me. He yelped but I carried on till I got to the second floor. I let go of his collar when we got to the landing and then tried the whole thing again. Whistle, clap, click. The fucker wouldn't move.

I stepped back and kicked him in his stomach, hard. He rolled down two steps, yelping. Again. Another few steps. And again and again. He kept yelping through it all. At some point I felt my right foot get wet as a sticky warmth seeped through my no longer white canvas shoe.

Max's yelps got louder and louder as I kicked him all the way to the bottom of the staircase, away from that filthy building. I kept kicking until all at once the yelping stopped.

Mr and Mrs Bansal came to our house that evening. They spoke in low tones and then my father took them into his study.

We left for the holidays the next day and when we came back, my father told me we were moving to a new house and that meant a new school for me. He wanted me to be excited but I wasn't.

I snuck out after my parents went to bed and ran to Sahil's place to tell him but his mother said he wasn't at home, which was strange because it was nearly midnight.

I noticed as I was leaving the Bansals' that the kennel was gone.

We moved to the new house the next day and I never saw my best friend again.

On Tuesday, 15 December, at 11.04 p.m.,
Roy Kapoor <roy_kapoor@me.com> wrote:

Mia,

I can understand that you're angry. I get it and I've been trying to give you some time to process everything. But it's been over a week now. I can't keep living like this. It's starting to affect my work and I don't know if that is something I'll be able to forgive. I NEED to come home. You don't have to speak to me – I'll tiptoe around you. But don't force me to do something I don't want to. Can't you see the only way we can make it out of this is together?

Remember the lavender fields? I'm still the same man, Mia.

I love you and I'm so sorry for what I've done to you. Let me in, please, so we can go back to our life.

Roy

MIA

Ma is here. In my living room. Sipping on *chai* and talking about her blood pressure as if this were any other day. I carry a bowl of *namkeen* and some biscuits back to the living room and sit down across from her.

I watch her assess the room and me. She puts her cup down on the coffee table and looks me straight in the eye.

'This has gone on long enough, Mia. I can see how upset you are. Siddhant's been miserable for days. I can understand what both of you are going through, *beta*, but it is high time we made some decisions.'

She gets up and crosses the two paces between us. Her *sari* rustles as she sits down next to me. Her bangles jingle as she places her hand on mine. It's sweaty. I don't think I've ever felt this uncomfortable before. My eyes flick to my watch; she's only been here fifteen minutes or so.

'Now, you've both made some mistakes. I just wish you had listened to me. It really is so important to have a baby within two years of marriage; couples need that to hold them together. And then living abroad, with these *goras* . . .' She trails off, shaking her head.

Oh.

Leave it to Roy's mother to find a way to blame me for everything. If only I'd done my duty and fallen pregnant, everything would be okay. Roy may still have strayed, but hey, at least I wouldn't have had the luxury of being angry about it. She pauses to take her hand off mine and I use all my energy to make sure I don't sigh with relief. But it gets worse. She turns to face me and places her palm on my head. She strokes my hair and continues. 'But ultimately, *beta*, you have to remember, *aap Indian ho*. Marriage means everything to us, not like these *goras* who can just throw one marriage away and move to the next one. *Aur beta*, you're almost thirty now. You know how difficult it is for a woman to remarry, you come from a broken home yourself. Just look at the life your mother's had to lead. Is that what you want for yourself?'

She pulls away and regards me for a second, as if to let the seriousness of my bleak future sink in. 'Beta, I don't think you realize how lucky you are. We are not like other Indian families. Siddhant is our only son, but did we ask for a dowry? No. You live away from us, you wear these western clothes, you work all the time, you travel so much that Siddhant even needs to cook and do the housework sometimes. Did we object? No. Siddhant's father and I always say, as long as the children are happy, we are happy. We have given you all the freedom. But this, *beta*? No, I cannot allow this. In our *samaaj*, marriage is a union for seven lives.

All these little things, they mean nothing in front of a marriage, Mia.'

She looks to me for agreement but I don't say anything. There's a pit at the bottom of my stomach and I can feel the tears coming. So much of what she's saying infuriates me, but there is so much that she's right about. Roy and I, we were meant to be for ever. We were supposed to make it through thick and thin. But adultery and violence – wasn't that where I was allowed to draw the line?

'Siddhant's father and I spoke about this already. It's perfectly okay for you to want some space; you've both been through a lot. But it's high time now. You must call Siddhant. The poor boy, he's under so much pressure already, but he is so attached to you, Mia, so loving, I know he will agree to come home.'

She picks up my phone from the coffee table and holds it in front of me. '*Chalo, phone karo.*'

She looks perplexed when I don't reach for it. A flash of realization. Perhaps she gets it finally.

'I see, I see. Don't worry, *beta*, I'll speak to him first. It may take some time but he will forgive you.'

He will forgive me? I thought Roy sent her to apologize on his behalf. But I can see now that his emails, progressively more desperate by the day, were just more examples of the tricks he'd used for years to control me. I feel the flicker of hope I had been protecting dissipate. I can't fix this, not when Roy can't see what he's done is wrong; that what he's been doing for years is wrong.

'Ma, I want to show you something,' I say. I get up and

walk to the kitchen. Roy's mother follows me and pulls up a chair at the kitchen table. I give it a few seconds. 'This is where I was sitting when I found out that your son was cheating on me.'

She sighs and nods.

I step back. I roll my sleeves all the way up to my shoulders. 'These are the bruises I have from when he grabbed me,' I say and she winces.

I walk over to the far end of the room and point to a spot on the wall. 'These marks you see here, these are from when he smashed his phone.'

I turn around, my back to her and pull the neck of my T-shirt to one side. It still feels sore. 'This bruise on my shoulder, it's from when he threw me against the wall. I have another one like that on my leg.'

I go back to face her. She's standing up now, her mouth set in a grim line. I can tell she's getting ready to launch into another one of her speeches. *You must have provoked him. He doesn't lose his temper often. He's been under a lot of pressure lately. It takes two to start a fight, don't blame him. Everyone gets angry sometimes.* The voices in my head sound a lot like Roy's mother. They sound a lot like Roy. I shake them away.

'He doesn't need to forgive me, Ma. I need to forgive him. And I don't think I can do that.' I pause, the words triggering a revelation. 'I don't think I should.'

I make a fresh cup of tea and sit at the kitchen table. I look up the number for the sexual health clinic and ring them for an appointment for a complete STI screening, and a urine and blood test. When the woman on the phone asks me if I'd like to pay for a private check-up or wait for an NHS appointment, I tell her I'll pay, it's urgent. I can't bring myself to tell her why.

I stay in the kitchen for two hours, drinking tea and reading through Roy's emails.

At half three my phone rings; it's Roy. I let it go to voice-mail and play it back as soon as he hangs up. He wants to know if I got his emails and texts. He wants to know if he can come home. If we can try to talk again. If I have for-given him. Funny thing is, he still hasn't apologized, not properly anyway. *I'm sorry for the way things have unfolded.* I can see how it's partly my fault that he thinks he can get away with it. And I'm scared that is exactly what will happen if I speak to him again. He'll cry, I'll crumble, and he will move back in. I tell myself it's okay to focus on myself for once.

I place my phone on the kitchen table and switch on my laptop. I'm looking at flights to India when it rings again. Private number. I sigh and pick it up. It's the estate agent in Bristol. As much as I still hate the idea, I hear him out, then ring James. After a few minutes of awkward conversation, I get to the point.

'Listen, James, the agent just rang. He's missing the free-hold certificate. Have you still got it kicking about somewhere?'

'I'm pretty sure Addi passed everything on, but hang on a second while I check.' I hear the sound of drawers opening and papers rustling. 'So I've been seeing all the news about that girl who's missing. She used to work with Roy, did she not? Were they close?'

'Just business acquaintances,' I say. I still haven't told Addi about any of this. She has enough to deal with right now.

'Still. Nasty business. I hope you guys are holding up okay?'

'Yes, it's all incredibly sad. We just hope they find her soon,' I say. It feels odd to refer to Roy and me as 'we'. Strange how quickly that happened.

'Well, it's not looking good now, is it? Terrible tragedy.' He pauses. 'Anyway, I've looked through the papers. Addi made copies of everything your mum gave us and I can't see a freehold certificate in there.' He hesitates. 'I can check if she's still got it?' he adds. I don't need to check the calendar. Mum's in chemo this week.

'Oh, don't worry about it, I'll sort it out. As a matter of fact, I've just thought of one more place I could check.'

'All right then. Tell the hubby I said hello and let's all catch up soon.'

'Absolutely,' I lie and hang up. I love James but I'm not ready to see him yet.

I set the box down on the kitchen table in front of me. I lost a few hours when I first went through it, trying to construct a memory to go with each newly discovered relic of a forgotten life. Focused entirely on the pictures and the cards, I didn't pay attention to the official-looking

documents in it. I open the box and start working through
the contents, stacking them all up on the table as I go.

A picture stuck to the back of a card catches my eye, the
Kodak stamp on the back faded and yellowed. I peel it back
and the edges curl inwards, as if to protect the picture. I
flatten it out and peer at the faded scene. I feel myself
deflate. It's just a picture of a beach. Anonymous. No
Daddy, no me. I tuck it into the album with the other
photos and put it to one side. I carry on emptying the box,
running through the medical records, bank statements, day
planners and letters. There are a couple of A4 envelopes at
the bottom. I pull them out and go through each one systematically. I hit gold with the third one: freehold certificate
and a copy of the house deed. I email the agent to let him
know I've found them and absent-mindedly rip through the
remaining two envelopes. The first one is Daddy's medical
degree from Cambridge accompanied by a single faded
photo of him and Mum with Uncle Bill and Aunty Jane.
Daddy is in the centre, squinting into the camera, one arm
thrown around Mum, her face eclipsed by a shadow, both
of them grinning in their graduation gowns. Aunty Jane is
at the edge of the frame and Uncle Bill, still a teenager, is
standing next to Daddy, looking frazzled, the camera clicking a second before he was ready. Daddy looks smug, as if
he's just got away with the ultimate prank. I try to picture
him goofing around, messing with a teacher, wooing
Mum, but I come up with a blank. My only claim to my
father is via a handful of memories and the bank of second-
hand knowledge I have of him.

I'm surprised to see that Aunt Laurel isn't in the picture. As one of my parents' best friends at Cambridge, she was there in almost all the other pictures I found earlier. I figure she must have been the one behind the camera and put the picture away.

Fragments of a memory flash past. Running through a house opening every door. Laughter. A garden. Butterflies. I try to piece it all together but it hovers, just out of reach. I shake the images away and open the last envelope. The legal writing is instantly familiar and I'm about to place the document with the freehold certificate I found earlier, ready to send to the estate agent, when I notice the address on it.

My father owned a house in Eastbourne?

ROY

Thursday, 17th December

I type up a quick cover note and press send on the *Wanderlust* piece. Not my best work, but it'll have to do for now, considering I can barely keep my thoughts straight. I pick up my phone and call you but once again it goes to voicemail. I send you yet another text. Where are you, my love? I haven't heard from you in days and I'm starting to get worried.

I lean back in the chair and hit refresh on the browser. No new email, either.

I get up and wander into the living room for want of something to do. The TV's on, and Emily's face fills the room. I can't seem to escape her. I turn it off.

My parents' bedroom door is ajar and I hear voices wafting out. They're talking about me, no doubt discussing how catastrophically I've disappointed them. I take a step closer and strain to make out the words.

'He wasn't a child then and he certainly isn't one now.'

'What do you mean?'

'He hit her. Do you understand what that means? He needs to take responsibility.'

'So what do you want to do? Leave him to rot in—'

'That's not what I'm saying. But perhaps if we had done something—'

'We did what was best.'

'A girl died!'

It hits me then. Her face flashes before me, the empty eyes, the blue lips, the blood trickling down her nose.

I move away from the door just as my father catches my eye.

'So now you eavesdrop too? Is it not enough to be a cheat, a wife-beater and a murderer?' he shouts, slamming the door shut.

I stumble out of the hotel and walk to the station. I've spent so long running and now that my past is catching up with me, I have nowhere left to go. I am back where it all began, haunted by a ghost.

I step off the tube when I reach Embankment. I get out of the station and go to the adjoining garden. It's still light, but the park is quiet. I buy a coffee from the kiosk and sit at a table overlooking the river. My thoughts, as always, find their way back to you; to the last time I was here with you.

You were sitting at the very table that I am at now. You stopped writing and looked at me as I sat down.

I set my coffee down and ran my fingers over your note-book – it was the same one you had accused me of stealing

– and at least for the moment, it was the closest thing to touching you. My fingers settled on the inscription. *LIKE THE SEA.*

'Did you have this inscribed?'

You nodded. You had that slight frown on your face that I had come to understand meant you were focusing on the present, making sure the past didn't pull you adrift.

'What does it mean?' I asked, my fingers trailing over the tiny gold letters.

You didn't say anything and I wondered if you'd heard me. I was about to repeat myself when you spoke, so softly I had to strain to hear you.

'It's my life. I've had such little control over everything, it often feels like I'm being swept up in the sea, as if the waves are carrying me towards the end.'

You looked down then, and reached over to touch the letters yourself. Our fingers grazed. The current that ran through me could have lit up the entire city.

'I don't know if I can make it out, if I ever will,' you whispered.

'You will.'

When you looked up again, your eyes were wet. You pushed your hair back and I noticed the fresh bruise snaking around your neck, the make-up only concealing it so much.

I knew how cautious you were, but in that moment, I didn't care. I placed my hand over yours. I squeezed.

'And if you don't, I'm okay with drowning,' I said.

You let my hand linger on yours for a moment and then you pulled away.

'I could never let you drown.'

I get up when it starts drizzling. I walk back to the station and get on the tube to Canary Wharf. The rain is in full form by the time I come out and I run the short distance to the hotel. The concierge stares at me as I shake the water off. I walk straight past him into the hotel bar. There's a fully stocked sideboard in my room but I'm in no mood to see my father and the thought of a semi-dark room full of strangers feels oddly comforting.

I sit at the bar and order a glass of Macallan 25. Double. At only £42 a pop, it seems reasonable to let my father foot the bill. He is constantly telling me how entitled I am; may as well prove him right while I have the chance. Mia once told me that she thought being around my parents turned me into a teenager, and it occurs to me now that she may have been right.

I turn my gaze to the TV screen angled in the far corner of the bar and lose myself in the mind-numbing banality of watching a football match on mute.

I'm on my third glass by the time the match ends and the barman starts flicking through the channels, running through old movies, more football and overtly cheerful commercials. It takes me a few seconds to register what I'm looking at when he finally settles on a scene at a beach.

There's tape everywhere and officers in high-visibility jackets are huddled around something in the background.

I don't need to read the text running across the bottom of the screen to know I'm looking at the beach in Littlehampton.

A reporter is squinting into the camera, the wind whipping her hair into her eyes. She's gesturing towards the drama unfolding behind her, one hand shielding her headset as she speaks into it.

'Turn it up,' I say to the barman.

'I'm sorry, sir, we aren't allowed—'

'Turn it up,' I yell. A few people turn to look at me. The barman does my bidding, then slithers off to the other end of the bar.

'That's correct, Martyn,' the reporter is saying. 'The police have now confirmed that the body of a young woman was found washed up on West Beach in Littlehampton early this morning. Littlehampton is, of course, just thirty miles from Seaford, where twenty-one-year-old Emily Barnett was last seen. I am being told that a formal identification is yet to take place, but the police are currently working on the belief that the body they've recovered is indeed that of Miss Barnett. We are yet to receive any confirmation on cause of death, but early investigations suggest Miss Barnett may—'

The screen goes black, cutting her off mid-sentence, and before I know it I have a security officer speaking into my ear, telling me I need to leave, one hand crushing my elbow, the other pressed firmly into my back, forcing me out of the bar stool. I try to push back, but he's too strong and I'm too drunk.

'What is the matter with you?' I slur. 'I'm trying to watch the news. This is important. Let go of me. Let go of me! I have the right to be here,' I scream, as he drags me out and deposits me in the lift.

'Go to your room, Mr Kapoor,' he says, pressing the button for floor twelve and handing me my room key.

I fall back against the brightly lit walls as the doors slide shut, my head spinning.

Even though I didn't hear the reporter finish her statement, I know what happened. Emily is dead.

She drowned.

MIA

Thursday, 17ᵗʰ December

Addi answers the third time I call, full of apologies. She spent the day in hospital with Mum.

'How is she feeling?' I ask.

'Weak. Nauseous. She's sleeping now. This round has been harder on her than the first one. She could barely walk out of the hospital after the chemo.'

I can feel a lump in my throat. I swallow it down. I can't stand to think about it too specifically, to picture Mum hooked up to machines, the medicines snaking up her arm, making her sick before they can make her better.

'Do they know if it's helping yet?' I ask. Something, anything to make the pain worthwhile.

'They hope so. She's got another round of tests to go through next week. Tomorrow . . .' Addi's voice catches. She takes a moment then carries on. 'Tomorrow I'm taking Mum to see a wig guy in Gurgaon. He's supposed to be the best, most lifelike.'

The phone line crackles while I take this in. This silence

is one too difficult to fill. I picture Mum with her waist-length hair. Hot oil every Friday night, followed by lime juice on Saturday morning and then herbal *shikakai* shampoo. Addi and I had scoffed at her when we were kids, turning up our noses at the stinky green paste, refusing to use anything but Pantene or L'Oréal. Whatever was being endorsed by the hottest new supermodel – because we were worth it, we'd claim, ponytails swinging. But Mum's hair had always looked glossier than ours and we'd both switched to her routine by the time we were in our twenties. I touch my hair, and feel tears spring to my eyes. It's silly. It's just cosmetic. The important thing is that she gets better.

'It's just hair. It'll grow back,' I say. My words sound hollow, even to myself.

'Oh yes, yes it will,' Addi replies, a beat too soon.

'Anyway –'

'Anyway –' We both speak at the same time. I have a vision of playing jinx when we were growing up. Poking and prodding Addi, tugging at her skirt, even pulling her hair to get her to say my name but to no avail. Addi was much better at it; she would just sit and wait till I slipped up. She always had a knack for keeping things quiet. I suppose it's my turn now.

'Applied for holidays yet? Do you think you and Roy will be here for Christmas?' Addi is saying.

'Yes, all signed off. We'll book our flights this week.'

'Okay, good. Check in with James every once in a while,

will you? He worries about you.' She hesitates. 'Are you okay, Mia? If any of this starts to feel overwhelming . . .'

'I'm fine, Addi. Stop worrying.'

'I miss you,' she says, a thousand emotions tied up in that simple statement.

Guilt fingers me. Addi sounds tired and lonely. She's the only one who might be able to explain the deed I found yesterday but I can't bring myself to ask her. I've been selfish enough already.

Come on, don't you want answers?

Not now. Not like this.

'I miss you, too. And Mum. Call me when she's strong enough to talk, will you?'

I chase sleep for a few hours. My thoughts circle back to Roy. I remember being scared. Thinking no one was allowed to be this happy. That something must be wrong. Then cursing myself for thinking it. Forcing myself to be happy. Feel happy. Act happy. Was I role-playing again? I've spent the past few weeks hoping and wishing I could go back in time, fix everything that went wrong, but now I find myself wishing it had never happened. The first date. The wedding. The marriage. Everything. I just want to hit undo. I want to unmeet, unkiss, unlove.

Undo.

It's pitch black. I twist and thrash, swallowing gulps of liquid darkness every time I resurface. It tastes salty. I adjust my eyes to the darkness. They sting. I look around; I'm in an ocean. The icy waves crash into me from all directions. The rocks move closer, sharp edges turned towards me. I try to swim but I can't. I'm clutching something; it's small, defenseless. I must protect it. I hold on tighter. I still can't find Roy but this time I know he isn't coming. There is no escape.

ROY

It's barely morning, but when the knock comes, we are all expecting it. My father gets up to open the door and steps to one side to let the officers in. The arrest itself is swift, lacking in the commotion that I've come to expect from watching too many detective dramas. My father rings Alistair, and then stands in the corner, refusing to react. My mother sits on the sofa, hands folded neatly in her lap, a lone tear working its way down her cheek.

The drive to the station goes by in a blur. It may have taken twenty minutes or three hours, I can't be sure. Robins opens the door for me when we arrive and I step out into the near darkness. It is raining and as the icy water drips down my face, I feel a familiar sense of dread envelop me. Her face flashes in front of me. The sound of her screams sickens me. I don't know if I can escape this any-more. My brain runs through the possibilities, but there is only one that seems plausible: prison. It feels ironic and fitting at the same time. I have spent my whole life seeking freedom, my travels and my career just a statement to that effect, yet here I am, handcuffed and under arrest. Do I deserve it, my love? Is it karma? I don't know. What I do know is that I cannot bear to be without you and that I must hold my ground, if for no other reason than to see you again.

As soon as we are inside, I am handed over to the custody sergeant. Over the next fifteen minutes, I am stripped of all my belongings, and with every article that's labelled and bagged, I feel the elaborate persona I have spent years constructing being chipped away, until all that is left is the crude teenager that has been lurking beneath the polished exterior.

I am photographed. I am fingerprinted. I am swabbed for DNA samples. Then I am taken into an interview room and told my solicitor will be with me shortly. This room is different to the one I was interviewed in the last time, I notice. It's bigger yet somehow feels more stifling. I shift in my chair. I wait. My brain whisks me back to that night. I think about the way she fought, all arms and legs, and then afterwards, her body just a mangled mess. I shake the image away. *Stay calm*, I tell myself, *what's done is done. Focus on the future.*

Something my fiction writing tutor used to say springs to mind: the only way to have a reader truly buy into your story is to believe it yourself, to talk to the characters and live and breathe the plot as if everything in the story is real, even if none of it happened. I try to remember this while I wait.

Alistair comes in after a few minutes. He sits down across from me and starts briefing me on the next steps. For the most part, I nod along while he explains the process. He tells me I have the right to silence but he recommends I don't use it. We have already prepared for this interview and he feels it would be best to get my new, corrected story on tape. He tells me he's gone through disclosure with DI Robins. They must be holding back for the interview but he reckons anything else they have on me will be circumstantial or they would have charged me straightaway. He thinks they'll interview me then bail me out in a few hours.

'Okay, you ready then?'

Alistair is already at the door, waiting.

I hesitate. They've found the body, they might already know.

You've got to tell me everything, Roy, however bad it may seem. That's the only way I can help you, Alistair had said in our first meeting.

In that moment, I can't fathom why I left it so late; why I gave him a new version of the same half-baked story I gave the detectives.

Perhaps I believed they'd never find her.

Or perhaps I thought I could get away with everything.

Whatever I thought, I was wrong.

'Roy?'

I take a deep breath and look Alistair in the eye. It's time.

'Sit down, Alistair, there's something I need to tell you.'

MIA

I wake up with a start and go down to the kitchen. It's past seven o'clock but the sun isn't out yet. There's a strange milky quality to the light. I put the kettle on and notice my phone sitting on the counter. I must have forgotten it downstairs last night. I pick it up and turn it on, the white light illuminating the room. Twelve missed calls. I scroll through until I see a number I recognize and press dial.

'Switch on the news. I'm on my way,' George says, his voice far too alert for this early in the morning.

Emily's face fills my living room. They've found her. Washed up on the West Sussex coast. They're running a special, all kinds of experts debating why it took so long for the body to wash up and why it ended up all the way in Littlehampton.

Perhaps that's where she was dumped, you idiots. They repeatedly flash to an old clip of Emily's mother weeping. The presenter keeps calling it tragic. It's infuriating.

The presenter interrupts herself and cuts to a reporter

in Seaford. She's standing in front of the cliffs, where they found Emily's car a couple of days ago.

I turn up the volume.

'It has just been confirmed that a thirty-one-year-old man has been arrested on suspicion of the murder of Emily Barnett. This follows after the body that washed up in the early hours yesterday was identified as Miss Barnett. A post-mortem was conducted last night. Cause of death has not yet been released but the police have confirmed that this is now a murder investigation. Additionally, we are able to confirm that Emily was pregnant at the time of her death. It is a tragic . . .'

I collapse on the sofa. All I can hear is the blood pumping in my ears.

A baby.

The one thing he never wanted.

The one thing he would have done anything to avoid.

I can't hide from the truth anymore. I take a deep breath and let the words dance around in my brain until they align themselves in the only logical order.

My husband killed Emily.

ROY

Friday, 18th December

'Emily rang me a few times after I broke up with her. I didn't know how to respond and let it go to voicemail. I figured she would stop calling eventually and she did. I didn't hear from her again until about a month ago. She sounded panicked. She said she had to see me right away, that there was something we needed to discuss. So we agreed to meet at the pub in Archway.'

'This was on Wednesday the second?' Alistair asks.

I nod. 'When I got there, she was already waiting at the booth. She started crying when I sat down. She told me she was pregnant.'

'How many weeks?'

'She wasn't sure. She said seven, maybe eight.'

'I told her we could take care of it quietly. She wouldn't have to go to the NHS or anything if she didn't want to. I even offered to book her an appointment at a private clinic and pay for the whole thing. But she wasn't sure she could do it.'

'Have an abortion, you mean?'

'Yes. We spoke about what her life would be like if she had the baby. You have to understand, Emily, she was very ambitious. She had that job in Australia lined up. She used to speak about travelling the world. She wouldn't be able to do any of that with a child. And I . . . I told her I couldn't be involved. I told her . . . I wouldn't acknowledge her or the baby so she would be totally alone. I was just trying to convince her.'

'What happened next?'

'She realized how stupid she was being. She agreed to have an abortion, told me she would ring the clinic the next day. She asked me to accompany her but I told her I was away. We went to the cash machine and I gave her some money. I thought that was that till she called me on Friday afternoon.'

I press my fingers into my temples, that phone call still fresh in my mind.

I was on the motorway when the phone rang. I turned down the music and answered. I could hear Emily howling on the other end.

'Ems? Are you okay?'

'I can't do it,' she stuttered.

'Oh . . . why?'

'I don't know. I just . . . this is all happening too quickly . . . I need to think about it. I can't just get an abortion because you want me to.'

'We spoke about this. There's no other option. What are you going to do? Raise it on your own?'

'I don't know . . . maybe.'

'Don't you want a life? A career? I've already told you, I can't be involved in this.'

'Well, guess what, that's your baby growing in me. You don't have a choice. What kind of a man are you?' she screamed down the phone.

'Come on, Emily. Calm down.'

'You can't just leave me in the lurch like this. I'll tell everyone.'

'You're right, I'm sorry. I overreacted. I'll stand by you whatever you decide, okay?'

'It is yours, Roy,' she whispered. I could hear the tears in her voice.

'I know . . . I know. Have you been to see a doctor yet? Your GP?'

'No.'

'Have you spoken to a friend?'

'No, but why—'

'Listen, we can't do this over the phone. Let's meet and discuss this properly. Monday?'

'I'm at my parents' next week,' she said between sobs. 'We can meet tonight.'

'I'm on a press trip,' I lied.

'Cancel it.'

I hesitated. Letting Emily sit on this was risky. 'Let me call you back,' I said.

I called Emily back after a few minutes.

'Listen, can you come down to Seaford? It's only an hour from your parents' so you can go there directly tomorrow morning. Ems?'

'I don't know. Why do I have to come all the way there?' she moaned.

I sighed audibly. 'I can't cancel last minute, Emily. I'm already halfway there. Look, I don't want this hanging over your head all week. I want you to enjoy your time at home. Please just come, okay?'

I could hear her breathing but she didn't say a word.

'Emily? Please?'

'Fine.'

'Okay, good. There's a train leaving Victoria at five twenty-five. You'll need to change at Lewes. Write that down. L-E-W-E-S. You can stay at the Seaford Head Hotel.'

'Seaford Head . . . we've been there before—'

'Yes, I know. Have you got it?'

'Yes, but why—'

'I'll meet you outside the Co-op on the High Street at seven. We can talk once you get there.'

I picked her up and we drove to the beach. It was cold, so we stayed inside the car, rehashing the same conversation we'd had at the pub. I reminded her of all the reasons to abort and she found ways to shoot them down. I didn't know what to do. She could be so challenging.

'You said you would stand by me, whatever I decide.'

'It's not that simple, Emily. I have a wife.'

'Leave her.'

'No,' I scoffed. 'I'm not going to let you dictate my life. Get rid of it.'

It had started to drizzle. Emily was staring outside the window.

'Emily?'

'It's not your decision to make. This is a baby we're talking about, Roy.'

'A fetus.'

'I won't do it,' she said, turning to face me. 'You can't make me.'

'Fine. Keep it. But don't think you or your kid will ever see me again.'

'You can't just walk away unscathed,' she said, tears coursing down her cheeks.

'Watch me.'

'I'll tell . . . Mia. I'll ring her . . . right now and tell her everything,' she howled. She picked up my phone from the dashboard.

'You really think anyone will believe you?' I smirked. I snatched the phone easily out of her hands. 'Wake up, Emily. You're a slutty, irresponsible girl who chased after a married man. You practically begged me—'

'How dare you?'

'—to screw you. Who the fuck knows how many others there were? You're lucky I agreed to pay for—'

'You're evil.'

'—an abortion. I don't even know if the thing is mine. You tell anyone, you'll be ruined.'

'No wonder your parents hate you,' she spat out.

The fucking cunt. I slapped her across her face and she shut up, the silence ringing through the car.

I was about to apologize when she struck back. Before I knew it, she was clawing at me, screaming. She grabbed my neck, her nails digging into my flesh. I felt a sharp burn and realized I was bleeding, just behind my ear.

I grabbed her wrists and twisted them behind her seat, pinning her down with one knee.

'You're hurting me,' she wailed.

I held on. I pushed my knee in further. I told her I wouldn't let her go until she stopped screaming. Gradually, her screams turned to sobs and I eased off of her. I handed her the box of tissues and told her to clean herself up. Then I drove her to the hotel and watched her go inside. That was the last I saw of her.

MIA

Hot tea seeps through my T-shirt. I put the cup down, grab some kitchen roll and dab furiously at my chest while straining to hear the voice coming through my phone. Roy was arrested on suspicion of murder last night, my father-in-law is telling me. They haven't charged him, but he's being interviewed in custody. They searched the hotel and his car last night. His laptop and phone have been seized. My questions, though logical, sound overdramatic in contrast to his matter-of-fact tone. Yes, he has a lawyer with him. Yes, a good one. No, we don't know how long they'll hold him. I'm still on the phone when the doorbell rings. I tuck the phone between my shoulder and my ear, unlock the door and head back towards the kitchen for some more kitchen roll. George can let himself in.

I stop when I hear the deep voice behind me.

'Mrs Kapoor, we're here from the Metropolitan Police.'

I tell Roy's father I'll ring him back and spin around to face the officers.

There are four of them. I stare at them, speechless, scanning their faces. Neither of the two detectives I know is here. Even as the thought crosses my mind, it seems ridiculous and I want to laugh out loud. Since when do I *know* detectives? I take a deep breath and focus on what the officer in charge is saying.

He reminds me that my husband, the man I thought was the love of my life, is under arrest on suspicion of the murder of the woman I invited into our lives. Then he tells me they need to search our home for evidence and that I am required to stay in the living room, where a female officer will babysit me, for the duration of the search.

I step aside. I let them in and watch them ransack what is left of my life.

In the two and a half hours that follow, they take special care to upturn everything they come across. Midway through, I tell the female officer that I want to use the toilet and get up. She gets up too and I frown. I sit back down, cross my legs and turn on the TV. Oprah's on; Christmas special. I lose myself in someone else's drama.

Through it all, I'm thinking about the slip of paper I found in Roy's car. It's still sitting in the dresser upstairs. I wonder if they'll find it. I find myself hoping that they don't and instantly hate myself for it. Someone died and I'm still protecting him?

As soon as they leave, I run upstairs to check. They found it. They found the receipt.

ROY

Robins marches in with an officer I haven't met before and sits down across from Alistair and me. She places a hefty file on the table and flicks through it, while the man introduces himself as DCI Patrick Dunmore, of the Homicide and Serious Crime Command. Wilson has been discarded for someone higher up.

'My client has prepared a statement,' Alistair says, pulling out a piece of paper from his folder, before they can begin questioning me.

'Sure,' Robins replies.

'On Friday, the fourth of December, my client, Siddhant Roy Kapoor, left his house in southeast London around four p.m. Emily Barnett called him at approximately five p.m. asking him to meet her. Roy suggested they meet on Monday but she sounded distressed and, therefore, he agreed to meet her that same evening. Roy drove to Seaford, arriving at approximately seven p.m. He picked Emily up from outside the Co-op on Seaford High Street and, subsequently, they drove to the beach. They stayed in the car throughout, talking. Roy dropped Emily off at the Seaford Head Hotel at about nine p.m. and then my client drove to the Grand Albion in Brighton. He checked in at approximately nine forty-five p.m. and went straight to his room, where Celia Brown joined him at approximately ten thirty p.m. Celia left around eight a.m. on Saturday, the fifth. My client checked out at midday and drove back to his house in Crystal Palace, London, arriving at approximately four p.m.'

I keep my eyes glued to the table while Alistair reads. When I look up both Robins and Dunmore are staring at me.

'Okay. Let's get this started, shall we?' Dunmore says. 'Why did Emily want to meet you that day?'

'To discuss the pregnancy. She said she was going to her parents' place on Saturday morning, and I didn't want to leave it till the next week . . .'

'Why not?'

'I was worried about her, I didn't want her to do something rash,' I improvise, thinking of all the reports that had been dominating newspapers last week.

'Something rash like tell her family? Were you trying to force her to terminate the pregnancy, Mr Kapoor?'

'No! I would never . . . Look, we discussed it. She wasn't keen on it to begin with, but after we spoke about it, she realized it was the most logical way forward.'

'By "it" you mean an abortion? She wasn't keen to kill her own baby?'

Alistair interrupts. 'That's a bit severe, DCI Dunmore. Need I remind you that abortion is legal in the UK?'

Dunmore smiles and moves on. 'Were you aware, Mr Kapoor, that Emily was Catholic? She went to church every Sunday. I find it hard to believe that she would want an abortion.'

'A Catholic would also be unlikely to go after a married man, but that didn't stop her, did it?' I say. Alistair shoots me a look and I reel myself in. Robins remains quiet. 'I didn't say she was without guilt or confusion. But she felt it was the best option.'

'The best option,' Dunmore repeats slowly. He leans forward, elbows on the table, and looks me right in the eye.

I shift in my chair. Her face flashes in front of my eyes. She was a fighter, right till the end.

'Well, it was the only option, though, wasn't it?' he says. 'I mean, it's understandable: it wasn't just her life that would change if she had the kid. Having a child with another woman . . . it would destroy your marriage. So when she told you she wasn't sure, it must have made you very angry. She was going to be with family the next day and you couldn't risk them finding out. Your best shot was convincing Emily when she was alone. It's one hell of a situation to have to deal with,' he says, shaking his head. 'So the way I see it, the logical thing to do, what anyone in that situation would do, is to ask Emily to meet you immediately, somewhere familiar, so she feels safe, but also remote, just in case, you know, things get out of hand. You try to talk some sense into her but she doesn't listen. We already know Miss Barnett was strong-headed, a real *per-sonality*. You argue, maybe get into a physical fight.' He looks at Robins and she nods. I feel my breathing change. Alistair puts a hand on my knee. Dunmore continues. 'When things calm down, you drop her off at her hotel and then you drive back to Brighton, check in. You order room service for two, tip the waiter, make sure you're seen there. And then you go back and deal with Emily. You couldn't convince her so you killed her. Isn't that what happened, Roy? Isn't that why you killed Emily?'

'The hotel waiter said he brought the food up at eleven thirty p.m. But instead of having him bring it in, you went out of your room to pick up the tray yourself,' Robins says.

I just look at her. Is there a question here? I want to ask, but I keep quiet.

'Why would you do that?'

'Celia and I, we were in bed, and she wasn't . . . um . . . dressed. I didn't want a waiter coming in.'

'I see. Were you dressed?'

'No, but I threw some clothes on.'

'What clothes?'

'I don't remember . . . the dressing gown, I suppose.'

'How long after the knock did you go outside?'

'A minute, maybe two.'

'Less than a minute by the waiter's assumption.'

'Okay,' I shrug.

'In his statement, the waiter said you were wearing a

black hoodie, jeans and white trainers when you went outside. You pulled out your wallet from your back pocket to tip him.'

'Like I said earlier, I don't remember.'

'Like you said earlier,' she frowns, 'the logical thing would be to throw on a dressing gown. I find it a bit strange that you would jump out of bed, presumably straight after sex, get fully dressed, lace up your shoes, just to go outside for thirty seconds.'

Alistair steps in. He focuses his gaze on Dunmore. 'Have you got a question for my client, Detective?'

Dunmore shakes his head at Robins and she moves on, a small smile teasing her lips. I can't imagine what she's playing at.

'Did you order breakfast in the morning?'

'Yes.'

'Room service for two?'

'Yes.'

'Did the waiter bring it in?'

'No, I did. Celia was in bed.'

'So no one saw Celia?'

'Look, we had to be careful about these things. We're both married. We were in the city that she lives in. It would be catastrophic if anyone saw her.'

'That's understandable. But then why did you book the room under both your names? Wouldn't it make more sense to use false names? That is what you did with Emily, right?' she asks, looking at her notes.

'Yes, I—'

Alistair puts a hand on my knee again to stop me babbling. I close my eyes and slouch down, resting my head on the back of the chair.

'Detectives, perhaps we can skip this,' I hear Alistair say. 'My client has already given you a statement about his whereabouts that evening. What he chose to wear or which name he booked the room in is irrelevant. Perhaps you should bring in the alibi witness for a statement if your area of interest is the motivation behind her discretion.'

'Ah, see, that's the problem. It isn't just discretion. The woman that your client claims is his alibi, his lover, she doesn't exist.'

The detectives step out and Alistair turns to me, his face red.

'She doesn't exist?' he hisses. 'You need to start talking. Right now.'

'I don't understand. Celia told me they'd been to see her.'

'Well, they clearly haven't.'

'They're lying . . .'

'Why would they lie?'

'You said yourself they would try to badger me for a confession. Isn't that what this is?'

'They wouldn't go this far.'

I try to think of why they would do this but I draw a blank.

'Have you got any proof of the relationship?' Alistair says after a moment.

'Proof?'

'Emails, photos, friends who can vouch for you? Anything we can show them?'

'No. There are no photos or emails. We used to text but we . . . we always deleted them afterwards. Mia can be quite nosy and Celia was worried; she didn't want to leave a trail because of –'

A thought occurs to me and I stop mid-sentence. *Nonono.*

'What?'

'What if he's done something to her? He's – he's hurt her before. She never filed a complaint but . . . Oh my god, he must have found out. That's why she—'

'Slow down, Roy. Who are you talking about?'

'Her husband, Dave. She's terrified of him. We need to talk to the detectives, they need to find—'

'Don't panic. I'll look into it.'

MIA

Friday, 18th December

George draws me into a hug as soon as he gets in.

'You okay?'

'Yes,' I mumble even as my tears wet his shirt. I hadn't realized how badly I needed a friend until now.

'Jesus, what happened in here?' he asks when I pull away. His eyes scan the room, taking in the upturned cushions, the littered floor, the open cabinets.

'Police search,' I say.

'The man they arrested, it's Roy?'

I nod.

He closes his eyes and takes a deep breath. 'Where's your coat?'

I don't want to risk running into any neighbours so we drive to a cafe in Forest Hill. It's the kind of quaint that was trendy five years ago – a wall of antique picture frames without pictures, Victorian knick-knacks and teacups masquerading as flower pots lining the shelves. I look around while we wait at the door for a table. The cafe is full of couples and young families having brunch, Christmas wishes floating in the air, mingling with the overbearing smell of bacon and eggs. I hear my stomach grumble and realize I haven't had anything to eat since lunchtime yesterday. A little boy runs past us, his mother trailing behind, struggling to push a buggy while juggling her shopping bags. George, ever the gentleman, holds the door for her, wishing her a merry Christmas as she walks past. I have a flash of envy and tear my eyes away. That should have been me.

The host shows us to our table in the back, and we sit down to look at the menu.

Five minutes later, he's back to take our order.

'Pancakes?' George asks me and I smile. It's nice to be looked after again.

'They haven't charged him yet?' George asks when the waiter leaves.

'No. I'm guessing that's what the search was about.'

'Did they take much?'

'Not really. I think they were quite disappointed.'

George runs a hand through his hair and shakes his head. 'I still can't believe it. Roy and Emily . . . I'm so sorry, Mia, I should have noticed something. I mean, I was right there with them.'

'Georgie, it's not your fault. Even I didn't notice anything for months. God, at the wedding I was convinced there was something going on between *you* and Emily.'

'Why would you think that?'

I shrug, and George looks away.

'You need to tell Addi. Whether or not he's charged, it's only a matter of time before the press get hold of Roy's name,' he says after a long pause.

'I know, I know. I just don't want her to worry about all this on top of everything with Mum, you know?'

He nods.

'I feel so guilty . . . I've been horrible to Mum, with the house sale, and . . .' I cover my face. I look up when the waiter reappears with our coffees. I give him a small smile.

'Do you think it was a mistake?' George asks when he's left.

'What?'

'Roy . . . your marriage . . .'

I sigh. Perhaps it was a mistake. The odds were always against us. We're very different, we got married way too young. But I loved him. Despite everything, I think I still do. Doesn't that count for anything?

No. Love fades.

And you screw everything up.

'It must have been,' I say finally, my eyes fixed downwards as I try to blink away the tears.

I'm deep into my third pancake when I hear a shrill voice behind me.

'Mia!'

I turn around. It's Alanna. Chris's tall, over-the-top, unseasonably bronzed wife, Alanna.

'Alanna.' I get up to greet her, our air kisses even more fake than our smiles. 'I forgot you still live nearby.'

'Never moved,' she grins, her words delivered in a sing-song manner, the Liverpool accent still thick after years of living in London. 'We just love it here.'

We? I wonder if she's with the Italian waiter now. I feel a pang of anger on Chris's behalf then snap it away. Not my problem, not after what he did.

'How are you holding up?' she asks, touching my arm and cocking her head to one side. I can sense the 'awww' coming. I panic. I haven't seen the news since we got here. Have they released Roy's name?

'I'm fine,' I reply, my words slow and measured. 'How are you?'

'Oh, you know.' She shrugs and I touch her shoulder on cue. 'I've started practising Buddhism. I chant every day and we have these great discussion meetings every few weeks. It's all about accepting your life force and forgiving yourself. You have to trust the . . .' She chats on and I feel myself glaze over. I catch a glimpse of a small TV every time the kitchen door opens. I sneak glances at it while nodding along to Alanna. Images of Emily flash past. The text at the bottom rolls on and I strain to read it. *A man is being held in custody for questioning* . . . it reads. The video cuts to a weather forecast and I let out an inward sigh. No name. I turn my attention back to Alanna.

'It's been tough, you know, especially with everything that's happened in the past few months,' she is saying. Her face breaks into a smile, her eyes fixed to a spot behind me.

I turn around just as she says, 'But we'll get through it, won't we, baby?'

'Of course, darling,' Chris says, walking around me to give Alanna a peck.

I try to mask the shock that must surely have taken over my face. Chris?

'Have you paid?' she asks and Chris nods.

'All done.'

George gets up and offers his hand to Chris and then Alanna. Introductions are made. Alanna's Liverpool drawl all but disappears when I mention George is a TV producer.

Chris pulls me aside when she begins telling George about her modelling career.

'I've been trying to reach you.'

'I've been busy.'

'Alanna and I . . . I decided to take your advice. We're giving it another shot,' he says, fiddling with the wedding ring that's now back on.

'Great.'

'Mia, is everything okay? Have I done something?'

'Excuse me?'

'You haven't returned my calls.'

'Like I said, I've been busy. You know, looking for a job and all.'

He gives me a strange look. 'It's hard on me too, you know.'

'It's hard getting promoted?' I scoff.

He stares at me, then shakes his head.

'I was asked to leave. Mike called me in right after you left. Thanks to *your* decision to issue those MDAs.'

It takes me a few seconds to process this. 'What? Why? I thought you told them about the tests.'

'I would never do that to you,' he says. The hurt on his face punctures through my bitterness. He steps away from me, and leans in to whisper something to Alanna.

A quick goodbye and they're off.

I turn on the TV as soon as we enter the house. Still no name, no charge. I leave it on, buzzing in the background, as I go upstairs to get changed. When I go back downstairs a few minutes later, George is in the kitchen, rifling through the cabinets.

'What are you doing?' I ask.

'You can't leave things like this,' he says, with a swoop of his hand across the kitchen – some of it the mess the police left behind, but most of it my own. I decide not to tell him that. I had forgotten what a clean freak George is.

'Leave it, I'll do it later.'

He starts loading up the dishwasher.

'You know, I was thinking, why don't you come back to Bristol with me for a couple of days? It'll make a nice change of scene and I really don't like the idea of leaving you here by yourself,' he says, wiping his hands and coming around to stand in front of me by the kitchen table.

'I don't know,' I answer. 'What if the police need me for something?'

'Like what?'

'I don't know . . . anything.'

'Well, you can always come back. It's only a couple of hours away.'

I hesitate.

'Come on, it'll be just like old times. You could do with a bit of fun, Mia,' he says.

He's right, I *could* use some fun. And I hate being in this house by myself. Plus I could go to see Uncle Bill and try and get some information about the other house. I nod. 'Okay.'

'Great. Why don't you go and pack and I'll finish up in here,' he says.

I'm already in the hall when he calls out. 'Oh, and Mia, a package arrived for you earlier. It's on the coffee table.'

I nip into the living room to see what it is, using a set of keys to tear open the packaging.

Roy's iPad is back from the dead.

ROY

They come back with a cup of milky coffee for me and a glass of water for Alistair. They remind me I'm still under caution and then the stream of questions resumes. Dizzying. Relentless.

'Do you have a credit card, Mr Kapoor?'

'I have two. A Mastercard and an Amex.'

'Are these the ones?'

'Yes.'

'Can we record that these were recovered from Mr Kapoor's wallet when he was brought in.'

'When was the last time you washed your car, Mr Kapoor?'

'I don't remember.'

'Hazard a guess, will you?'

'November sometime, after my parents left.'

'Are you sure?'

'I already said I don't remember,' I bite back.

'This was recovered from your house earlier today,'

Robins says and slides a piece of paper towards me. It's a photocopy of a car wash receipt. Seaford, 3 a.m., Saturday, 5th December. Paid for by my Amex.

'My card must have been cloned. That happened to my frien—'

Dunmore raises a hand and I shut up. 'We've already requested CCTV footage. Shouldn't be long,' he says.

'Can I confirm what you were wearing that evening, Roy?'

'Blue jeans and a black sweatshirt.'

'With a hood?'

'Yes.'

'And remind me which car were you driving?'

'Vauxhall Astra, black.'

'Registration?'

'LD61 TXM'

'Where did you park?'

'In the hotel car park,' I say, mimicking her intonation.

'The hotel has two car parks, does it not?' she asks, irritation lining her voice.

'Yes.'

'Which one did you use?'

'The one in the basement.'

'Why that one?'

'It was freezing, I didn't want icy wheels in the morning.'

'There was a notice there, at the entrance of the basement car park. Do you remember it?'

'No.'

'This might jog your memory,' Robins says, placing a picture on the table.

It's a notice saying the CCTV in the basement car park was broken and guests were advised to use the car park behind the hotel.

'I don't remember seeing this.'

'That's interesting.'

'Detective—' Alistair begins but Robins cuts him off with the flick of a hand.

'Could you confirm the time you entered the car park and the time you left?'

'I was in the hotel from nine forty-five p.m. on Friday till around midday Saturday, so obviously, my car was in the car park for the same duration,' I cut back. I am starting to get tired of this.

'Perhaps you can explain these then,' Robins says, pulling out a picture from her file and sliding it across the table as Dunmore glares on.

I peer at it. Screen grabs from CCTV footage. There's mud smeared on the number plate, hiding the last digit, but it's unmistakable. It's my car. On the Brighton seafront. The time stamp says 1.35 a.m., Saturday, 5th December.

I rub my eyes. This can't be happening. It isn't possible.

'This is a mistake.'

'Here's another.'

Marine Drive, Saltdean. 1.52 a.m., Saturday, 5th December.

I place my elbows on the table and press the heels of my

hands into my eyes. I black out the images. I don't understand how they got these.

'Perhaps we should call it a night, Detective. My client is visibly tired,' I hear Alistair say.

I stay like that, head in my hands. I breathe deeply.

'No problem, Mr Stanton. We'll pick this up first thing tomorrow. Lots more where these came from. You left breadcrumbs all the way to Seaford, Mr Kapoor.'

I hear the door shut and then I look up. Spots of red and blue dance in front of my eyes, then slowly the room reappears.

'I don't understand—'

Alistair holds up a finger, pointing to the red light flashing above us. We both stare at it for a few seconds.

Alistair nods when it finally goes off.

'Roy, this is the last time I'm going to ask you this. Have you told me everything?'

'Yes! I don't understand why they're asking me all this. I have an alibi! You need to find Celia. She will confirm I was with her all night.'

'They have pictures that prove you weren't.'

'I don't know how they got those. Maybe they've faked the photos. Can they do that?'

'No.'

'Then someone obviously stole my car.'

'And put it back?'

'Yes. Maybe it was one of Emily's ex-boyfriends. Those men they released didn't look right.'

Alistair gives me a wry look and gets up. He doesn't believe me.

'I didn't do it, Alistair. I promise you.'

'I'll see you tomorrow,' he says before the door slams shut again.

MIA

'Wine?' George calls out, going straight into the kitchen.

'Just some water, please,' I say, dumping my bag on the floor. The living room is warm, the old radiators ticking along noisily. George had got here before me; I'd insisted on bringing my own car, a little assertion of independence. I walk up to the brick fireplace that dominates the room and look at the photos on the mantelpiece.

'There you go,' he says a minute later, handing me a glass of water. He pours out some wine for himself. 'Sure I can't tempt you?'

I shake my head. 'Where is this?' I ask, picking up a picture of George and a brunette from the mantelpiece. She's pretty.

'Cambodia.'

'You travel so much! I always wonder what things would have been like if I hadn't moved into sales. Do you remember how much fun we had when we went to Senegal for that artist exchange?'

'You mean when you got wasted on that fifty-pence wine, threw up all over the group leader's backpack and then passed out in the bathroom?'

'I forgot about that!' I say and we both laugh. I put the picture back. The laughter dissipates and an unexpected panic takes its place.

'Oh Georgie, what am I going to do? It's all just so . . . I mean, how did I even get here? Fired, running from my own home, married to a man who's accused of murder?' I sigh. 'And Mum . . .'

'Hey, don't go weak on me now, Mia. You're one of the smartest, most independent women I know. You'll figure it out.'

I nod. There's more, I want to say. I want to tell him about what I discovered the other day but I can't seem to form the words.

'Look, let's attack this one thing at a time, okay? We'll come up with a plan,' he says. 'You're brilliant, you'll get a new job the minute you start looking. But maybe this is a good thing. You clearly need a break, Mia. You need to go to India, spend some time with your mum, and then you need to get back to being yourself. As for Roy, I don't know if he's guilty or not, but he's an arsehole for the way he's treated you, and Emily. I know it might not seem like it right now, but you were right to leave him.'

I take a deep breath and smile. I feel my heart rate go back to normal. The buzzing stops. I start to feel solid again. 'Thanks, George.'

'Anytime. You're better than him. Don't forget that. Now, how does pasta sound for dinner?'

'Sure, it's the only thing you know how to cook,' I attempt, my eyes still wet.

He squeezes my arm and turns to go to the kitchen. I start to follow but he steers me towards the sofa instead. 'Sit down, chill out. And have some wine. You know where the glasses are.'

I sink into the sofa, the cream leather folding around me in habitual creases. I feel myself relax for the first time in days. I lean back and close my eyes. I'm exhausted. I haven't been here in years but it feels like I never left.

I flick through a copy of the *National Geographic* on the coffee table. By the time George comes back, I know the top ten holiday destinations for the next year. Cambodia and Peru top the list. I can't imagine ever visiting either of them. Not the way my life is going.

'So, I was thinking about that deed you told me about,' he says. 'Remember Phil Buckley?'

'Vaguely. Tasha's brother?'

'That's the one. He works at the land registry, he's quite high up. I can ask him to look into it if you want?'

'That'll be great.'

'Sure, just give me the papers tomorrow and I'll pass them on.'

'Okay.' I look down at my spaghetti. I twirl some on the fork.

'Hey, you'll be all right, I promise,' he says.

I fight to hold back the tears.

This isn't the life I wanted. None of this is right. In a matter of days, my whole life has fallen apart. Everything has changed. I'm drained, exhausted, and alone.

George puts his bowl down, then takes mine and places it on the coffee table next to his own.

He pulls me into a hug and for the second time in one day, I cry into his shirt. His sturdiness feels safe and I don't want to let go.

I pull away slightly when the anxiety passes. I attempt a smile. 'I'm sorry,' I say, my voice hoarse from the crying. 'I've ruined your shirt.'

'It's fine,' he whispers.

His breath feels hot on my face and it occurs to me how close we are. The atmosphere changes in that instant.

'Remember when you crashed your bike when we were little? You totalled it, twisted your ankle and then went home to find that Scooby had died. You wept for a week straight. You were convinced your whole life was over.'

'Uh-huh,' I murmur. His hands feel warm on my back.

'That's what this is. I know it feels like the end but you'll make it out, stronger,' he says, looking me straight in the eye, his brows knitted together. 'I promise.'

It all seems so familiar – the way he smells, the way I fit into his arms, the way his eyes droop after a few glasses of wine. He's still the same. He's still here. He's still *dependable*.

It would be so easy.

I allow myself to lean into him once more. I close my eyes. It feels exciting and comforting at the same time. Like coming home. His mouth brushes mine, soft, gentle. Delightful.

Slut.

I jerk away. I flop back on the sofa, clutching on to the armrest to regain my balance. My head begins to throb.

George has hurled himself to the other end of the sofa. He looks lost.

We sit like that for a minute, staring at each other, me in shock, him in . . . I don't know, disgust?

He speaks first, his voice muffled. 'Mia, I'm so so sorry. I didn't mean for that to happen. Not like this.'

I nod. I don't know what to say. I look at the bottle of wine in front of me. It's empty.

'Nothing happened,' I say.

George nods from the other end of the sofa. 'We just got lost in the moment, that's all.'

I get up and go to the guest room.

'Mia, please. Can we just talk about this . . .' I hear George call out.

I close the door. I rip off the bedspread and climb into bed.

I close my eyes. George was drunk but I hadn't even touched the wine. That was all me, sober as day.

Look at that. You're a slut too.

Just like Emily.

Nothing happened, I tell myself.

Nothing happened.

ROY

My cell is on the fourth floor of the police station. 'Penthouse suite,' the jailer smirks as he opens the cobalt blue door to let me in.

The door slams shut and the stench of urine fills my head. I take a look around. It's tiny, smaller than my bathroom at home, all the walls covered in light grey tiles. Masquerading as a bed along the right wall is a narrow concrete bench. A steel sink and lavatory with no lid take up the corner of the opposite wall. I peer at the pot. Skid marks all over. I shudder. I can hold it in till the morning.

I cover my nose with my hand and lie down on the bed. I stare at what is meant to be a skylight – it's no more than an eight-inch-by-eight-inch square. It's too dark to see anything out of it, but I suspect even during the day it would be foggy at best. It doesn't look like this cell has been cleaned in years.

I toss and turn. The blue plastic mattress is too limp to

provide any real comfort but I suspect tonight would be hard even in a *real* penthouse suite.

Dunmore's and Robins's words echo through the airless cell.

They say you aren't real. They say that I made you up to protect myself. That Celia Brown is nothing more than a figment of my imagination.

How do I explain to them that you are more real than any of them could ever hope to be?

I see a shadow pass across the rectangular window in the door and I prop myself up to try and decipher who it is but it's too dark to make out. I lie back down and turn on my side. The mattress slides to the other side and I pull it back in. I think back to that night in Brighton, how we luxuriated in the king-size bed, falling asleep in each other's arms. When I woke up, I could hear the water running in the bathroom.

'Come back,' I called out, still in bed.

A moment later you appeared, all wrapped up in a towel, beads of water trickling down your neck.

'What's that?' you asked, leaning on the bathroom door.

I don't think you could ever look more beautiful than you did in that moment. Your head cocked to one side, sunlight streaming in from the bathroom windows, turning your pale skin luminous.

'Come back,' I repeated, pulling the duvet over me so you wouldn't see how hard I was.

You smiled. You let the towel drop to the floor. You walked over slowly and drew the duvet away. All while you held my gaze. You climbed into bed and lay down next to me, close enough for me to feel the warmth of your skin but far enough to drive me wild with desire.

'You're driving me crazy,' I croaked, propping myself up on my elbow so I could look at you. You smiled, but stayed put.

'What if we don't go back?' you said, looking at the ceiling.

'Back?'

'To our homes, our marriages.'

'Where would we go?'

'I don't know, we could go anywhere. Everywhere.'

'We could.'

'We could travel. Write. Build a life together.'

You closed your eyes, lost in this fictional paradise. I knew how seductive it could be, that promise of opportunity, the chance to be different. I wanted to tell you how much I wanted it as well. But I didn't. We were suspended in an alternate reality, one where this was real, where we could be together. The silence allowed the dream and I let it.

I reached over. I ran a finger down your neck and you smiled. I kissed your nipples and you stirred. I fingered you and you moaned. I entered you and you cried.

Afterwards as we lay tangled in the sheets, your legs, pale and smooth, entwined with my own, your fingers running across my chest, you whispered, 'Maybe there is a way.'

MIA

He's in the water with me. The pool, it has no walls. The water's swirling, trapping me in a whirlpool. I can sense him behind me. Strong hands on my shoulders, the comforting voice in my ear. I turn to look at him but the current is too strong and I only manage to catch a glimpse of his hand before the water sucks me under. I struggle upwards, telling myself not to panic. He's here. He'll pull me out. But I am stuck under the surface, sinking. I thrash around, flailing my arms, kicking my legs, but it doesn't help. The water stills. Why am I still sinking? Why isn't he pulling me out? Then I feel it, the sharp push downwards, the hand over my mouth. I am drowning.

He is drowning me.

I push the front door open and blink twice. The house is flooded with light. I step inside to find that all the blinds have been taken down. I walk around. The rooms have been cleaned, walls painted, all the furniture removed. The house looks new, ready for another family to fill with their own stories. I set my bag down on the kitchen counter and check my phone. There's a text from George to say he's emailed Phil the deed, we should hear back later today.

I didn't see George this morning. I waited in the guest room, pretending to be asleep, until I heard him leave. I wasn't ready to see him, not yet. It was all too confusing. I haven't thought of George like that in a long time and I don't want to give him the wrong idea. It was hard on him when we split up. He refused to accept it, proposing to me three weeks later as he drove me to the airport. I laughed, thinking he was joking – I was only nineteen, after all – until I looked at his face. I backtracked immediately; George was my best friend and I didn't want to hurt him. So I let him kiss me when we said goodbye. 'Wait for me,' I whispered in his ear before I pulled away. 'Wait for me.' Even though I didn't mean it.

A knock on the door jerks me back to the present.

'It's open,' I shout out and the agent appears after a minute.

He called me last night to say everything was in place; all he needed was the original freehold certificate. A young couple had put in an offer. Cash buyers, so there was no survey or mortgage approval to worry about.

'What happens now?' I ask after he's inspected the document I hand him.

'All the paperwork is drawn up. I just need you to sign the contract. The buyers are wanting to move quickly so we should be able to complete the sale early next week.'

He pulls some papers out of a folder and lays them out on the kitchen platform.

'I see.'

'Your sister's solicitor's already looked through these.'

'Uh-huh.'

I pick up the contract and have a read through. I pause when I see the buyer's name.

'I thought you said it was a couple?'

'It is but the girlfriend's the one with the money.'

I shudder inwardly. Recipe for disaster.

I gather the papers up into a pile and turn to the agent.

'Look, why don't you leave these with me and I'll drop them off first thing tomorrow?'

'It's Sunday tomo—'

'Monday then.'

'No, no, it's fine. I can pop into the office tomorrow. Ten a.m.?'

'I'll let you know,' I say. I shove the papers into my bag and take one last look around.

Let it go, Mia, this isn't home anymore, I tell myself.

The voices correct me instantly. *If this isn't home, then where is?*

Even without any trace of our life here, memories crowd the house, drumming a frantic, relentless beat. I'm not ready to let go, I realize. Not yet. There's one last thing I have to try.

ROY

The door rattles and I sit up with a jerk. My back feels stiff and when I turn my neck to the right a sharp pain shoots through my whole body. I've been up all night, listening to the footsteps and voices filtering through from outside.

The hatch clatters again and I realize it is the jailer. I grab the blue plastic tray he shoves through and inspect it.

A handful of beans and something that looks like a sausage float in the watery orange sauce from last night. A piece of stale bread and a cup of tea accompany it. I dunk the bread in the tea and attempt a bite. Disgusting.

I set the tray down on the floor and go back to lying on the concrete plinth and staring at the flaking paint on the ceiling.

The plan was simple. I would wait till after Christmas to tell Mia I wasn't happy. She would cry, and I'd hold her hand. I'd explain to her that my heart wasn't in our marriage anymore. I'd tell her I needed to pursue the Arctic project, that maybe that would fill the hole in my life. Maybe that was all I needed, some space and time to do my own thing, recalibrate. I wouldn't mention divorce, not yet. She would let me have the money. Just come back, she would beg and I'd hug her and let her cry. It would work. All I had to do was make sure Mia never found out the truth.

Your husband was a little more complicated. Dave wouldn't let you go willingly, so the only way was to run. I wanted you to leave him immediately but you were terrified that he would track you down before we had the chance to get away. I won't let him hurt you, I said, but you shook your head. Dave is going to Oxford for a job in January, you told me. He'll be gone for three days. If I can just keep him calm till then, you said, that will give us all the time we need. It was killing me, but I knew your mind was made up. No contact till then, you said. Once Dave left, you'd text me and I was to come and pick you up. We'd fly out the same day, somewhere in Europe at first, and then Africa and finally somewhere in South America. No pre-bookings, you insisted, no trail. By the time Dave got back, we'd be on the other side of the world, with enough money to set us up for at least a year, two if we were prudent. This will work, won't it? you asked me, the ever-present fear in your eyes seeping into your voice. It broke me to see how scared you were and I pulled you in closer. It'll work, I promise, I said and you smiled, burrowing your head in my shoulder.

It was a good plan. It would have worked.

But of course Emily had to fuck it all up.

I hear the jingle of keys and the cell door swings open. The custody sergeant tells me they are ready for me.

How long till they figure it out, my love?

MIA

Saturday, 19th December

Stepping into Uncle Bill's home feels like stepping into a time machine and going back twenty years: the heavy curtains, the floral-patterned sofas, the mahogany dining table . . . it is exactly as I remember it. Right down to the custard tarts and milky tea Aunty Jane places in front of me as soon as I sit down.

'It's good to see you, love,' she says, pulling up a chair next to me. She positions the chair diagonally, stretching her left leg out to one side when she sits down. 'Bad knee,' she explains.

I smile and ask her about Uncle Bill. He got called in for an emergency surgery, she tells me. We talk easily over the next hour: about me, my job, Roy, Roy's job, Aunty Jane's good knee, her bad knee, Uncle Bill's practice, James's practice, her hair, the cost of butter, my hair, the cost of jam, Kate Middleton's hair, all while I work my way through the dozen or so custard tarts arranged prettily on the baby pink two-tier cake stand. Turns out even at twenty-nine, I can't leave one sitting in front of me.

'I'll pack some for you to take back. It's lovely having you here after all these years, Mimi,' she says, using her special nickname for me.

'I'm sorry I don't come over more often.' Even as the words leave my mouth I try to figure out just what went so wrong that we all but cut off from Aunty Jane and Uncle Bill. 'It's a shame we lost touch over the years.'

'Yes, well, I wish things had turned out differently. After David, everything just sort of crumbled, didn't it?'

I nod quietly.

'Why didn't you ever come to visit us in India?'

'Rekha never invited us.' Her words scissor through the room, snipping away any ties I'd restored in the last hour.

'I remember how close you and Mummy were,' I say tentatively.

She nods slowly. 'She needed time to heal. So did we.'

We sit in silence for a few minutes.

'Will Uncle Bill be back soon?'

'I don't know, Mia,' she says, her exasperation evident. 'He'll come when he comes. Do you need to speak to him about something?'

It's unlikely she will know much but I recall Uncle Bill's face the last time I saw him and decide to take my chances with Aunty Jane.

'Do you know anything about a house in Eastbourne, Aunty J?'

'Eastbourne?' She tenses up, her spine pulled taut.

'Yes,' I say slowly. 'I was clearing out some things at the old house and I found a copy of a deed for a—'

'I don't know what you're talking about.' She pulls her leg in and places both hands on the table, shifting her body weight to her left, preparing to get up.

'I need to know, Aunty J. Please. Maybe we can keep the house in Bristol. Wouldn't Uncle Bill like that?' I try to appeal to the husband-pleaser in her.

'You should really ask your mother about this,' she says.

My mother? So it did have something to do with her affair.

I take a deep breath. I pick my words carefully. 'Mummy's ill . . . it's cancer. We just found out. I can't ask her right now and I really need to know.'

'Rekha's ill? Oh Mimi.' She reaches over and squeezes my hand. 'Is she going to be okay?'

'They're doing what they can, but it's stage four.'

She nods, the hint of tears in her eyes. She labours up and goes into the kitchen wordlessly.

'It's really not my place to talk about all this,' she says when she comes back, two mugs of tea in hand. 'William will be furious.'

'I know why Mum and Dad were fighting in his last few months, Addi told me.'

'Ah,' she says, unconvinced.

'I know about the affair, Aunty J.'

She nods, massaging her knee.

'What do you need to know, Mimi?' Her voice is clipped, as if she fears saying too much.

'The house in Eastbourne – did we sell it already? Is that why Mum is selling the one in Bristol now?'

She shrugs. 'I suppose Rekha needs the money. William's furious, but to be honest, I get it. It's her house and she has the right to do whatever she wants with it. I'm surprised she's waited this long to sell it. It can't be easy raising two girls on your own while holding on to those memories.' She shudders. 'As far as selling the house in Eastbourne goes, she can't. David didn't leave it to her.'

'Oh. Did he leave it to Uncle Bill?'

'No, Mimi. William tried to contest the will, he thought it should have gone to Rekha or him, but David had made sure there were no loopholes. It was shocking but what can you—'

'Then who did he leave it to?'

'Laurel.'

Aunt Laurel?

I stare at the mug of tea in my hand. I don't want it. I hold it out and Aunty J reaches forward to take it from me.

'I don't get it. He must have been upset with Mum about her affair but why would he—'

'Her affair?' The shock in Aunty Jane's voice is genuine. She puts her cup down on the table and puts a hand on my knee. 'Mimi, love, your mother wasn't the one having an affair.'

MIA

Saturday, 19th December

I stare at her, stunned. She's lying. She has to be. What she's saying is not possible. It can't be. I press my fingers onto my eyelids and try to process her words. The room goes black. It just doesn't make any sense.

Aunt Laurel had been at Cambridge with Uncle Bill, two years behind Mum and Dad. She was one of Daddy's best friends and featured in every story my Dad ever told me about Cambridge. She had been there for nearly every birthday party, every Christmas, every ill-advised barbecue when I was little. And then one day she stopped coming.

'Daddy and Aunt Laurel?'

Aunty J nods.

'But . . .'

'I was equally shocked, Mimi. Laurel was like a sister to me.'

'How long . . .'

'I'm not sure. A few years, I think. Since Cambridge. Rekha didn't find out till much later, of course.'

'There was a barbecue . . . at your house. The summer before Daddy's accident . . .'

'That's when you – I mean, that's when I found out,' Aunty Jane says, shaking her head.

I grip the chair, my fingers closing around the rough upholstery as the memory that's been eluding me for years hits me out of nowhere.

Addi and I were playing in the garden with the other kids. Uncle Bill had set up a trampoline for us. It was the sort of summer day when everything slows down. The grown-ups were scattered in groups around the garden, sipping their drinks and chatting. Mum was in the kitchen helping Aunty Jane with the food.

I hopped off the trampoline and wandered over to the conservatory. Uncle Bill was walking around passing drinks to everyone. I stared up at him. I used to think he was the tallest human on earth when I was little. I would beg him to carry me on his shoulders so I could be tall too.

'Are you tired, Mimi?'

I shook my head. 'I want to pee.'

'Okay, run along, you,' he said, ruffling my hair and smiling down at me.

I ran up the stairs to the bathroom and peed. I remember taking my time washing my hands. Aunty J always had the coolest soaps. The one I used that day looked like a butterfly. It gave me an idea for a new game to play on the trampoline and I wiped my hands quickly, excited to show everyone. I heard Daddy's voice when I stepped out of the bathroom and decided I should find him first, so he could see me be a butterfly. I knew I would be the best. I ran from room to room, looking for him. The first door was locked – Aunty Jane's bedroom. The second door revealed a very frazzled-looking woman, ancient to my six-year-old eyes, reapplying her lipstick. There was only one room left, that's where he must be! I threw the door open with a flourish and met with a sight, the memory of which, even today, years later, feels like a punch in the stomach.

She saw me first. Her blouse was open, the front still tucked into her skirt. Her arms were looped around my father's neck. His back was to me, head bent into her neck, hands on her hips. Aunt Laurel looked at me for a minute. 'David,' she said quietly. 'David,' she repeated, pushing him away. Her bra was red. He turned. I don't know why, but I shrieked.

He was kneeling beside me, telling me to be quiet, but I kept at it, my shrieks getting louder and louder until they stopped all at once.

'Behave yourself, Mia,' he whispered. I stared at my shoes, tears pooling in my eyes, too afraid to say anything. I ran down the stairs, straight into Aunty Jane.

When I open my eyes, Aunty Jane is sitting next to me, with one arm around my shoulder. I allow myself a moment and then when the sobs subside, I wipe my face with the serviette and turn to her.

'How did you find out?'

'I heard screams. I was about to come up when I saw

you running downstairs. David and Laurel weren't far behind.'

'Did you tell Mummy?'

'No, I couldn't – I couldn't believe it myself for some time. I knew your parents were having problems but it was David and Laurel. I didn't even tell William. But then I went to see Laurel a couple of weeks later, and when I asked her it all came out. She made me promise not to say anything. David wanted to speak to Rekha himself.'

'But he didn't?'

'Things between your parents got worse. I tried to speak to David but he blew me off. Then one day, a couple of months later, your mum turned up here. She was hysterical. First I thought it was one of you, that there had been an accident of some sort. But you were both at school. She – she'd found out. One of her friends from work saw David with Laurel and—'

'Why didn't she leave?'

Why didn't you?

'It wasn't that simple for her, Mimi. She had two little girls to look after and her family, your grandparents, they were all the way back in India . . . David bought the house in Eastbourne for Laurel and he started spending more and more time there. He didn't even bother lying once Rekha knew. Your mother . . . she came to William as well, but he didn't want to get involved. David had always been so strong-minded, trying to talk him out of something only made him more stubborn. William tried to explain that to

Rekha but she didn't want to give up. She asked me to speak to Laurel. I tried, but Laurel . . .'

I lean back on the sofa and close my eyes.

It all falls into place, the memories completing themselves. The house, the garden, the stairs.

And then his voice, just a whisper in the air.

Unbreakable.

'Aunty J?'

'Yes, love?'

'Did Daddy . . .' My throat closes up, the words refuse to come. 'I mean . . . was he violent?'

Aunty J strokes my cheek. My tears wash over her wrinkled fingers.

After a long pause, she nods, her own eyes watering.

I walk, first slowly, and then break into a scramble towards my car. Doors bolted, hot air blasting out of the vents, I drive around aimlessly, circling the neighbourhood. Aunty Jane's words crowd the car, suffocating me. I lower my window, drawing in gulp after gulp of the crisp air I grew up with. I keep my eyes fixed to the road, focusing on the cars in front of me, but it doesn't help. My brain is exploding. Every familiar bend in the road brings something back but the memories no longer belong to me.

I tighten my grip around the steering wheel, my fingers cramping with the effort. She's lying, I tell myself. Of course she is. She has to be.

Why would she do that?

He wasn't like that. My father was a kind, honest and

generous man, I repeat to myself over and over again. That is how I always describe him to strangers. It's an easy routine. A cock of the head, a sad smile, the smattering of 'awws' afterwards. But the more I think about it, the more practised it sounds. A past manufactured to protect my future.

Your whole life is a lie.

Do you even know who you are?

The voices race through my childhood, ripping every memory to shreds, until I realize that the idyllic childhood, the loving father, all of it is simply fiction.

ROY

Saturday, 19th December

I get a few minutes alone with Alistair before the detectives come in. 'I looked for her. I checked the electoral roll, the phone directory, had a contact at the Eurostar look into their records for the day you took it . . .'

'You found her?'

'I found a Celia Brown.'

'Is she okay? He hasn't hurt her, has he?'

'Celia Brown is ninety-two and living in a care home for people with dementia.'

'Do you think you can ever really know someone?' I asked you, tracing my fingers along the bottom of your breasts.

You shivered and turned to face me, pulling the duvet over you.

'No.'

'Okay,' I laughed. 'So you don't think you know me, I suppose? Bit risky to go off into the sunset with me then.'

You angled your head back and gave me one of your

serious looks. 'How can we know one another when we barely even know ourselves most of the time? We're constantly changing. All we can hope for is to find someone who loves us enough to say, I'll ride out the waves with you,' you said, intertwining your fingers with mine, 'And then we hope for the best.'

I pulled you into me. 'I'll never let you go,' I whispered into your hair.

You were right, of course, like you so often were. I simply didn't realize until now that you were talking about yourself, not me. I know nothing about you. Nothing that's true, in any case.

Hindsight is a vicious thing, isn't it, my love?

MIA

I tiptoe into the hall and head straight to George's guest room. I collapse on the bed and close my eyes. Sleep eludes me. Images from the past circle my brain, each one stronger than the last. Shaking my head, I climb out of bed and turn on the light. I need something to do. I reach for my laptop and listen to the familiar whirring of the fan while it powers on. It switches on for a second, then tells me it's out of battery and dies. I get up and root through my bag for the charger, then realize it's still sitting in my living room in London. Roy's iPad catches my eye. I've been avoiding opening the box. It will just give me more evidence to torture myself with. I look at the books in the display case. I flick through a novel about a woman presumed dead who turns up years later to avenge the lover who was framed for her murder. It's a gritty crime thriller and I tire of it quickly. My eyes dart back to the iPad. I give in. Perhaps torturing myself with Roy's infidelities is better than with my father's. It asks me for Roy's code. I hesitate, and then punch in his birthdate. Surprisingly, it works.

I prop myself up in bed and click on to his emails. Nothing. I do the same with his messages and draw a blank. He was obviously clever enough to delete everything. No wonder he didn't bother changing the code.

I put in George's wifi password and click on to Netflix. I set the iPad on the bedside table and scroll through my phone while Neil Patrick Harris babbles on in the background. There's a new email from George. He's forwarded Phil's email about the Eastbourne house to me. My eyes dart through the chain of ownership. David F. Parker to Laurel B. Smith in 1996, and then to Alice Doughty in 1999, and then to a yet-to-be registered cash buyer two weeks ago. Alice Doughty. The name rings a bell but I can't place it.

I check the time. It's nearly morning. I really should get some sleep. I reach for the iPad to switch it off when I notice several new message notifications come up. The iPad must be syncing to Roy's Apple iCloud account, I realize. I wait for the notifications to stop, then work my way through the texts, hundreds between him and Emily, going all the way back to September. Times, dates, hotels, fake names. It's all in there. I scroll up to the most recent. October 23rd. They met at a B&B in Surrey.

picked up some new knickers for tonight
Oh?
crotchless. but maybe I shouldn't wear them at all . . .
Nausea. I scroll down quickly. There are no more

messages after that. I look for any mention of Celia but find none. My brain tells me Roy made her up for an alibi, but it doesn't make sense. If he did kill Emily, why do it in a place they could so easily link him to? He had hidden the affair for months; he could have come up with a better way to do it.

He didn't hide the affair. You just chose to ignore the signs.

I tap into the pictures folder. A quick scroll through the thumbnails proves there are no pictures of Emily or ghost woman Celia. I spot a picture of Roy and me at the wedding and tap on our faces to enlarge it. Roy's behind me, his arms wrapped around my waist. We're both looking into the camera, our smiles perfectly matched. That picture was taken the day after the wedding. We hadn't been speaking to each other but we'd put on an act in front of the family. The perfect couple. I wonder how long we'd been doing that, pretending to be happy instead of really being happy. Perhaps we were doomed from the start, him a compulsive liar and me the enabler. I flick through the pictures, hundreds from the wedding, from Roy's press trips, from the Diwali dinner at home. I keep flicking mindlessly till I get to the picture of a pebbled beach. There's no one in the frame but the pier in the distance tells me it's been taken in Brighton. I check the date. Friday, 4th December. The night Emily disappeared. I swipe to the next picture; this one is a hotel room. There are pictures of it from every angle, panoramas, close-ups, arty shots. Perhaps Roy was hoping to use them for an article. I scroll through. It is a beautiful room. High ceilings, a large picture window, gorgeous bedding, marble bathroom, generous dressing area. A shadow in the corner of the frame catches my eye and I zoom in to look at Roy's reflection in the bathroom mirror. I blink quickly when the picture enlarges, the shadow behind him now discernible. I peer closer, certain that my mind is playing tricks on me.

No. No. No.

I hug myself as panic takes hold of me.

It isn't.

I pant. I shut my eyes.

It can't be.

I rub my eyes and blink the room straight.

I look at the picture again. It's blurry, but there is no doubt about it. The sharp jaw, the drooping eyes, the high forehead. I've stared at that face for hours. I know every curve, every line, every mark on it by heart. I stumble out of bed.

I need to get out of here.

I'm already at the door when I hear him behind me.

'Where are you going?'

I turn around, the front door open, my hand still on the handle.

'George, I – I didn't want to wake you. I'm just going to get some . . . um . . . breakfast.'

'With your bags?'

'Yeah . . . I . . .'

He takes a step towards me. I drop my bag on the floor, between us.

'Is this about last night? I know it was sudden and confusing, and I never meant for it to happen, not – not like this anyway . . . but I don't regret it. I – I love you, Mia. I always have.'

'George, I'm still—'

'You asked me to wait for you, Mia, and I did. And then when you came back, you started seeing Roy. Roy! I should never have let you go.'

'He's—'

'He doesn't deserve you. But you and I, we fit, we always have. Let me take care of you, Mia.' He moves closer. 'We can build a life together. Just think about it, we—'

'I have to go,' I snap. I bolt out, slamming the door shut behind me.

ROY

We're in the same interview room as yesterday, the same biro graffiti on the desk, the same black box ticking along, the same Dunmore and Robins sitting opposite Alistair and me, yet something feels different. The air. It has a charge to it that permeates through the stale stench of tobacco.

Robins places a photograph in front of me. 'Do you recognize this?'

'Yes.'

'Care to elaborate?'

'It's my disposable phone. The one . . . the one I used for Emily and Celia.'

'Was this in your possession over the last six weeks?'

'Yes.'

'We had our digital forensics team look into this.'

I nod. Alistair had already warned me they would do this after they found it in my car. That is a good thing. It will prove I was in Brighton throughout.

Alistair reads my mind. 'I will presume you managed to recover enough to establish my client's alibi?'

'Or the lack thereof,' Dunmore scoffs.

He nods to Robins. 'There was very little of note on your regular phone, but we hit the jackpot with this one. Everything we need for a conviction . . .'

She lays out a series of A4 papers on the table in a neat row. Maps. Key locations have been circled with a red marker. Below them she places another set of A4 papers. Texts to Emily.

Texts that shouldn't exist.

I don't need her to tell me just how bad this all looks.

12.30 a.m., December 5th, Brighton.

I'm so sorry about earlier, Ems. This is all just so sudden, I don't know how to react. Still, I shouldn't have lost my temper and I want to make it up to you. I'll be done here in twenty minutes. Say you'll meet me? Please?

12.45 a.m., December 5th, Seaford.

just for a bit Roy. i'm tired.

12.48 a.m., December 5th, Brighton.

I'll be there in 30. Will text you when I arrive, meet me in the car park. We'll go for a drive. The pier is gorgeous at this time of the night.

01.27 a.m., December 5th, Seaford.

Ems, I'm here. Come out.

'Is there anything you'd like to say, Roy?' Robins asks me softly.

I look at Alistair. I shake my head.

Robins sighs. 'Let us help you, Roy.'

I keep my eyes fixed on the scratched graffiti on the table. Words leap out at me.

Cunt.

Innocent.

Prison.

Life.

'Very well,' Dunmore says. 'We've had the results of the DNA and forensics profiling back this morning. The blood splatters and strands of hair that were found in the boot of your car on Wednesday have been matched to Emily. We also recovered fibres matching the rope that was used to strangle Emily on the dashboard.'

I look up at this. Strangle?

'Why don't you tell me what happened, Roy?' Robins repeats. 'I know you aren't a bad guy, not really. You must have felt like you had no other option. Perhaps she pushed you too far?'

Robins leans forward and places her hand on my arm. 'We are prepared to make certain recommendations when it comes to trial and sentencing but I need you to talk us through that night, explain to me what happened.' She pauses, pulls her hand back. 'Emily's gone. We can't bring her back but we can provide the family with closure, spare them the pain of a very public trial. This is your chance to make amends. Show them some respect, Roy; let them mourn their loss in the privacy of their homes.'

I clutch the chair, the cold metal edges digging into my skin. I can't feign innocence anymore. They're going to make me pay for what I did.

My head spins. This is what everything has been leading up to. The lies, the guilt, the karma, it's all catching up with me, making sure I pay. For a crime I didn't commit and a crime I did. Biblical justice.

My life for hers.

Everything happens very quickly after that. I am charged with killing Emily. I'll be presented before the Magistrates' Court tomorrow afternoon, I am told. Alistair leaves, and before I know it, I'm being escorted back to a cell for the night.

As the metal door swings shut, I find myself back where it all began. Trapped. Staring at the body splayed out at my feet and wondering what to do next.

MIA

Sunday, 20ᵗʰ December

I rush into my car and lock the doors. I see George run out of the flat in the rear-view mirror but I look away. I skid out of the driveway and swerve onto the T-junction. I turn right, away from George, away from my father, away from the city I thought of as home.

The road blurs as my eyes prick with tears. I blink them away. I press my foot down on the accelerator and switch lanes. The driver in front of me honks as I zip past him onto the M5. I need to get away.

I end up back in the one place where my perfect family lives untarnished. The last place we were all together. Berrow Beach. I turn off the ignition and rest my head on the wheel, and then, with my arms wrapped around myself, I cry. I cry for the father who doesn't deserve my tears, the mother I never understood, the husband who shattered my heart, and the boyfriend who never let me go.

*

I feel faint when I step out of the car a few minutes later. I steady myself, take a deep breath and walk down to the beach, my feet sinking into the golden sand that stretches out for miles. The tide has dragged the water out, and the beach is streaked with hard ridges of sand encasing tiny pools of water. The Norwegian shipwreck that Addi and I played on as kids is still there. I look for a dry spot and sit down. The disconnected images that build up the narrative of my life flash past as the threads begin to unravel, all the lies and betrayals revealing themselves one by one.

Every time I asked George if he had found someone, he brushed it off. I don't have the time for a serious relationship right now; I love being single; none of these women seem right. Lies. All lies. He had been waiting to pounce on me all along and I had walked right into it.

A dog-walker waves at me from a distance and I look away. Go away, I will him silently. Go away.

I lie back on the sand and close my eyes. I try to focus. Perhaps if I keep still, I can slow my brain down. My thoughts hammer on relentlessly.

Roy. The love of my life. The boy who cried wolf. How was I to know this was the one thing he wasn't lying about?

Now it's too late and I'm too weak.

How had I managed to surround myself with liars? When did it start?

I think back to all the PTA meetings and dance recitals Mum had missed when we were growing up, Daddy attending them alone, telling the other parents that Mum was sick again. All the times we were shipped off to Uncle Bill's without any explanation. It all adds up. She missed so many school events that after a point I just presumed she skipped them because she didn't care and Daddy never corrected me.

Because that's what he wanted me to believe.

That day, when I scraped my elbow under the stairs, Mum hadn't been keeping Dad from kissing me better; she had been keeping him from hurting me, his unbreakable little girl.

I close my eyes as it hits me, the realization clenching my throat with a vice-like grip. Addi. The elder sister. First in line for everything. No wonder she never grieved him. And I punished her for it. I punished them both for it.

I gasp for air as the panic grabs me out of nowhere. I sit up. I claw at the powdery sand, counting to regulate my breathing. How could I be so blind?

Out on the horizon, the sky is darkening quickly, the sun long gone. I have been sitting here for hours. Inky blue patches blur the sky into the sea. Every few minutes the clouds part, and the sea glimmers, silver sequins dancing on black water. I stare at the waves and imagine myself floating away with them, letting them carry me to the middle of the ocean before closing my eyes and breathing in deeply, sinking slowly and not quickly enough, soft bubbles escaping to the surface until there is no air left in my lungs, until all that is left is the ocean. It would be so simple. Peaceful.

Coward.

I'm tired.

You're weak.

My gaze settles on the shipwreck. It still stands, jutting out skywards, the ocean pounding and smashing against it.

You're a burden. That's why everyone leaves you behind.

It's not my fault.

It is your fault for putting up with it.

I push myself off the sand and walk towards the shipwreck.

I thought he loved me. They loved me.

No one can ever love you.

The timbers that remain are covered in moss and seaweed, but they are still there, fighting the waves.

The voices eat away at me. 'Go away,' I whisper.

You didn't try hard enough.

The problem is you.

You're worthless.

I feel the darkness building inside me. Pulsing. Burning through my skin.

Daddy. I looked up to him. I *worshipped* him. He has defined every relationship in my life. Yet I never even knew who he really was.

I let Roy get away with so much because I had been conditioned to it as a child. After every lie came an elaborately charming excuse; after every bout of violence, a teary apology; after every argument, a grand romantic gesture. The pattern never jarred. How could it, when it reminded me so much of my father? Roy's version of the truth was so clear that mine began to get blurry. I started believing him when he told me I was being unreasonable, that I was crazy. I started believing that I was broken, and the only one who could make me whole again was my husband.

I wonder if that's what it was like for my mother.

I run into the ocean, the icy waves crashing into my legs, pushing me three steps back for every step forward. I take off my father's watch and hurl it into the water. A deep wordless scream tears through my throat and bounces over the waves.

You did this to yourself.

Shut up.

There is only one way out.

'Leave me alone,' I say, but the voices persist. I stand there, the water up to my knees.

It would be so easy.

It would.

I take a few steps forward, the water up to my thighs.

I breathe in.

My waist.

I close my eyes.

It's quiet. All I can hear is the sound of the water.

A wave crashes into me, knocking me backwards. My head hits the ocean bed. It's surprisingly hard. There's water everywhere. I can't breathe.

Just let go.

Mummy. I never told her how sorry I am.

She'll understand.

Addi. Roy.

I'm the only one who knows he didn't do it.

They want you to be at peace.

No. They need me.

I struggle to stand up. The waves are too strong. The world contracts; it refocuses.

I don't want to die.

The waves roll forward, dragging me further. A moment of calm as the sea prepares its next assault. I use all my strength and push myself to my feet. My head breaks the surface and I take in a deep gulp. Clean, fresh air. The water is up to my shoulders. I can still make it back.

I can see another wave approaching.

Things will never get better.

This is the only way out, the easiest way out.

Just close your eyes.

'Shut up, shut up, shut up!' I scream out loud. I stagger backwards, then turn and break into a run away from the water.

I collapse on the sand, panting. I stare at the waves. The tide washes away my footsteps in an instant.

For a moment, all I can hear is the waves. It unnerves me. Then I get it, they're gone.

The voices are gone!

I have barely let out a sigh of relief when they start again. I close my eyes and push my fingers into my ears but it's getting too loud inside my head.

Why won't they go away?

Breathe.

I open my eyes. I lower my hands. I listen.

Just breathe.
You can do this.
I smile. This time the voice is mine.

ROY

After the argument, I stormed out of my father's house and straight into Ajay and Rahul's flat in Green Park. I was seventeen; how dare he try to tell me what to do? Didn't he know how difficult it was to get into Columbia? Did it not matter that I hated med school? Did *I* not matter? I hurled questions at my friends and they passed me beers. You're awesome, man. Chill. Parents don't get it. Here, I'll cut you a line. You'll win a fucking prize one day. Pul-something, what's that prize called? I nodded along, the cocktail of drugs and booze softening my edges. Fuck him. I was going to make it on my own. More beer. Coke. Grinding in nightclubs. An endless summer. Girls. Have you got a hit? Not here, come with me. A bathroom somewhere. My first time. I didn't last. It's the coke. Always blame the coke. Here, have more. Better the next time, Rahul's classmate, Ajay's sofa. Much better. More booze. Parties. Girls. A friend, a tourist, someone's cousin, no names register, the faces blur. They all want the same thing.

Then the email from Columbia. There are no scholarships this year. My father laughing. Go back to med school. Fuck that, man. Writing can't be taught. You're a natural. Have some more. Cut me another line. Suddenly sober. We've run out. Call Karan, we need more.

Karan honked downstairs. He called the dealer and set it up. We drove to Hauz Khas Village. The smattering of artist studios and designer shops shut down at six and then the dealers and junkies came out, the columns of the derelict fort the perfect spot for a fix, and with a view of the lake to top it all. We picked up a bottle of rum and some more beers on our way. Ajay and Rahul waited by the lake while Karan and I went to meet the dealer. We cut two lines and I slipped the bag in my pocket. We wandered back to the lake. We could hear Ajay and Rahul singing all the way from the fort. *Tu cheez badi hai mast mast.* I can still hear them, drunk and slurring, eating up half their words.

It was so dark, I could barely see. The coke had kicked in, it was good stuff, and everything was blurry; the stars were flashing green and blue at me, an open-air disco. Rahul and Ajay came into focus, their backs to us. Rahul was thrusting, his beer abandoned at his feet, and Ajay was cheering him on. Drunken bastard. Karan laughed. We were a few paces away when I saw the shape in front of Rahul. A girl, young, must be fourteen or fifteen, dressed in rags. She was cowering on the floor, her back pressed up against the fence circling the lake.

'Rahul, what the fuck, man?' I said. I could hear Ajay and Karan laughing in the background.

He turned and I saw he had his dick out. The arsehole was wanking off on her.

'Leave her alone, man. She's a kid.'

'Dude, I'm just having some fun.' He turned to look at me, staggering.

Her leg came out of nowhere. He fell back and she jumped up. By the time any of us realized what was happening, she had picked up his beer bottle and smashed it. She was waving it at Rahul, hurling abuse at him, threatening to kill him. He nudged away, half sitting, half lying on the floor. Calm down, we're leaving, okay, we're leaving, Karan hollered, while Ajay and I dragged Rahul back to his feet.

She was doing a kind of *kabaddi* step, bent down into a half-squat and moving from side to side, pointing the bottle at each of us in turn. She was guarding her space, lunging out every few seconds to make sure we retreated.

The high disappeared. My heart plummeted. I don't remember being that scared ever before or since.

We stepped back slowly.

Karan kept speaking, moving back little by little so Rahul was at the front again.

Rahul turned to us and smirked. '*Hot hai, saali*. And I haven't even touched her yet.'

He was still laughing when she leapt at him.

Someone screamed and we all ran. Karan was way ahead of us; he had the car up and running. Rahul was behind him. He was laughing manically, blood dripping down his arm.

I tripped. They were screaming at me to hurry, all three of them in the car by then. She was only a few feet away. I got up and ran towards the car. I could hear the engine running. Almost there. I willed my legs to speed up.

A sharp pain in my shoulder. I screamed. I flipped around and there she was. I snatched the bottle from her hand. I shoved her into the wall on my left and dug the glass into her neck.

I don't know what I heard first, the crack of her skull or her gasp, that quick release, before she fell to the floor, blood colouring her grey *kurta* red, a distorted mess in an alleyway.

I dropped the bottle and turned to run to the car but they were gone.

I was sitting next to her when my father arrived. I didn't mean to, I sobbed, as I watched him pick up the bottle and throw it in the lake.

I didn't mean to, I repeated on loop, as he drove me home and to the airport the next morning.

I didn't mean to.

MIA

Sunday, 20th December

I lock the doors and switch on the ignition. The heating blasts into life. I turn the vents towards me and strip down to nothing, dumping my wet clothes in the back. I find a set of used but dry underwear, a jumper and some jeans in my bag. That'll have to do for now.

I turn on the radio and rummage through my bag for my phone. I have a few messages from George, a voicemail from James asking me to call him back immediately, and fourteen missed calls from unknown numbers.

'. . . *A thirty-one-year-old Indian man, Siddhant Roy Kapoor, has been charged with the murder of student Emily Barnett. He is due to appear at the Westminster Magistrates' Court on Monday for the initial hearing. In a statement issued . . .*'

I turn it off. I can't believe it. I place the phone on the seat and grip the steering wheel, trying to decide where to go. The contract for the house sale catches my eye and I pull it out of my bag.

I can't keep putting this off. I find a pen and skim

through it, signing at the bottom right-hand corner of every page. Done. I'll go to James's, I decide. I put the car in reverse, then jerk to a stop. I scroll through my phone until I find the email from Phil. I run through the chain of ownership on the Eastbourne house, skimming through the names. David F. Parker, Laurel B. Smith, Alice Doughty. I double-check the buyer's name on the contract I just signed.

Alice Doughty.

It's too much of a coincidence. I stare at the contract till the letters begin dancing, jumping, rearranging themselves.

The picture from Roy's iPad pops into my head. She wouldn't even have realized she was in it.

I rummage through my bag and fish out the estate agent's card. I ring the number at the back.

'Hello.'

I hesitate.

'Hello? Who is this?'

I take a deep breath. I have to do this; I know I do.

'Hi, it's Mia Kapoor. I need your help. The buyer, Alice, what does she look like?'

I hang up and rest my head on the wheel. I can't believe it. I found her.

I found Celia.

ROY

The journey from the police station to the Magistrates' Court takes little over twenty minutes, but it's twenty minutes of bumps, jerks, swerves and breaks. The van turns a corner and I sway sideways on the bench.

The two guards across from me smile and hold on to the bar behind them, 'Almost there,' the one with an elaborate tattoo snaking up his neck says and I nod.

Aren't tattoos better suited to armed robbers than coppers?

I turn my head to look outside. The high window offers glimpses of London as we drive through. It's all grey. Grey blocks of council flats, grey sky, grey drizzle trickling down the windowpane. Even the iconic red London double-decker looks a dirty maroon when seen through the tinted glass. I wonder if this is what my life will be like from now on? Endless versions of the same day, the same view, the same food, again and again and again.

As we approach the court, we are greeted by a bevy of

press people waiting behind barricades on either side of the street, their cameras flashing pointlessly at the darkened windows as we whizz past, sirens blaring, into the heavily guarded rear entrance. I am hustled out of the van without ceremony and the walk to the court cells is somber in contrast, no cameras or microphones, just a long dark corridor and the sound of metal doors opening and closing.

Nothing happens today. The Mags, as Alistair calls it, will hear the case and send it on to the Crown Court. Murder doesn't fall within their jurisdiction. I will be remanded in custody until the judge at the Crown Court is ready to see me. It's unlikely I will be granted bail, he has explained.

Do you remember that afternoon, my love, when we walked from Blackfriars to the cafe near St Paul's? You pointed out the Old Bailey when we passed it. I asked you how you knew and you shrugged. I like old buildings, you said.

Had you known then that I would end up there? Had you been planning it?

There is this strange heaviness in the centre of my chest. It appeared when Alistair told me the only Celia Brown he could find was an old woman in a care home, and it has stayed lodged there firmly since, twisting itself around my heart. It's the sting of betrayal. I trusted you and you destroyed me.

I wonder if this is how Mia felt.

When she found out about Emily, Mia asked me when I had made the decision to betray her. It wasn't a choice I made, Mia, I yelled, not everything is a decision. Some things just happen.

But it was a decision, wasn't it? Having a drink with Emily after pack-up, leaving the party to wait for a taxi in a dark alley with her, going to her hotel in the middle of the night, taking her to the maze. It was a series of insignificant choices, innocuous if viewed separately, but each of them leading me here, to this moment, held in an airless cell, charged with a murder I didn't commit.

I wonder when it happened for you. When did you decide you were going to betray me? Was it quite early on, a plot you hatched when we first met, or did you, like me, make a mistake that you couldn't come back from? Was it me that you were after all along or am I just collateral damage in some score you had to settle with Emily?

MIA

Monday, 21st December

Dorset

The door is green. A bright, primary green that reminds me of art class. I stare at it for a long time. It's a solid wood door. No stained-glass panel or peephole. The curtains on the windows are drawn, affording not even a peek inside. I've driven like a maniac to get here, but now that I am here, it feels surreal. I worry I'll burst into laughter. I turn around and look at the car. Still there. I can leave whenever I want. I'm the one in control here. I finger the little brass circle on the wall. It feels cool, springy.

Come on, you can do this.

I take a deep breath and press my finger down. A retro jingle fills the air, taking me back to summer afternoons and ice cream vans. I wait.

Nothing.

I am about to press the bell again when I hear footsteps. I lower my hood and step closer to the door.

The door swings open and I take another step forward,

keeping my head bent low. I jam my foot in the door frame and then look up.

The only thing I have to work with here is the element of surprise.

She sways backwards, her already pale skin a deathly white, and I use her momentary confusion to push my way inside.

'Hello, Celia,' I say.

I pull my hood down.

I look straight at her.

'Or do you prefer Natalie?'

I hear the sound of the door closing, locks turning, bolts going in. I spin around to face Natalie but her face is obscured by a shadow.

'Did you think you'd just get away with it?' I say.

She doesn't respond. She turns towards the console table and slips a set of keys into the drawer.

My head buzzes. This doesn't feel right.

'Why did you do it?' I go on. 'All these years, I trusted you and you manipulated me. You destroyed my marriage, my confidence, everything. Why?'

I stop talking as my eyes take in the surroundings.

The drawn curtains, the solid door, the remote location.

Natalie steps out of the shadows.

It's so obvious it's unnerving.

None of this is to keep intruders out. It's to keep hostages in.

She walks towards me and I take a few steps back.

She smiles. 'You must be tired. It certainly took you a while to get here.'

I feel my bravado from earlier slip away. What have I got myself into?

'Tea?' she asks, taking my elbow and steering me inside. 'Milk and one sugar, right?'

The kitchen is light and airy. Whitewashed walls. Wooden floor. There is a glass door opening directly into a small garden. No blinds or curtains on this one. She doesn't need them here. The back of the house sits almost directly on the cliff edge and the sound of the waves crashing into rocks rings through the room. A mantra. Nowhere to run, nowhere to hide.

The kettle boils. Natalie moves around in the kitchen, pulling out cups, teabags, biscuits, as if this is just a regular social visit. I stare at her. Her hair is different; the long black hair is gone. She's a tousled redhead now. Alexa Chung meets Florence Welsh. I feel a giggle bubbling up inside me and I squash it. I remind myself that this is the same woman who has been manipulating me for years, who has so systematically ruined my marriage and framed my husband for murder. I remind myself that I am here to confront her, to claim my life back.

'Why are you doing this?'

'What? Making tea?'

Her coolness is disorientating and I lose my train of thought. She finishes making the tea, squeezing each teabag out carefully, and sets my cup on the table along with a plate of biscuits.

My eyes flick up to the picture hanging on the wall to my left. It tugs at my brain. It's the same anonymous beach I used to stare at while baring my soul to this woman. I've seen it somewhere else as well.

Natalie follows my gaze. 'Gorgeous, isn't it? I've always had a thing for the ocean,' she says wistfully. 'But then so have you.'

She leans back on the counter. 'I know you have some questions, but why don't you get comfortable before we speak?' She smiles, the perfect hostess. 'I'll take your coat,' she says, arm outstretched.

'I'm okay,' I say.

Everything about the way Natalie's acting is bizarre but it's her smile that terrifies me. 'That wasn't a request. Now, please.'

I slip off my coat and hand it over, straining to keep my expression blank. I watch as she checks the pockets, my heart hammering against my ribs. Even though I am fully clothed, I have never felt as exposed.

She shakes her head. 'I knew I couldn't trust you,' she says, pulling out my phone. She switches off the recording mode, and deletes the audio file.

She slings my coat over a chair and places my phone and keys behind her on the kitchen counter.

'Sit down,' she says, nodding towards the table.

I do as I'm told.

Natalie regards me for a minute, sips her tea, then says, 'You know, when I was working on my dissertation, I came across an experiment they conducted in America in the eighties. An actor went up to a pedestrian and asked for directions. While the pedestrian was giving the directions, two men carrying a large wooden door passed between the actor and the pedestrian, completely blocking their view of each other for several seconds. During that time, another actor replaced the original actor. Different height, build, outfit, haircut, the works. They tried this on a few hundred people. Over sixty per cent of the participants didn't even notice the substitution. People will ignore what's right in front of them if it doesn't tally with how they choose to see the world.'

She puts her tea down and looks at me. 'Just think about it, if you can understand how people think, how their brains function, you can make them believe anything you want without them even realizing it. Isn't it amazing? The only thing is, sometimes it can get boring if it's too easy. And you and Roy, you were both so easy. But then Emily came along, and that girl, she was a challenge. She put the fun back in it.'

Even though it's now obvious that Natalie is deranged, I am appalled. 'Fun? Emily was pregnant! You killed her, killed her baby, framed Roy for murder . . . for *fun*?'

'Don't be so dramatic. Of course it wasn't for fun. And it wasn't about Roy. Or Emily. Or her goddamn baby. It was about you,' she says, reaching out to run a finger along my cheek. 'Everything has always been about you.'

I jerk back. 'What the hell are you talking about?'

'I saw you in the park in Bristol, years ago. You were having one of your panic attacks. I was going to come up to you to help, but before I could, your sister and her boyfriend got there and you drove off with them. I knew I had to see you again, so I tracked James down at a conference, introduced myself, made sure we rubbed shoulders. Fast-forward a couple of years, your previous therapist left,' she smiles, 'and I stepped in.'

She leans forward, her face inches from mine. 'This, however, is all about fun. So let's slow down, shall we?'

'You know it always annoyed me how ungrateful you were,' she says. 'You had it all, a family, a job, a husband, a *good* life. But you weren't happy, were you? All these people, things, and you still weren't happy. Always playing the victim. Always moaning. Even the first time that we met, at James's fundraiser, you were completely off your face and still, all you could do was moan. James had to practically carry you out of his own event, and that useless sister of yours, faffing about, trying to make light of it.'

I wince but I don't say anything. She knows I don't like thinking about that.

'But even after you gave up the drugs, it just didn't stop, did it? I mean, I should know, I've had a front row seat to the Mia show for years now. They aren't giving me a promotion. He's cheating on me. She's selling the house. They're leaving me behind. It was infuriating, having to sit there and listen to you go on and on. Some people don't have any of that, you know. They don't have anyone in their lives to complain about.'

'So that's it then?' I say, my patience wearing thin. 'You were jealous of me?'

'No,' she scoffs, 'I wasn't jealous. I was intrigued. I wanted to know everything about you. I wanted to understand how someone who had everything could hate her life that much.'

She walks back the few steps to her spot by the kitchen counter and picks up her tea. She looks at me coolly. 'I've always been fascinated with that little brain of yours. I mean, you're practically the reason I became a psychotherapist.'

My head is spinning. 'How long have you—'

'Known you?' she finishes for me. 'Ever since you were a baby.'

'So you see, as I was saying . . .' she continues, and for a second I have a vision of her presenting at a conference or seminar. She speaks with such authority, she could convince anyone she's an expert and I wonder if that is how she lured James in, how she convinced him without a shadow of doubt that she was an excellent therapist. 'I'd been observing you for years, before we ever met each other, and I became obsessed with understanding how someone who had it all could be so unhappy. I wanted to see what would happen if I took it all away. I wanted to see for myself how *unbreakable* you were.'

Natalie paces in front of me, buzzing with a frantic energy. Her words bounce around the room, dizzying me as I try to make sense of them, until a single word centres me.

Unbreakable.

I never told her that. I never told anyone that.

My eyes flick back to the picture and I remember coming across another one just like that not so long ago.

My gaze settles on her and the realization hits me in my stomach even before the thought completes itself. Of course. It all adds up.

'Who are you?' I ask, even though I know the answer already.

Something passes over her eyes. The slightest shift in the dynamic as my words settle in. Her smile creeps off her face and sends shivers through my spine.

'Why, Mia, I'm your sister, sweetie.'

MIA

'You're Laurel's . . .' I stutter.

'And she finally gets it.'

'Laurel?'

Natalie's lips tighten. She turns around to look out of the window and for the first time in all the years that I've known her, I hear her voice quiver. 'She died. Less than a year after Dad. You ruined my life,' she says, her back still to me. 'My father had always been my secret. Mama, Dad and I, we weren't like any other normal family. We couldn't just go for a film or a picnic anytime we wanted. He was the most amazing father, but in hiding. Before the start of the new term, he'd sit with me and help me cover all my new notebooks. When I did well in a test, he would bring every ice cream flavour in the shop home so I could have whatever I wanted. Once, when I was upset because he'd missed the school play, he spent the entire weekend setting up the house like an auditorium so that the three of us could put on our own show. He was perfect.

'But then, a couple of years later, it was like he just lost interest in me. He'd be gone weeks at a time. He even missed my birthday once. Mama said he had forgotten about us because he had a shiny new daughter. You. And for a few years, that was all there was to it. I kept trying to make him stay, but he kept leaving. Then one day, he announced that everything was going to be different. He said he was going to leave your mother and marry Mama. We were going to be a real family. No more hiding. And then, he finally left and came home. *To us*. Brought his clothes and everything. This is it, he said. I've left her, I've done it. Mama and I . . . we were ecstatic. The next day we went to the beach. All three of us. He said he wasn't worried about being seen with me anymore. The waiter at the cafe commented on how much I looked like him, he said I was a spitting image of my father,' she says, the memory filling her face with pride.

I look at her properly. The pale skin, the wide mouth, the flecked grey eyes. The resemblance is uncanny. She resembles him more than Addi and I put together. How had I not seen it before?

'For years, the girls at school had teased me. I hated it. But everything was going to change. I couldn't wait to take him with me to all the school events, shut those girls up for good.' She starts pacing. 'But then, of course, you had to ruin everything. Your mother had always tried to come between Mama and Dad, but she'd never dared to ring the house. But you. *You* found the number and called . . . and when I answered the phone, you just demanded to speak to your daddy. *Your* daddy. As if you owned him. He hadn't even wanted you. Mama told me – you were an accident. But there you were, howling down the phone, lying, saying you'd taken a tumble down the stairs, that you'd had stitches. He was livid with guilt, kept telling you that you were unbreakable. He'd been drinking already. He made a big speech about how it was your birthday and he had to get you your perfect doll's house. I begged him to stay, to pick me, but of course he picked you. He always picked you,' she spits out.

Even now, that brings a smile to my face. I hide it away quickly. He picked me! Then I remember that phone call. I had forced Addi to do it. Told her if she didn't find Daddy and make him speak to me, I would go out and find him myself. And then when I spoke to him, I had lied so he would come back. All these years, I had blamed myself for that. Perhaps I always will.

'Mama tried to convince him to stay, to wait till he sobered up at least, but he wouldn't hear of it.' She pauses to steady herself. 'He stormed out.'

I hold my head in my hands. I know the rest of it.

She grabs my hair and yanks me back, my spine crashing into the wooden chair with a thud. 'Look at me,' she screams, bending over so her face is inches from mine. 'When Jane called the next day, Mama refused to believe that he wasn't coming back. At the funeral, your mother and William, they didn't let us near him. We were his real family, the one he loved, but we had to watch from the car. Your mother didn't give a damn about what he would have wanted; all she cared about was you. Protecting you. I didn't even get to say goodbye. For months afterwards, Mama just sat there on the sofa, drinking herself into a stupor. There was no room for my grief. I was only eleven years old, and I was looking after my mother, who had gone, in one week, from being the most wonderful mama to a drunk who couldn't even wipe her own snot. I bathed her, I cooked for her, I did everything I knew how to do, but none of it helped. I'd come home from school and find her lying in a pool of her own piss. But even that was better than having no one. When she died . . . I was eleven. I was eleven and I was alone. They called William and Jane, but they refused to even look at me. Just left some money and drove off, like I was some filthy little secret, not their niece.'

She takes a breath and for the first time, I see a flash of genuine emotion in her eyes. My father's eyes.

'I lost both my parents,' she says, 'because of you.'

'Where did you—'

'Foster homes, five in as many years. No one wanted me. I was too sad, too angry, too broken. I couldn't wait to leave, to start training as a therapist.'

'Like Daddy,' I say. Despite everything, I feel a swell of emotion for her. No child should have to go through that. 'In therapy, you kept asking me if I felt guilty . . .'

'I was trying to give you a chance. But you're just an entitled little bitch, aren't you? If you hadn't insisted on seeing him that very night, he would be here. I would have had a family, a life. You stole everything from me,' she hisses.

'So you took everything from me,' I say, finally understanding what this has all been about, why Emily had to die and Roy had to become collateral damage. Affairs dwindle but a life sentence is forever.

'You and Roy . . . did you two . . . did you have . . .'

'Sex? Of course we did. We spoke about it beforehand. Planned it. He wanted it to be meaningful, poetic; he wanted us to make love,' she sneers.

I picture them together. *Making love.* He was like that with me, once. Kind. Gentle. So, so romantic.

'Of course he never hit me. That was reserved only for you. Because he could see you for what you really were.'

I close my eyes. I try to mute her out.

'Still listening to those voices in your head, are you?'

'How long have you and Roy . . . I mean . . .'

'Not long, a couple of weeks, if that. Surely you've heard that the most intense loves are the ones left incomplete? I first met him when he was going to Paris, on the Eurostar.'

'But how . . .'

'His emails,' she shrugs. 'And yours.' She looks at my face and scoffs. 'I just told you I've been observing you for years, and hacking isn't exactly rocket science. Keep up, will you?

'You led me right to him. By the time I met him, I knew everything about him, what he liked, what he craved, his trigger points. He thought we were soulmates. I played hard to get to begin with, but I didn't have to do much, not really; he was so sick of you, he was happy to do all the chasing. He was already feeling torn up about Emily, so when he told me he wanted to be with me, I asked him to choose – empty sex or true love. You know what he chose, don't you?

'I was counting on Emily not to let him go easily. But the pregnancy, that was sheer luck. When Roy told me she was having second thoughts about an abortion, I played the supportive girlfriend. I encouraged him to meet her straightaway; said we could delay our own date by a few hours. I even suggested the hotel he booked her into – the Seaford Head. The barmaid there owed me a favour. I met Roy at our hotel in Brighton and made him a drink after we, you know, made love. When the Temazepam kicked in, I texted Emily from his phone. I dressed in his clothes, took his phone and car and drove there. I smeared the licence plates, made sure it looked like he was trying to cover his tracks,' she says.

'The barmaid had slipped Emily a sedative as well. By the time she came outside, she was already pretty out of it. She got in the car without even checking who was in it. All I had to do was wrap the string around her neck,' she continues, her words becoming more and more animated. 'She fought for a bit, but she died easily, the poor girl. I put her in the boot, made sure they would find her DNA there, and then dropped her off the cliff.'

She stops pacing and looks at me. Her expression turns sour. 'That's when things got complicated. The barmaid was supposed to report her missing the next morning, but she chickened out. She ran away, didn't even turn up to collect the rest of her money.'

'So you tipped the police off. You were the caller who identified her on the train,' I say, finally catching up.

'Bingo. But even then they took too long,' she continues. 'By the time they started the search, the tide had washed her too far out. But I had other things going on. Your marriage was only one part of your life.'

It takes me a moment to grasp what she means.

'The Eastside order. I told you about the tests . . .'

'You always did talk too much for your own good,' she smiles. 'Next came the situation with your family, but all you needed there was a little nudge. You destroyed that one all by yourself. The only thing left to tackle then was your – what do you like to call them? – episodes. After I rejected you too, I knew it wouldn't be long till you crawled back to drugs, and of course, you didn't disappoint.'

'I trusted you,' I say. 'I thought you were trying to help me.'

'You killed my father.'

'It wasn't my fault!' I scream out before I can stop myself. I take a deep breath. I cannot live with the guilt of his death anymore. He got into the car drunk. It was his fault, I tell myself.

'He was my father too, you know,' I say out loud. I get up. 'I need the loo.'

She grabs me by the elbow and leads me up the stairs to the bathroom. It's the only room in the house that looks lived in – a pale grey towel hangs over the bathtub, a box of paracetamol and a toothbrush sit on the sink, healing crystals and toiletries line the ledge of the bathtub. My eyes come to rest on a pair of scissors on the windowsill. I turn to close the door but she shakes her head. My heart sinks. I sit on the loo and will myself to pee under observation.

All sorts of things occur to me as Natalie escorts me back downstairs. It shocks me to think how long she must have been planning this. How ready she was when the opportunity arose and how easily I had led her into my life, my marriage. I don't need her to tell me that if it hadn't been Emily, it would have been someone or something else. And there I was congratulating myself on my cleverness, thinking I was going to confront her, when all I was really doing was following the breadcrumbs Natalie had so carefully laid down for me. The fact that I thought I'd be able to outsmart the woman who had manipulated me for years is downright laughable.

'I think I should leave now,' I say when we get back to the kitchen.

'Do you?'

She returns to her spot by the kitchen counter, keeping watch over me. A block of knives sits behind her, next to my phone. A documentary I watched about kidnapping pops into my head.

'You can't keep me here, Natalie. People know where I am,' I try.

She just raises her eyebrows, calling my bluff. 'Do they now?'

'What about your husband? Aren't you worried he'll find out?'

'See, this is what gets me about you every single time. You're so completely self-obsessed; it's no wonder Roy went looking for attention everywhere else. There is no husband, Mia. Not yet, anyway. There is a fiancé, but he's given me something of an ultimatum. Because of you. He says he can't be with me until I'm ready to commit to him fully – no distractions, no causes, no needy, clingy patients taking over my whole life.'

It builds slowly, the dread, until I am completely in its grip. I can't believe I thought this was going to be a simple conversation I'd be able to walk away from. I take a step back. I try to calculate the distance from the back door to the street. I notice the narrow path along the cliff edge leading down to the beach. Not impossible, if I didn't fall off trying, that is.

'Why are you telling me all this? Why now?' I ask her.

She smiles.

'Because you see, little sister, as much as I love torturing you, I have one shot at happiness left, and I'm not about to let it go,' she says, slipping her hand into her pocket.

I stare at her dumbfounded as I realize what she has in her hand.

I need to get out, right now.

Addi's words from earlier echo in my ears.

'Don't be stupid, Mia. If what you're saying is true, this woman could be dangerous. We need to call the police,' she had insisted.

'And tell them what? That I've found my husband's mistress, who happens to be my therapist, and coincidentally, my brother-in-law's known her for years? So what? All that proves, Addi, is how gullible we are.'

'Fine, then let me call James. Take him with you. I don't like this, Mia. It just doesn't feel—'

'This has nothing to do with James. This woman has been controlling me for years; I need to see her. I need to know why she did this to me.'

Addi continued to fight me on it, but she was thousands of miles away and my stubbornness and stupidity knows no bounds.

I try to slow my breathing down as I attempt to work out how long it would take me to get to the front door, and then I remember all the locks and bolts. Even if I manage to get there, I'll never get out. And trying to run out of the back door would be a death wish; one wrong step and I'll be over the cliff. I have only one option.

'You don't have to do this, Natalie,' I say, inching towards the table. 'Daddy would want us to be happy. Both of us. We can work this out. I'm the only family—'

'Don't you dare talk about him. You have no idea what he would want.' She pauses to pull herself back. 'We're going for a walk,' she says.

'What?'

'Now,' she screams, closing the distance between us in two strides, her fingers wrapped tightly around a gun that's pointing straight at me.

'Natalie, please . . .'

'Shut the fuck up! This is what you deserve,' she says, her face contorting into an ugly scowl, and I have a moment of recognition. I can see my father in her.

I am prepared for the panic to take over, for my life to flash before my eyes, but instead a strange calm takes over.

It's up to me now. No one is coming to save me.

I hold her gaze and, with the smallest of movements, I reach for the cold tea sitting on the table. In one quick motion, I throw the murky liquid in her eyes and shove her hard. It's not much but it buys me a few seconds. I push her again as she stumbles backwards, then grab my phone from the counter and run into the hallway and up the stairs. I've barely dialed 999 when I hear her behind me, pounding up the stairs. I run into the bathroom but before I can close the door, I feel a sharp pain in the back of my head. My knees buckle and before I know it, I am being dragged across the bathroom floor. My eyes search out my phone and just as she steps around me to kick it out of my reach, I grab both her ankles and pull her towards me. She lets out a scream as she lands on the floor and the gun gets knocked out of her hand. I lean on her with all my weight and press my knees into her back as she struggles underneath me. I push her shoulder down with my left hand and, with my right, I reach for the first thing I see. The jarred edges of a healing crystal dig into my palm as I swing it down on her with all the strength I can muster.

The silence that follows chills me. I drop the pale pink crystal on the floor and reach for my phone. It slips out of my grasp. There's blood on my fingers.

'Hello? Hello?' I pant into my phone when I finally manage to pick it up. I am hoping that the operator's still on the line and that she's somehow figured out what's going on but real life is messier than the movies.

I scramble up and run out of the bathroom and down the stairs, leaving Natalie on the floor, unsure if the blood on the floor is hers or mine.

I dial 999 again and speak as quickly as I can while I rummage through Natalie's console table for her front door keys. I practically scream with relief when the first one I try unlocks the bottom lock.

I'm on the third lock when I hear her behind me.

'You're not going anywhere.'

I spin around. I set the phone down on the console table. Natalie is standing at the foot of the stairs. The gun is back in her hand.

'The police are on their way,' I say, slowly trying to wrestle some control back. 'If you kill me, you'll never get away with it.'

She steps closer. 'You think that's what I care about? You think after all of this – strangling Emily, framing Roy, being your fucking therapist – you think I care about getting away? You killed my father!'

Our father, I want to scream, but I force myself to stay calm. 'Killing me won't bring him back. But if you leave now, you can still have a life.'

'You ruined any life I could ever have,' she says, and I stare at her as she points the gun at me, the metal glinting where it catches the sun.

I take a step back as I realize this is it, the end of the line. There is nothing left for me to try now.

I hear the click as she unlocks the safety switch.

We both hear the distant wail of sirens get closer.

A loud crash.

A frenzy of footsteps.

A microsecond of distraction.

I lunge at her. But it's too late.

I'm too late.

The sound of the gunshots rings through the room while I lie on the floor trembling.

ROY

Monday, 21st December

London

I have been waiting all day. The cell door swings open and a guard escorts me to a different room. Save for the metal desk and chairs that take centre stage in this room, the cell is almost identical to the one I've been sitting in for the last few hours.

It's hard to believe that when this all started, all I was worried about was Mia finding out about the affair, or at worst the pregnancy. And yet here I am, less than a month later, sitting in a chair that's bolted to the floor, waiting for my solicitor to come in and tell me just how much worse everything is about to get.

Alistair comes in after a few minutes, looking flustered. I want to smack him. He doesn't have the barrister he promised me with him, I note.

'Sorry to keep you waiting,' he says, 'but I wanted to come here when I knew what was happening.'

I raise my eyebrows at him.

He grins. 'The charges against you have been retracted pending review.'

'What?'

'The official line is that you're no longer the chief suspect, but after a fuck-up this huge, I'd say it's pretty unlikely that they'll come after you again. There's some paperwork to be completed, and you may still need to stay overnight, but as of four p.m. today, you are a free man.'

He says something about discontinuance and section twenty-three, about the prosecution withdrawing charges based on new evidence, then places a massive folder on the table and starts flicking through it, talking me through procedure, timelines, everything. I sign wherever he asks me to but I'm not listening. I'm already somewhere else.

I'm free.

MIA

Monday, 21ˢᵗ December

I am shaking as I wait outside. Someone has wrapped me up in an oversized coat and I am thankful for the warmth that instantly envelops me. An officer escorts me to the back of an ambulance. Someone brings me a cup of tea. Another two officers are setting up a cordon, blue and white tape sealing me off from the rest of the world. I have never seen so many police officers in one place. They're everywhere. Noises assault me from every direction: the whir of radios, sirens going off, medics screaming for backup, officers asking me question after question. I can see James across the street. He's speaking to a large officer, gesturing emphatically.

A woman approaches me and flashes her badge. CID.

She tells me that Addi called them from India so when I rang 999 they were aware of a potentially risky situation in Dorset. By the time I called them the second time, a team was already on its way.

She tells me I'm lucky and I stare at my right hand. I'm still not sure if the blood is Natalie's or mine. I want to ask the policewoman but she has questions. So many questions.

I just shake my head. Later, please, later. She nods, apologizes, and then asks me if I can accompany her to a station to give my statement. I nod absent-mindedly.

I ask her about Roy, about what happens to him now, and she tells me that they heard enough on my second call, that in those three sentences Natalie confirmed everything Addi had told them. What they need from me now is context.

The large officer speaks into a radio and James runs across the street, appearing next to me in less than a second, hugging me and talking all at once. He's rambling and I tune him out.

A medic turns up and starts asking me more questions, looking at my hand, checking my pulse, tightening a tourniquet around my arm.

I'm fine, leave me alone, I want to scream but I don't. I clench my fist and let him do his job. I am polite if nothing else.

I am also numb.

A flurry of activity to my left catches my eye. Two men in white suits carry a stretcher into the ambulance parked next to the one I'm in. I push myself forward and crane my neck to get a better view.

I breathe easily for the first time in days. Tears prick my eyes.

I can't see her. It's over.

She never stood a chance once the armed officers barged in.

She's in a bag.

PART THREE

Two months later

India

MIA

Friday, 26th February

Haridwar

Cold, grey water laps at my feet as I step in. Flames erupt on the far end of the bank and I stop to look at them. Smoke fills the air. I rub my eyes. They are raw, but not yet dry.

Next to me, Addi has also stopped in her tracks. She's looking at the funeral pyre in the distance but her eyes are glazed. I take a step towards her and hold her hand. We descend further, following the priest down the steps till we are standing on either side of him, waist-deep in the Ganges. I adjust my *dupatta* over my head and nod to him.

He stands erect, eyes closed, holding the clay urn out in front of him. The sun is going down, casting a pink glow over everything. He begins chanting and Addi and I release fistful after fistful of our mother's ashes, watching the river carry her away, our sobs and the priest's hymns drowned out by the sound of the Ganges rushing past.

*

Mummy didn't make it to the end of the six months the doctors had promised us. She went quickly, quietly, her death as unobtrusive as her life had been.

'*Aur kuch*, madam?' the waiter asks, placing my *chai* on the table and handing me a small leather dossier. I sign my name, thank him and give him thirty rupees. I take my tea and stand by the fence, looking at the river in front of me. It hurries past, the current hauling the water through. Across the river, devotees in saffron clothes are clustered in small groups. Their chants fill the early evening air, all of them performing the same holy ritual: bending down to cup the water in their hands, standing up and letting it fall through their fingers; offering roses and magnolias to the river; lighting *diyas* and placing them in the water; and then watching it all glide away.

I wonder where she is now.

My thoughts drift back to an evening less than a week before we had to rush her to the hospital. We had just come back from another round of tests. James was flying in for a few days and Addi had gone to the airport to pick him up. It was one of those rare occasions when Mum and I were alone.

'Shall we go out?' I asked after she'd taken her medicines. She had little stamina but being outside in the fresh air lifted her spirits so Addi and I tried to take her for a walk every evening.

She nodded. 'Perhaps we can go to the lake today?'

I put on my jumper and draped a shawl around her shoulders. It was still light outside. The lake was less than a ten-minute walk away, but I took the car, parking right by the promenade. We walked for a few minutes then sat down on a bench facing the lake.

'You'll need to go back soon,' Mum said, her eyes focused on all the activity in front of her.

'There's no rush.'

In front of us, young couples strolled past, hand in hand, and wives haggled with the peddlers selling *chana jor garam* and *masala* corn-on-the-cobs while their husbands hung back and the children wailed for ice cream.

'What was she like?' she asked, after a few minutes.

'Natalie?'

She nodded.

'She had his eyes, and the same sharp jawline.'

'Your father had beautiful eyes,' she said. 'But always full of conflict.' Mum smiled and leaned back. She looked so peaceful.

'Did you still love him, despite everything?' I asked.

'I used to think so. I did in the beginning. Whenever he got angry, I would tell myself that it was just a little argument. I convinced myself it was normal. And in the beginning, it wasn't much, a small push here, a shove there. But over the years, it got worse. Our arguments grew more frequent and every time it would end the same way. My injuries would be more severe each time and I was calling in sick so often, I lost my job, and with it, any shred of dignity I had left. I started believing him when he told me I deserved it. Things might have carried on like that but everything changed when he hit you. Up until then, he was hitting me, throwing verbal abuse at Addi, but not you. Never you. He adored you. He used you as proof that the problem wasn't his temper; that Addi and I provoked him,' she said, her gaze pointing downwards.

I looked at my mother. How long had she suffered alone?

'The relationship you had with your father . . . it was so . . . pure, it made me believe we could still fix things. But after the barbecue at William's, something changed. I'd never seen you that upset. You refused to speak to David for days . . . And then, when I found out about Laurel and their little girl, it all fell into place. It took me a long time but I knew I had to leave him, if not for myself, then for the two of you. One of my friends from Cambridge was a divorce lawyer and he started drawing up the paperwork. I should have left it at that but I don't know why I felt like I had to warn them.' She paused to wipe away the tears that had escaped her eyes. 'I hadn't been able to protect you and Addi, but I felt like if I could at least protect the other little girl, Laurel's girl, I might be able to live with myself. I couldn't bring myself to speak to her so I wrote to her.' She looked up. 'David found the letter.'

'The night he left . . . that's what you were arguing about?'

She nodded. 'He came in completely drunk. He was furious. He kept saying that I was just trying to manipulate Laurel with that letter; he would never hurt either of them. He said he only hit me because I drove him to the point of madness. When I told him I wanted him to leave, he started punching me. Addi saw us and ran upstairs. I couldn't see you; I thought you must be upstairs as well. It was then that I heard you, under the stairs. I don't know what you were doing there but—'

'Hide and seek. We were playing hide and seek.'

She nodded.

'I wanted to reach you before he did. I had never seen him like that and I was scared. Terrified. But you kept crying out for him and he kept asking you to come to him. I wedged myself in between the two of you and yelled for Addi to come down. I pulled you out and she took you upstairs. He left when Addi threatened to call the police. I thought it was over, but then the next day . . .'

'The next day, I called him back. I'm sorry, Mummy,' I whispered, my tears blurring the world.

Mum held me till the tears stopped.

'It wasn't your fault, darling,' she said. 'We didn't talk about these things back then, but I always knew your father was an alcoholic. And he had a terrible temper. That's what caused his accident, not you.'

'Why didn't you ever tell me what he was like? I punished you. I gave you so much grief about the house, about everything . . .'

'By the end . . . I hated him, but he loved you. You were the only thing that was left of my marriage that was still pure, and I couldn't bear to destroy that. I always thought I'd tell you everything when you were older, but after your father's death, you became so withdrawn. You started having panic attacks. And then . . .' She broke off, unable to continue.

'Then the drugs started.'

'You were already so vulnerable, I couldn't forgive myself if anything happened to you, especially after your accident . . .'

'I know.' I paused, thinking back to that night when, in a way, it all started. 'That's when I first met Natalie, you know. At James's party.'

'She was there?'

'Yes,' I said, that phase of my life painful even in its memories, but James's fundraiser felt like it had been etched into my brain, and no matter how hard I tried, I couldn't rub it out. It was my nineteenth birthday, and I was celebrating the only way I knew how, dosed up on a cocktail of so many pills, all the doctors at that party could probably have treated a week's worth of patients with just the drugs coursing through my body. James had carried me out kicking and screaming. I woke up the next evening in Addi's flat. It had been swept clean. Not even an aspirin in sight. I managed to feign sleep for a few hours, and as soon as I knew Addi was asleep, I snuck out. I had no money, and no phone, but I knew I only had to get to the hospital nearby and I'd be able to get my hands on something, even if it was just hand sanitizer.

I made it to the hospital, but via the scenic route. I got hit by a car on the corner of Addi's street and ended up first in A&E, and then in rehab, where they kept me for the best part of the year. When I came out something had changed in me; the accident had scared me enough that I was off the pills, but I was more broken than ever. I met Roy almost immediately after and he was just so charming, it felt like he was everything, like he could save me from myself. Thinking about the early days still brings a smile to my face.

'Do you remember what it was like when I first met Roy? I was so happy, we both were.'

'I remember, sweetie.'

'And then our life together, we had everything. It was perfect. What if Natalie had never happened?'

'But she did happen, Mia. And Natalie may have inched him along, but your father, Roy, men like that, they bully women so they can live with their own insecurities. You deserve so much better than that.'

I nodded, even as a small voice inside me told me that without my marriage my life was over. It wasn't as bad as I first thought. He hadn't killed Emily. And the rest of it . . . we could work on it, couldn't we?

'Everyone always thought your father and I had the perfect marriage, Mia. But it wasn't real. Don't make the same mistakes I made, darling,' Mummy said quietly.

'Why didn't you ever remarry?' I asked her as we drove back.

'It took me so long to stand up for us, I didn't want to give that power away. I wanted to get to know myself again. And once I did, I realized I liked what I saw.' She smiled. 'I had both of you and that was all I ever wanted. I never saw us as a broken family, Mia. I saw us as an independent one.'

MIA

Udaipur

I take my *chai* on the terrace and wave my cousins off as they climb into their car. A light breeze carries the smell of the season's first mangoes from the garden. It will be too hot to sit outside in a few days.

It's been odd being back in India for such a long stretch, contradictory, almost like being reunited with an old lover. For the most part, this is where I grew up, where I went to school, had my first kiss, my first heartbreak and, yes, my first pill. But this is also the place we called home after Daddy died and for years, that simple fact tortured me. How could I allow myself to love anything that was a result of my father's death?

But somehow, the ambiguity doesn't sting as much anymore. I'm enjoying the quiet of the valley. The fresh air and the long walks by the lake have allowed me a sense of stillness that's hard to come by in London, and being around my extended family has been strangely restorative. Yet there are moments – every time there's a power cut or a relative drops in unannounced or I have a craving for sushi – when I just want to jump on the next flight out. I could go anywhere – Bristol, where I was born, or London, where I built my career and bought my own house – or I could just stay here, peaceful and sushi-less. It feels like I've left little pieces of myself everywhere, and for the first time ever, it doesn't bother me.

In the distance, I see the lights go on around the lake and I get up. Mosquitoes start prickling my skin. I take my empty cup and go inside.

I switch on my laptop and scroll through my emails. I sent my CV to a couple of recruitment agents last week but so far I haven't come across a role that feels right. I skim through the new email from Daphne at Style Jobs.

Sales Director

Niche brand retailing via Colette, Galeries Lafayette, Selfridges and Harvey Nichols

Generous salary + relocation package, private healthcare

Flexible working hours

Paris

Paris.

It has always been a dream.

I run through the pros and cons in my head. Ultimately, it comes down to one thing: Roy. He hates Paris.

Roy has been calling me non-stop for weeks now and I have been stalling, delaying giving him an answer. He's apologized more earnestly than ever before, sworn he's changed, told me he's seeing an NHS-recommended therapist. He's doing everything I wanted him to do. And I want to believe him, I do. It would be so easy to step back into my life in London, the one I so meticulously created. But I don't know if I fit into that life anymore. It feels small, somehow.

I think back to what my mother said. It isn't love that's been holding me back, I realize. It's the memories. Love is fleeting; it's the forgetting that takes forever.

I type up a quick reply to Daphne and send it off before I can change my mind.

Maybe I do deserve more.

MIA

Tuesday, 19th April

Delhi

I'm about to lift my carry-on and put it in the overhead locker when the man in front of me speaks. 'Let me get that for you.'

French men really are quite cute.

'Thank you,' I smile and sit down, eyes glued to the window.

I put on my seat belt, the conversation from last night replaying in my head while the overhead speaker crackles. I had finally told Roy I wanted a divorce. Predictably, he wasn't happy but I held my ground. I knew I would still have to see him; to cut him off completely would be wrong. But all the same, it was time to stop putting him first.

A moment later, the air hostess appears. I glance at her drinks tray.

'They do say one glass is okay,' she says, following my gaze. I peel my eyes away from the wine and shake my head.

'I'll be fine, thank you,' I say. I lean back and close my eyes, my hand resting lightly on my stomach. I smile.

We'll both be just fine.

ACKNOWLEDGEMENTS

Thank you

To my agent, Annette Green, who believed in my writing from the beginning and made it all so *so* real. I couldn't have wished for a kinder or more enthusiastic agent.

To my editor, Vicki Mellor, who knew exactly what I was trying to say even when I didn't and, with her talent, insight and patience, made Roy and Mia's story come to life.

To my very first reader, Anvi Mridul, who took time out of her very busy life to read multiple early drafts and quickly went from being my little sister to my most astute critic and tireless cheerleader.

To Richard Skinner, whose wisdom and encouragement gave me the confidence to think of myself as a writer.

To everyone from the Faber Academy June 2016 Writing a Novel class for their enthusiasm and continued support.

To my early readers Anjola Adedayo, George De Freitas,

Alice Feeney, Giles Fraser, Maria Ghibu, Daniel Grant and Alison Marlow for their friendship and generosity, and for asking all the right questions.

To Manesh Mistry, Sally Romartinez and Rodney Shek for the laughter and for reminding me to (occasionally) have some fun.

To Samara Brackley and Tony Wong for helping with police and procedural matters.

To my family in India for putting up with all the un-answered Skype calls and texts and treating me like a bestselling novelist before I had written a single word.

To my family in London, Linda and George De Freitas, for holding my hand in my darkest moments and cheering me on through the happiest hours. I wouldn't last a day without you.

And finally, to Mummy, Papa, Rishabh and Prachi. Everything I have and everything I am is because of you. This book is as much yours as it is mine.